**W9-BLS-581**

*Praise for the novels of Robert Charles Wilson*

## THE HARVEST

"Reads like a combination of Arthur C. Clarke and Stephen King." —*Rocky Mountain News*

"May join the ranks of the classics." —*Chicago Sun-Times*

"Literate and satisfying . . . The characters seem as real as your next-door neighbors." —*The Knoxville News-Sentinel*

"One of the best new writers . . . [Wilson] conveys [his] story on a very personal level with rich characters and a page-turning plot." —*The Denver Post*

"Science fiction at its best." —*The Toronto Star*

## A BRIDGE OF YEARS

"I very much doubt you'll find a finer, more compelling science-fiction novel this year than *A Bridge of Years*." —*Star Tribune*, Minneapolis

"In [*A Bridge of Years*] there is beauty, and in it there is truth. . . . [Wilson is] a storyteller of astonishing compassion and understanding." —Orson Scott Card, *The Magazine of Fantasy & Science Fiction*

"[A] rewarding time-travel fantasy." —*The New York Times Book Review*

## THE DIVIDE

"A literate thriller, a superbly crafted novel of character." —*The New York Times Book Review*

**Books by
Robert Charles Wilson**

*A Bridge of Years*
*The Divide*
*Gypsies*
*The Harvest*
*A Hidden Place*
*Memory Wire*
*Mysterium*

# Mysterium

ROBERT
CHARLES
WILSON

BANTAM BOOKS
NEW YORK    TORONTO    LONDON    SYDNEY    AUCKLAND

MYSTERIUM

A Bantam Spectra Book

PUBLISHING HISTORY
Bantam trade edition published May 1994
Bantam paperback edition / March 1995

SPECTRA and the portrayal of a boxed "s" are trademarks of Bantam Books, a division of Bantam
Doubleday Dell Publishing Group, Inc.

ISBN 0-553-56953-8

Published simultaneously in the United States and Canada

Bantam Books are published by Bantam Books, a divison of Bantam Doubleday Dell Publishing Group,
Inc. Its trademark, consisting of the words "Bantam Books" and the portrayal of a rooster, is Registered in
U.S. Patent and Trademark Office and in other countries. Marca Registrada. Bantam Books, 1540 Broad-
way, New York, New York 10036.

PRINTED IN THE UNITED STATES OF AMERICA

RAD    0 9 8 7 6 5 4 3 2 1

for jo:
parallel worlds

# Before

**THE REPUBLIC OF TURKEY, 1989.**

On a dry inland plain, under a sky the color of agate, a handful of Americans scuffed at a rubble of ancient clay masonry.

The Americans, mainly graduate students doing field-work toward their degrees and a few tutelary spirits in the form of faculty members, had arrived three weeks ago. They had driven from Ankara by Land Rover, away from the Kizil Irmak and into the heart of the dry central plateau, where a neolithic Anatolian townsite had lain dormant for almost nine thousand years. They had erected their tents and Porta Potties in the shade of a rocky hill, and in the cool of the morning they worried the soil with wire brushes and whisk brooms.

The site was ancient, but small and not very productive.

A graduate student named William Delmonico was nibbling his way through a string grid that had produced only a few flaked stones, the prehistoric equivalent of the cigarette butt, when he uncovered what looked like a shard of polished jade—an anomalous substance, and immensely more interesting than the flints he had already cataloged.

The jade fragment was deeply embedded in the stony earth, however, and no amount of toothbrushing would free it. Delmonico alerted his adviser, a tenured professor of archaeology who welcomed this respite from what had begun to seem like a wasted summer of fruitless and repetitive fieldwork. Delmonico's nubbin of glass (not jade, certainly, though the resemblance was marked) represented at least an intellectual challenge. He assigned two experienced diggers to the grid but allowed Delmonico his proprietary excitement. Delmonico, a lanky twenty-one-year-old with a shine of sweat on his face, hovered over the site.

Three days later a jagged spar of dull green material the size of a tabletop had been uncovered . . . and still it remained embedded in the earth.

That was odd. Even more peculiar, it looked as if they would have to call in a materials expert to identify this substance. It was not jade, not glass, not pottery of any kind. It retained its warmth long after sunset—and nights were often brutally cold on this high, arid plain. And it *looked* strange. Deceptive to the eye. Slippery. From a distance, it seemed almost to shrink—to disappear, if you stood a few yards outside the dig, in a stitch of air and sand.

On the fourth day after his discovery Delmonico was confined to his tent, vomiting every twenty or thirty minutes into a half-gallon mason jar while a wind storm battered the canvas and turned the air to chalk. He had come down with the flu, everyone said. Or common dysentery—he wouldn't be the first. Delmonico accepted this diagnosis and resigned himself to it.

Then the sores appeared on his hands. The skin blackened and peeled away from his fingers, and the bandages he applied turned yellow with suppuration. Blood appeared in his stools.

His faculty supervisor drove him to Ankara, where an emergency room physician named Celal diagnosed radiation sickness. Celal filed a report with his chief of staff; the chief of staff notified an official of the Ministry of Public Health. The doctor was not surprised, given all this, when the delirious young American was taken from the ward by a military escort and driven into the night. It was a mystery, Celal thought. But there were always mysteries. The world was a mystery.

Delmonico died in a closed ward of a U.S. Air Force medical complex a week later. His companions from the dig were quarantined separately. The two postgrads who had labored over the jade fragment lived another day and a half before dying within an hour of each other.

The rest of the expedition were treated and released. Each was asked to sign a paper acknowledging that the events they had witnessed were classified and that divulging those events to anyone for any reason would be punishable pursuant to the Official Secrets Act. Shaken and at a loss to make any sense of what had happened, all fourteen surviving Americans agreed to sign.

Only one of them broke his oath. Seven years after the death of William Delmonico, Werner Holden, formerly an archaeology major and now an auto parts dealer in Portland, Oregon, confessed to a professional UFO researcher that he had witnessed the recovery of a portion of the hull of a flying saucer from an archaeological site in central Turkey. The UFO researcher listened patiently to Holden's story and promised to look into it. What he did not tell Holden was that the whole crash-fragment approach had grown unfashionable—his audience expected something more intimate: abductions, metaphysics. A year later, Holden's account appeared in the researcher's book as a footnote. No legal action was taken as a consequence. Holden died of a runaway lymphoma in January of 1998.

The Jade Anomaly, as Delmonico had thought of it before his death, was retrieved from the soil of the abandoned archaeological site by a platoon of military men equipped with spades and protective clothing. They worked at night under floodlights so the sun wouldn't cook them inside their lead-lined suits. Over the course of three nights they succeeded in unearthing a gently curved piece of apparently homogeneous material 10.6 cm thick and irregular in shape. One observer said it looked like a piece of an egg shell, "if you can imagine an egg big enough to hatch a stretch limo." The fragment was highly radioactive in the wavelengths around 1 nm, but the intensity of the radiation fell away to undetectability at distances greater than a meter or so, an apparent violation of the inverse-square law that no one attempted to explain.

Arrangements were made with the Turkish government to have the material quietly removed from the country. Blanketed in lead and packed in an unmarked shipping flat, it left a NATO airbase in a Hercules transport bound for an undisclosed destination in the United States.


Alan Stern, a professor of theoretical physics and recent recipient of the Nobel prize, was approached at a conference on inflationary theory at a hotel outside Cambridge, Massachusetts, by a young man in a three-piece suit—quite an anomaly, Stern thought, among this rabble of thesis-writers, academic hacks, bearded astrophysicists, and balding cosmologists. Stern, both bearded and balding, was intrigued by the younger man's air of quiet authority, and the two of them adjourned to the bar, where the younger man disappointed Stern by offering him a job.

"I don't do classified work," he said. "If I can't publish it, it's not science. In any case, defense research is a dead end. The Cold War is over, or hasn't that news reached your Appropriations Committee?"

The younger man displayed an impenetrable patience. "This isn't, strictly speaking, a defense project."

And he explained further.

"My God," Stern said softly, when the young man had finished. "Can this be true?"

That evening, Stern sat in the audience as a Lucasian Professor of Mathematics read a paper defending the anthropic principle in the language of set theory. Bored by the lecture and still excited by what the young man had told him, Stern took a notebook from his pocket and opened it across his knee.

*God is the root of the All,* he wrote, *the Ineffable One who dwells in the Monad.*

*He dwells alone, in silence.*

The Two Rivers Physical Research Laboratory was constructed over the course of six months on a parcel of uninhabited land in northern Michigan deeded to the government by an impoverished Ojibway band.

The nearby town of Two Rivers accepted the facility without complaint. Two Rivers had begun life as a mill town, survived as a hunting and fishing town, and had recently become an alternative to the suburbs for white-collar workers who commuted by fax and modem. The main street had been refurbished with imitation brickwork and gas lights, and a gourmet coffee shop had opened up next to the Baskin-Robbins. Lately there had been complaints about water-skiers chasing the ducks out of Lake Merced. Sports fishermen complained and hired charter planes to carry them farther from the encroachments of civilization, but the town was prospering for the first time in thirty years.

The construction of the research facility provoked little comment from the Town Council. Construction crews and equipment came up the highway and approached the site from the west along a corduroy logging road, often at night. There had been some expectation that the project would create employment among the townspeople, but that hope soon flickered and dimmed. Staff were trucked in as quietly as the concrete and cinder blocks; the only local work was temporary and involved the laying of high-capacity water and power lines. Even when the facility was up and running—doing whatever clandestine work it did—its employees stayed away from town. They lived in barracks on federal property; they shopped at a PX. They came into Two Rivers to arrange fishing trips, occasionally, and one or two strangers might stop by the bars or take in a movie at the Cineplex in the highway mall; but as a rule, they didn't mingle.

One of the few townspeople who expressed any curiosity about the facility was Dexter Graham, a history teacher at John F. Kennedy High School. Graham told his fiancée, Evelyn Woodward, that the installation made no sense. "Defense spending is passé. According to the papers, all the research budgets have been slashed. But there they are. Our own little Manhattan Project."

Evelyn operated a bed-and-breakfast by the lakeside. The view, particularly from the upper bay windows, was pure postcard. Dex had ducked out of a Friday staff meeting for a session of what Evelyn called "afternoon delight," and they were savoring the aftermath—cool sheets, curtains twining in long sighs of pine-scented air. It was Evelyn who had turned the conversation to the Two Rivers Physical Research Laboratory. She had a new boarder who worked at the plant, a young man named Howard Poole.

"Amazing," Dex said, turning his long body lazily under

the cotton sheets. "Don't they have their own quarters out there? I never heard of one of these guys boarding in town."

"Don't be so cynical," Evelyn scolded him. "Howard says there's a housing problem—too much staff, short accommodation. Musical chairs, I guess, and he was left standing. He's only here for a week. Anyway, he says he wanted to see the town."

"Admirable curiosity."

Evelyn sat up and reached for her panties, vaguely annoyed. Dex possessed a deep, automatic cynicism she had begun to find unattractive. He was forty years old, and sometimes he sounded a little too much like the toothless janitor at his school, the one who was always mumbling about "the government."

The question was, would Dex give Howard Poole a hard time over dinner?

Evelyn hoped not. She liked Howard well enough. He was young, shy, bespectacled, vulnerable-looking. She was charmed by his accent. Bronx, perhaps, or Queens—places Evelyn knew mainly from her reading. She had never been east of Detroit.

She dressed and left Dex in bed, went downstairs to the kitchen and began to prepare a coq au vin and salad for herself, Dex, and her two boarders, Howard and a woman named Friedel from California. She hummed to herself as she worked, a tuneless little song that seemed to arise from the memory of what she and Dex had done in the bedroom. Sunlight tracked across the linoleum floor, the wooden chopping board.

Dinner went better than she had expected. Mrs. Friedel, a widow, did most of the talking, a gentle monologue about her trip across the country and how much her husband would have enjoyed it. The coq au vin put everyone in a benevolent mood. Or maybe it was just the weather: a fine spring evening, the first warm evening of the year. Howard Poole smiled often but spoke seldom. He sat opposite Evelyn. He ate sparingly but paid attention to the food. The vivid sunset through the dining room window was reflected in his oval glasses, disguising his eyes.

Over dessert, a cinnamon cake, Dex raised the forbidden topic. "I understand you work out at the defense plant, Howard."

Evelyn tensed. But Howard seemed to take it in stride. He shrugged his bony shoulders. "If you can call it that—a defense plant. I never thought of it that way."

"Government installation is what they call it in the paper."

"Yes."

"What exactly do you do out there?"

"I'm new to the place myself, Mr. Graham. I can't answer the question."

"Meaning it's classified?"

"Meaning I wish I knew."

Evelyn kicked Dex under the table and said brightly, "Coffee, anyone?"

"Sounds wonderful," Howard said.

And Dex just smiled and nodded.


Curiously, Mrs. Friedel had packed her bags and announced her intention to leave as soon as dinner was over. Evelyn settled the account but was worried: "You're driving after dark?"

"I wouldn't ordinarily," the widow confided. "And I don't believe in dreams—I really don't. But this one was so vivid. I was taking a nap this morning. And in the dream I was talking to Ben."

"Your husband."

"Yes. And he told me to pack and leave. He was not upset. Just a little concerned." Mrs. Friedel was blushing. "I know how this sounds. I'm not such a lunatic, Miss Woodward—you don't have to stare like that."

Now Evelyn blushed. "Oh, no. It's all right, Mrs. Friedel. Go with a hunch, that's what I always say."

But it was strange.

She took her evening walk with Dex after the dishes had been washed.

They crossed Beacon and headed for the lakeside. Gnats hovered under the streetlights, but the mosquitoes weren't a menace yet. The breeze was gentle and the air was only beginning to cool.

She said, "When we're married, you have to promise not to harass the guests"—more in reference to what *might* have happened than what *had* happened.

And Dex looked apologetic and said, "Of course. I didn't mean to badger him."

She admitted that he hadn't. It was only her apprehension: of his unyielding nature, of the grief he carried deep inside him. "I saw you biting your tongue."

"Howard seems like a nice enough kid. Bright university grad. Probably drafted by some headhunter. Maybe he really doesn't know what's going on out there."

"Maybe nothing *is* going on out there. Nothing bad, at least."

"It's possible."

"Whatever they do, I'm sure it's perfectly safe."

"So was Chernobyl. Until it blew up."

"God, you're so *paranoid*!"

He laughed at her consternation; then she laughed, too. And they walked a silent distance along the shore of Lake Merced.

Water lapped at wooden docks. The stars were bright. On the way back, Evelyn shivered and buttoned her sweater.

She said, "Are you staying over tonight?"

"If you still want me to."

"Of course I do."

And he put his arm around her waist.

Later, Dex would wonder about the remark he had made about Chernobyl.

Did it represent a premonition, like Mrs. Friedel's dream? Had his body sensed something, some subliminal input his conscious mind failed to grasp?

And then there was Evelyn's tabby cat, Roadblock. Roadblock spent the evening in a kind of frenzy, tearing around the bedroom in tight circles until Evelyn lost patience and put her out. Had the cat sensed some tenuous radiation coming across the dark water of the lake?

Perhaps. Perhaps.

He woke a little after midnight.

He hovered a moment on the fragile edge of awareness, dimly conscious of Evelyn beside him, of the way she breathed in her sleep, long delicate sighs. What had woken him? A sound, a motion . . .

Then it came again, an irregular metallic tapping—a tapping at the window.

He turned and saw the moonlit silhouette of the cat. Roadblock, out for the night, had climbed onto the garage roof and up the shingled slope to the bedroom window. Now she wanted back in. Claws on the plate glass. *Tackscratch.* "Go 'way," Dex mumbled. Wishful thinking. *Tack tack.*

He stood up and pulled on his underwear. The warmth of the day had evaporated; the bedroom was chilly. The cat stood on her hind legs, arched against the windowpane in an eerie stretch. Moonlight fell on Dex, and he turned and saw his reflection in the vanity mirror. He saw the thatch of dark hair across his chest, his large hands loose at his sides. His gaunt face lay half in shadow, eyes wide and bewildered by sleep. He would be forty-one years old in August. Old man.

He unlatched the window. Roadblock leaped inside and raced across the carpet, more frantic than ever. The cat jumped on the bed and Evelyn stirred in her sleep. "Dex?" she murmured. "What—?" And rolled over, sighing.

He leaned out into the cool night air.

The town was silent. Two Rivers closed down after midnight, even on a warm Friday. The sound of traffic had faded. He heard the warble of a loon out on the deeps of Lake Merced. Trees flush with new leaves moved in tides of night air. Somewhere down Beacon Road, a dog barked.

Then, suddenly, inexplicably, a beam of light flashed across the sky. It came from the east, across the lake, far away in the abandoned Ojibway reserve—from the defense plant, Dex realized. The light cast sudden shadows, like lightning; it flickered on the lake. The bedroom was aglow with it.

A spotlight? A flare? He couldn't make sense of it.

Evelyn sat up in alarm, all the way awake now. "Dex, what's going on?"

There was no time to answer. He saw a second beam of light cut the meridian of the sky, and a third, so sharply defined he thought they must be laser beams . . . maybe some kind of weapon being tested out there . . . and then the light expanded like a bubble, seemed to include everything around it, the lake, the town, Evelyn's bedroom, Dex himself. The room, bathed in light, began abruptly to spin, to tilt on an invisible axis and slide away, until his awareness dwindled to a point, a pulsating singularity in a wilderness of light.

The town of Two Rivers, Michigan, and the federally funded research project on its outskirts vanished from the earth some hours before dawn on a Saturday morning late in May.

The fires began not long after.

The fires were useful when it was time to explain what had happened. The obliteration of a town the size of Two Rivers requires a great deal of explanation, and the existence of the military facility on the abandoned Indian lands had not been a secret (though its purpose had never been revealed). It was the desire of the Defense Department that these awkward truths not be connected. Both the town and the research project were lost in the fire, officials announced. It had not been one fire but several; unseasonal, unexpected, the product perhaps of freakish heat lightning. The fires had surrounded the town and grown with unprecedented speed. There was no defense against such a holocaust. Most of Bayard County was simply incinerated. More lives had been lost than in any natural disaster in American history, tens of thousands of lives. Commissions of inquiry were established and carefully staffed.

Questions were inevitable, of course. An American town the size of Two Rivers represents a substantial deposit of stone, asphalt, concrete, and steel—it can't simply burn to the ground. Where were the foundations, the chimneys, the stonework, the bricks? Where, in fact, were the *roads*? Barricades had been thrown up before the fire was extinguished, and they stayed in place long after. Battalions of federal bulldozers had moved in immediately—to clear the highway, officials said; but one retired civil engineer who lived east of the fireline said it looked to him like they were *rebuilding* that road.

And there were other mysteries: the sighting of curious lights; the interruption of phone service to and from Two Rivers long before the fire could have grown to threatening size; the fifteen civilian witnesses who claimed they had approached the town from the east or west and found the highway cut cleanly, as if by some enormous knife, and nothing on the other side but trees and wilderness. Power lines had been severed just as neatly, and it was the loose lines, some said, that were the real cause of the fire.

But these were clues that defied interpretation, and they were soon forgotten, except by the fringe element who collected stories of ghosts, rains of stones, and the spontaneous combustion of human bodies.

Never officially connected with the Two Rivers disaster was the case of Wim Pender, who was found wandering in a dazed condition along the grassy verge of Highway 75. Pender claimed he had been on a fishing/camping expedition in "the north of the Province of Mille Lacs" with two companions, from whom he had been separated when there was "a blast of light and flames to the south of us late one night."

Pender gave as his home address a number on a nonexistent Boston street. His wallet and identification had been lost in his flight from the fire. His pack contained only an empty canteen, two cans of something labeled THON PALE EN MORCEAUX (tuna fish, it turned out), and an apocryphal testament of the Bible entitled *The Secret Booke of James in the English Tongue,* printed on rice paper and bound in imitation leather.

When Pender's claims grew even more fantastic—including the accusation that both the Forest Service and the Michigan Department of Welfare were "Mohammedans or servants of Samael or worse"—he was remanded for psychiatric evaluation to a facility in Lansing.

Mr. Pender was deemed not to be a danger to himself or others and was released on June 23. He made his way to Detroit, where he spent the summer in a shelter for the homeless.

November was cold that year, and during an early snowfall Pender left his bed and spent his last money on a city bus, because the buses were heated. The bus carried him downriver to Southgate, where he got off in front of a bankrupt and abandoned retail lumber outlet. In the upper story of that building he tied his belt into a crude loop and hanged himself from a rafter.

Pinned to his shirt was a note:

THE KYNGDOM OF DEATH BELONGS TO
THOSE WHO PUT THEM SELVES TO DEATH.
JAMES THE APOSTLE.
I AM NOT INSANE.
SIGNED, WIM PENDER OF BOSTON

# Mysterium

PART
ONE

The void that precedes the creation of the universe is an imponderable, unknowing emptiness—lacking matter, vacuum, time, motion, number, or logic. And yet the universe derives from it according to some law not yet understood—a law which, governing nothingness, yields everything!

Call it Nous. Perfect Mind. Call it the Protennoia. The Uncreated God.

—from the secret journal of Alan Stern

# CHAPTER 1

Dex Graham woke with the sun in his eyes and the weave of Evelyn Woodward's bedroom carpet printed on the side of his face. He was cold and his body was stiff and knotted with aches.

He sat up, wondering what had caused him to spend the night on the floor. He hadn't slept on a floor since college. The morning after some nightmarish frat party blowout, drunk on the floor of a dorm room and wondering what happened to the strawberry blond grad student who had offered him a ride in her Mustang. Vanished in the haze. Like so much else.

A breath of cool air made him shiver. The bay window was wide open. Had he done that? The curtains tossed fitfully and the sky was as blue as china glaze. It was a quiet morning; there was no sound louder than the honking of Canada geese in the shallow water under the docks.

He stood up, a slow operation, and looked at Evelyn. She was awkwardly asleep under a tangle of cotton sheets. One arm was flung out and Roadblock lay stretched at her feet.

Had he been drunk? Was that possible? He felt the way he remembered feeling after a drunk—the same sensation of bad news hovering just out of reach, the night's ill omens about to unreel in his head.

And he turned to the window and thought: *Ah, God, yes —the defense plant.*

He remembered the beams of light stabbing the sky, the way the bedroom had begun to pinwheel around him.

Beyond the window, Lake Merced was calm. The docks shimmered under a gloss of hazy sunlight. The masts of pleasure boats bobbed randomly, listlessly. And due east— beyond the pines that crowded the far margin of the lake— a plume of smoke rose from the old Ojibway reservation.

He stared for a time, trying to sort out the implications. The memory of Chernobyl came again. Obviously, there had been an accident at the Two Rivers plant. He had no way of knowing what *kind* of accident. What he had seen had not looked like a nuclear explosion but might have been something just as catastrophic, a meltdown, say. He watched the smoke make a lazy spindle in the cool air. The breeze was brisk and from the west; if there was fallout it wouldn't travel into town—at least not today.

But what happened last night had been more than an explosion. Something had rendered him unconscious for most of six or seven hours. And he wasn't the only one. Look at Beacon Road, empty except for a scatter of starlings. The docks and boat ramps were naked in the sunlight. No boaters or dawn fishermen had taken to Lake Merced.

He turned to the bed, suddenly frightened. "Evelyn? Ev, are you awake?"

To his enormous relief, she stirred and sighed. Her eyes opened and she winced at the light.

"Dex," she said. "Oh-um." She yawned. *"Pull the drapes."*

"Time to get up, Evie."

"Um?" She raised herself on an elbow and squinted at the alarm clock. "Oh my God! *Breakfast!*" She stood up, a little unsteady on her feet, and pulled on a housecoat. "I *know* I set that alarm! People must be starving!"

The alarm was an ancient windup model. Maybe she *had* set it, Dex thought. Maybe it went off smack at seven, and maybe it rang until it ran down.

He thought: *We might already be dying of radiation poisoning. How would we know? Do we start to vomit?* But he felt all right. He felt like he'd slept on the floor, not like he'd been poisoned.

Evelyn hurried into the en suite bathroom and came back looking puzzled. "The light's out in there."

He tried the wall switch. The bedroom light didn't work, either.

"House fuse," she pondered, "or it might be a power failure . . . Dex, why do you look so funny?" Her frown deepened. "You were at the window last night, weren't you? I remember now. You let Roadblock in. . . ."

He nodded.

"And there was lightning. An electric storm? Maybe that's why the power is out. Lightning could have hit the transformer over by City Hall. Last time that happened we were in the dark for six hours."

By way of an answer he took her hand and led her to the window. She shaded her eyes and looked across the lake. "That smoke is the defense plant," he said. "Something must have happened there last night. It wasn't lightning, Ev. Some kind of explosion, I think."

"Is that why there's no electricity?" Now her voice took on a timorous note and he felt her grip tighten on his hand.

He said, "I don't know. Maybe. The smoke is blowing away from us, anyway. I think that's good."

"I don't hear any sirens. If there's a fire, shouldn't there be sirens?"

"Fire company may be there already."

"I didn't hear any sirens during the night. The fire hall's just down on Armory. It always wakes me up when they run the sirens at night. Did *you* hear anything?"

He admitted he hadn't.

"Dex, it's *way* too quiet. It's a little scary."

He said, "Let's do something about breakfast. Maybe we can run that little battery radio in the kitchen, find out what's going on."

It seemed as if she weighed the suggestion and found it weak but adequate. "Everybody needs to eat, I guess. All right. Let me finish dressing."


It was the off-season, of course, and with Mrs. Friedel gone, Howard Poole was the sole remaining guest—and Howard hadn't come down to breakfast.

The stove was electric. Evelyn rummaged in the warming refrigerator. "I think we're reduced to cereal," she said. "Until the milk spoils, anyway."

Dex opened the utility cupboard and found Evelyn's Panasonic radio. The batteries weren't fresh, but they might still hold a charge. He put the radio on the kitchen table, pulled its antenna to full length, and switched it on.

There was a crackle of static where WQBX used to be. So the batteries were good, Dex thought, but there was no broadcast coming out of Coby, some fifty miles west, where the relay tower was. The nearest actual radio station was in Port Auburn, and neither Dex nor Evelyn cared for its round-the-clock country-and-western music. But it would do, he thought, and he turned the dial clockwise.

Nothing.

Evelyn said, "There must be something wrong with it."

Maybe. It seemed unlikely to Dex, but what other explanation made sense? Ten years ago he might have guessed there'd been some kind of nuclear war, the doomsday scenario everybody used to dread, that it had wiped out everything beyond the horizon. But that possibility was slim. Even if some Russian had pushed some antiquated red button, it wouldn't have destroyed the entire civilized world. Surely it wouldn't have wiped out Port Auburn or even closed down the radio station there.

An explosion at the Two Rivers plant and a radio with a dead transistor. He wanted to make a logical connection between the two, but could not.

He was still turning the dial when Howard Poole came into the kitchen. Howard was wearing a white T-shirt, Saturday jeans with a rip starting at the left knee, and an expression of sleepy bewilderment. "Must have missed breakfast," he said.

"Nope. Cold cereal," Evelyn said briskly, "and we haven't really started yet. The power's off, you may have noticed."

"Trouble at the defense plant," Dex put in.

Howard's attention perked up instantly. "What kind of trouble?"

"Some kind of explosion during the night, from what I could see upstairs. There's smoke coming off it now. The town's pretty much still asleep. And I can't find anything on the radio."

Howard sat down at the table. He seemed to have trouble absorbing the information. "Jesus," he said. "Fire at the research facility?"

"I believe so."

"Jesus."

Now Dex caught something on the radio. It was a voice, a masculine rumble distorted by static, too faint to decipher. He turned up the volume but the intelligibility didn't improve.

"Put the radio on top of the refrigerator," Evelyn said. "It always works better up there."

He did so. The reception was marginally better, but the

station faded in and out. Nevertheless, the three of them strained to hear what they could.

And for a time, the broadcast was quite clear.

Moments later it faded altogether. Dex took the radio down and switched it off.

Evelyn said, "Did anyone understand *any* of that?"

"It sounded like a newscast," Howard said cautiously.

"Or a radio play," Evelyn said. "That's what I thought of."

Dex shook his head. "There hasn't been a radio play on the air since 1950. Howard's right. It was a news broadcast."

"But I thought—" Evelyn gave a small, puzzled laugh. "I thought the announcer said something about 'the Spaniards.' A war with the Spaniards."

"He did," Dex said.

For a few moments, the announcer's bored voice had risen from the rattle of noise and distance into rough intelligibility. *Issued* was the first word Dex had understood.

*. . . . issued reports of great successes along the Jalisco front in the war with the Spaniards. Casualties were light and the cities of Colima and Manzanillo are under Allied control. In the Bahia, amphibian landings—*

Then the swell of electronic noise buried the voice.

"Pardon me," Howard said, "but what the hell kind of accent was that? Guy sounds like a Norwegian funeral director on Quaaludes. And excuse me, but *Spaniards*? It's like the news from 1898. It has to be a joke. Or, Evelyn's right, some kind of radio drama."

"Like last Halloween," Evelyn put in, "when they played a tape of the old Orson Welles *War of the Worlds*."

"It's not Halloween," Dex said.

She gave him an angry glare. "So what are you saying, that it's legitimate? We're suddenly at war with *Spain*?"

"I don't know. I don't understand it. I don't know what the hell it's about, Evie. But let's not make up an explanation when we don't have one."

"Is that what you think I'm doing?" She raised her voice, and it might have become an argument—not a real argument, Dex thought, but one of those peevish debates with more of fear than hostility in it—but she was interrupted by the keening of the Two Rivers Volunteer Fire Department, both trucks rolling out of the Armory Street fire hall and speeding past on Beacon Road.

"Well, thank God," she said. "Somebody's doing something at last."

"Wait a minute," Howard said, and there was an expression of sick foreboding on his face.

"It's the fire department," Evelyn told him. "They must be headed for the Indian reserve."

"God, no," Howard said. And Dex watched in perplexity as the younger man stood and ran for the door.


Dick Haldane struggled out of a confused sleep at eight A.M., and from the front window of his house, with the view overlooking the brickworks and the west end of Lake Merced, he saw smoke rising from the old Ojibway reserve.

Haldane had the misfortune of being the acting chief of the Two Rivers Volunteer Fire Department. The chief and most of the Fire Board trustees were in Detroit until Monday for a conference on ISO grading policy. And it looked as if an emergency had fallen into his lap in the meantime: the electricity didn't work and neither did the phones. Perhaps worse, there was no water pressure in the bathroom— the toilet gave a sad last gasp when he flushed it. Two Rivers took its water pressure from a reservoir in the highlands north of the Bayard County line, so this might be a local problem . . . but it might not, and the idea of a major fire without the means to fight it was one of Haldane's personal bad dreams. Lacking alternatives, he hopped into his aging Pontiac LeMans and drove like hell to the Beacon Road fire hall.

The Two Rivers Physical Research Laboratory—obvious

source of the smoke—was supposed to have its own fire control team, and certainly no one had told Haldane the facility was inside his response area. Quite the opposite. The Department of Defense had had a long talk with the Municipal Fire Service. They didn't want volunteer brigades on the property unless they were specifically called for, and according to the DOD's Man in a Suit, that was about as likely as a 911 call from God Almighty.

Still that smoke kept on curling into a lazy sky.

Haldane kept the night shift on duty and waited for the morning crew to arrive. A couple of Honda generators in the basement provided AC for the dispatcher's radio, but there was nobody talking back. He made a couple of attempts to reach City Hall and the mayor at home, but it was no go. This whole mess was squarely on his back.

There had been a fire in the National Forest land north of town in 1962, when Haldane was twenty years old, and he had been among the men cutting the firebreak. He had witnessed many fires since, but none as terrifying. He imagined the Ojibway reserve as it had been before the feds moved in: weedy meadowland and tall wild pine, a few shacks where the traditionals still persisted in their old ways. Those shacks had been razed and a perimeter drawn on the county maps: DOD, Enter at Your Own Risk, Here There Be Tygers. But a fire, as Haldane told his troops, observes no limits. A fire goes where it feels like.

This fire didn't look all that serious, at least not yet, not from here, but still—he didn't want anybody saying a forest burned down because Dick Haldane was waiting on a telephone call.

He kept the engine company at home but dispatched a ladder company to survey the scene. He followed behind in the chief's car, a red station wagon with a roof light.

The siren cut the Saturday quiet like a hot, sharp knife. Not that there was much traffic to get in the way. Two Rivers was slow to wake this peculiar morning. He saw a few people on their porches out to stare at the ladder truck, a few kids in their PJs. No doubt they were wondering whether the TV would begin to work pretty soon—or the telephones. Haldane was troubled by the same question. There was no sign of an emergency except that smoke from the federal project, but how could a fire out there, even a bad fire, shut down so much of Two Rivers? Some kind of power surge, he supposed, or maybe a dead short across those kilovolt lines that had gone in last year. But he had never seen anything like it in his career, that was for sure.

They were quickly out of the crowded part of town, three miles down the highway and then east along the wide dirt road. All the federal money pouring in, couldn't they have paved the access? Haldane's kidneys protested this rattling. The woods were dense here, and although he saw the plume of smoke now and again, there was no clear line of sight to the plant itself until the road crossed a ridgeline overlooking the site.

He topped the rise and stood on the brake too hard. Even so, he only just managed to avoid ramming the rear end of the ladder unit. Who was driving? Tom Stubbs, as he recalled. Stubbs, too, was probably transfixed by what he was suddenly able to see.

The Two Rivers Physical Research Laboratory was a nucleus of low concrete bunkers in an asphalt-paved flatland where the old social hall used to be. At the extreme north of this paved space stood a tall administration building; at the south, a residence that looked like a stucco apartment complex misplaced from some L.A. suburb.

Two of the bunkerlike buildings had been damaged in some kind of explosion. The walls were blackened and the roofs were in a state of partial collapse. From the most central and badly damaged structure, that pall of oily smoke curled into the sky. No open flame was visible.

But that wasn't the astonishing thing. The astonishing thing, Chief Haldane thought, was the way all of this property was enclosed in a veil of diaphanous blue light.

A few years ago Haldane had taken his vacation time in

northern Ontario, along with two guys from the fire hall and a realtor from the west side of town. They went fly fishing in the lake country north of Superior, and for a solid week they had achieved a nearly ideal balance of sport, intoxication, and masculine bullshit. But what Haldane remembered best was a chilly, clear night when he looked up into a sky jammed with stars and saw the aurora borealis dancing on the horizon.

It was this same kind of light. Same elusive haze of color, now here, now there. He had never expected to see it in daylight. Certainly he had never expected to see it enfolding this collection of bunkers and brickwork like some kind of science fiction force field.

It was a smoky, uncertain light. Mostly you could see through it, but it obscured a detail here and there. And Haldane noticed another peculiarity: the longer you stared at something inside that glow, the less you seemed to see of it. He fixed his eyes on the burning building, perhaps a thousand yards down this hill and across the asphalt. It wavered in his sight. After ten seconds, he might have been staring at a blank scrim of color.

He shook his head to clear it.

The radio crackled. It was Stubbs, calling from the truck ahead. Haldane picked up the microphone and said, "You scared the piss out of me, I hope you're aware of that."

Stubbs's voice came crackling out of a deep well of static. He sounded like he was miles away, not a couple of yards. "Chief, what the hell *is* that? What do we do, turn back?"

"I don't see anybody fighting the fire."

"Maybe we should wait for the state cops or somebody."

"Grow some balls, Tom. Take your foot off the brake."

The ladder company inched forward.


Clifford Stockton, twelve years old, spotted the smoke about the same time Chief Haldane did.

Clifford, who was still called "Cliffy" by his mother and a mob of aunts, saw the smoke from his bedroom window. He stood in his pajamas watching it for a while, not sure whether it was important. He wanted it to be some dire omen, as in the disaster movies he loved—like the flaky pressure gauge nobody notices in *The Last Voyage,* or the snowstorm that just won't quit in the first *Airport* movie.

It was a great beginning for Clifford's Saturday, cue for any number of Clifford-scripts. He began orchestrating the movie in his head. "Little did anyone suspect," he said out loud. Little did anyone suspect . . . *what?* But he hadn't figured that out yet.

His mother always slept late Saturday. Clifford pulled on yesterday's jeans and the first T-shirt in his T-shirt drawer, cleaned his foggy glasses with a Kleenex, and went downstairs to watch TV. Whereupon he discovered the electricity didn't work. Not just in the living room, either, but in the kitchen, the hallway, the bathroom. And for the first time Clifford paused and wondered if it was possible, not in the world of wouldn't-it-be-cool-if but in the real dailiness of his life . . . if something *really weird* might actually be happening.

He remembered being awakened by lightning, a diffuse lightning without thunder; remembered drifting in and out of a confused sleep with light all around him.

He decided to check on his mother. He padded back to the dim upstairs of their rented house and eased open her bedroom door. Clifford's mother was a thin and not very beautiful woman of thirty-seven years, but he had never looked at her critically and he didn't do so now. She was only his mother, dangerous if awakened too soon from her Saturday morning sleep-in.

Saturday morning drill was that she was allowed to sleep till ten o'clock, and if Clifford was up early he could do whatever he wanted—get his own breakfast, watch TV, play outside the house if he left a note and was back by noon for lunch. Today was different, obviously, but he guessed the rules still applied. He wrote her a message—*I have gone to ride my bike*—and stuck it to the refrigerator with a strawberry-shaped magnet.

Then he hurried outside, locked the door, grabbed his bike and pedaled south toward the bridge over Powell Creek.

He was looking for clues. There was a fire on the old Ojibway reserve and the lights didn't work. A mystery.

Two Rivers seemed too quiet to yield any answers. Then, as he crossed the creek and rolled toward downtown, Clifford wondered if the very quietness was itself a clue. No one was mowing his lawn or washing the car. Houses brooded with their drapes still drawn. The sun shimmered on an empty road.

He heard the sirens when the fire engines went screaming along Beacon and out of town.

It was, he thought, almost *too much* like a movie.

He stopped at Ryan's, a corner grocery that had been taken over last year by a Korean family named Sung. Mrs. Sung was behind the counter—a small, round woman with her eyes buried in nets of wrinkles.

Clifford bought a candy bar and a comic book with the money from yesterday's allowance. Mrs. Sung took his money and made change from a shoebox: "Machine not working," she said, meaning the cash register.

"How come?" Clifford said. "Do you know?"

She only shrugged and frowned.

Clifford rode away. He stopped at the public park overlooking Powell Creek to eat the candy bar. Breakfast. He chose a sunny patch of grass where he could see the north end of town. The town was waking up, but in a slow, lazy way. A few more cars were prowling the streets. More shops had opened their doors. The distant plume of smoke continued to rise, but it was unhurried and unchanged.

Clifford crumpled the paper candy bar wrapper and stuffed it into his shirt pocket. He took the cardboard liner down to the creek and let it float away. It tumbled over a rock and capsized. It was the *Titanic* in *A Night to Remember*. The unsinkable ship.

He climbed the embankment and looked again at Two Rivers—the town where nothing much ever happened.

The *unsinkable* town.

He checked his watch. Twenty after eleven. He rode home, wondering whether his mother was up and had found the note; she might be worried, he thought. He dropped the bike in the driveway and hurried inside.

But she was only just awake, tangle-haired in her pink bathrobe and fumbling over the coffee maker.

"Damn thing doesn't work," she said. "Oh, hello, Cliffy."


Between breakfast and lunch, Dex Graham formulated the same idea as Clifford Stockton: he would go out and survey the town.

He left Evelyn in the kitchen and promised he'd be back by noon.

He drove west on Beacon to his own apartment, one bedroom in a thirty-year-old building, sparsely furnished. He owned a sofa bed, a fourteen-inch TV set, and a desk where last week's history papers waited to be graded. Yesterday's breakfast dishes were stacked in the drainer. It was a collation of postponed chores, not a home. He checked to see whether his lights were working. They weren't. So the problem wasn't confined to Evelyn's house or street—it wasn't only local. Somehow, he had doubted that it would be.

He picked up the phone, thought about calling somebody from the school—but his phone was as dead as Evelyn's had been.

Back to reconnaissance, he thought. He locked the door behind him.

He drove downtown. The streets were still too empty, the town sluggish for a Saturday morning, but at least a few

people were moving around. He supposed the blackout had
kept a lot of people home. The big stores were closed by the
power outage, but some of the smaller businesses had managed to open—Tilson's Grocery was open, illuminated by
daylight through the broad glass front windows and a couple of battery-powered lanterns in the dim corner where the
freezer was. Dex stopped to pick up some groceries. Evelyn
had asked for canned goods, anything nonperishable, and
he thought that was a good idea; there was no way to pre-
dict how long this crisis might last or what its nature might
turn out to be.

He filled a handbasket with canned vegetables and was
about to pick up a bottle of distilled water when a man
shoved in front of him and took two jugs. "Hey," Dex said.

The stranger was a big man in a hunting jacket and a
John Deere cap. He gave Dex a blank look and took the
bottled water to the checkout counter, where he added it to
a formidable stack of canned goods—the same sort of thing
Dex had come for, but more of it.

The girl behind the counter was Meg Tilson, who had
graduated from Dex's history class last year. She said, "Are
you sure you want all this?"

The man was sweating and a little breathless. "All of it.
How much?"

The register was down, of course, so Meg began to total
everything on a pocket calculator. Dex lined up behind the
man. "You seem to be in a hurry." Another blank look. The
man was dazed, Dex thought. He persisted: "So you know
something we don't know?"

The man in the John Deere cap turned away as if the
question frightened him, but then seemed to relent: "Shit,"
he said, "I'm sorry if I got in your way. I'm just . . ."

"Stocking up?"

"You bet."

"Any particular reason?"

"A hundred seventy-six eighty," Meg announced. "At
least I think so."

The man pulled two hundred-dollar bills out of his pocket while Meg, stunned, rummaged in a shoebox for change.

"I was supposed to drive to Detroit this morning," the man said. "For my sister's wedding. I wake up late, so I throw the tux in the back seat and I drive out Beacon and turn south on the highway, right? But I only get about a mile and a quarter past the city limits."

"The road's blocked?"

The man laughed. "The road's not *blocked*. The road just ain't there. It *stops*. It's like somebody cut it with a knife. It ends in trees. I mean old growth. There's not even a trail through there." He looked at Dex. "How the hell could that happen?"

Dex shook his head.

Meg put the groceries in two boxes and gave the man his change. Her eyes were wide and frightened.

"I think we're in for a long siege," said the man in the John Deere cap. "I think that's pretty fucking obvious."

Meg toted up Dex's bill, all the while casting nervous glances at the man as he loaded his boxes into the back of an old Chevy van. "Mr. Graham? Is what he said true?"

"I don't know, Meg. It doesn't seem likely."

"But the electricity doesn't work. Or the phones. So maybe—"

"Anything's possible, but let's not jump to conclusions."

She looked at his collection of canned goods and bottled water, not too different from the previous order. "Should we all be—you know, stocking up?"

"I don't honestly know. Is your father around?"

"Upstairs."

"Maybe you should tell him what happened. If any of this is true, or even if rumors start flying, there might be a crowd in here by this afternoon."

"I'll do that," Meg said. "Here's your change, Mr. Graham."

He put the groceries in the trunk of the car. It might

have been wiser to go straight back to Evelyn's, but he couldn't let the matter rest. He drove past the house on Beacon, connected with the highway and turned south.

He passed a couple of cars headed in the opposite direction. Through traffic, Dex wondered? Or had they hit the mysterious barrier and turned back? He decided he didn't believe the John Deere man's story; it was simply too implausible . . . but *something* might have turned the man around, perhaps something connected with the power failure and the explosion on the old reserve.

The state highway wound through low pine punctuated with back roads where tar paper shacks and ancient cabins crumbled in the noon heat. He saw the city limits sign, LEAVING TWO RIVERS; a billboard ad for a Stuckey's ahead where the state road met the interstate; LEAVING BAYARD COUNTY. Then he rounded a tight curve and almost rammed the back end of a Honda Civic parked with one wheel in the breakdown lane. He stomped the brake and steered hard left.

When the car came to a stop he let it idle a few minutes. Then, when it occurred to him to do so, he put it in park and switched off the muttering engine.

Everything the man had said was true.

Three vehicles had arrived here before him: the Civic, a blue Pinto with a roof rack, and a tall diesel cab without a trailer. All three were motionless. Their owners stood at the end of the road, huddled in confusion: a woman with a toddler, a man in a business suit, and the truck driver. They looked at Dex as he climbed out of his car.

Dex went to the place where the road ended. He wanted to make a careful observation; wanted to be able to describe this with scientific accuracy to Howard Poole, the graduate physics student back at Evelyn's. It seemed important, in this senseless moment, to register every detail.

The highway simply stopped. It was as if someone had drawn a surveyor's line across it. On this side, two-lane blacktop; on that side—old-growth forest.

The road seemed to have been cut by something much finer than a knife. Only a few particles of asphalt had crumbled. The graded road was lower than the forest floor on the other side. A hump of loamy soil rose above the road surface and had dropped crumbs of moss and composted pine needles onto it. The smell of the soil was rich and strong. Dex picked up a handful. It was moist and compacted easily in his fist. It had been here a long, long time.

An earthworm crawled across the white divider by his knee, sublimely indifferent.

The truck driver ground a cigarette under the heel of his boot and said, "It's real, all right. Nobody's driving south today."

Beyond this line of demarcation there was no road and had never been any road. That much was obvious. The forest was deep and trackless. Not so much as a deer trail passed through here, Dex thought.

"It doesn't seem possible," said the woman from the Pinto. She was hugging herself and kept glancing at the forest, furtively, as if it might disappear between peeks. The toddler pressed at her thigh.

"It *isn't* possible," said the man in the business suit. "I mean, there it is. But it's not, I mean, *possible*. I don't think *possible* has anything to do with it."

Still cataloging details, Dex went to the side of the road where a string of telephone poles followed the right-of-way. The phone lines had been sliced as neatly as the road. The wires dangled limply from the poles.

"That's not all," the truck driver said. "Even the trees don't match. This side's been burned off a couple of times, I think. Over there it's all old growth. Go a little ways in that direction, there's an old pine sliced right up the middle. All the heartwood exposed and the sap leakin' out. The bugs aren't at it yet, so it must have happened just recently. Like last night."

Dex said, "You come from out of town?"

"Yeah, but I spent the night in Two Rivers. Had the

alternator replaced. I sure as hell wish I could leave, but it's
the same at the other end of the highway, about three miles
beyond the quarry. Dead end. I think we're locked in, unless there's some side road they missed."

"They?"

"Whoever did this. Or *what*ever. You know what I
mean. Maybe there's still a way out of town, but I doubt it."

The woman repeated, "How is that possible?" By the
expression on the truck driver's face, Dex guessed she had
been saying it for a while now.

He couldn't blame her. It was the right question, he
thought. In a way, it was the *only* question. But he couldn't
answer it; and he felt his own great fear treading on the
heels of the mystery.


Howard Poole chased the ladder company as far as the
old Ojibway reserve. As he came over the rise where Chief
Haldane and his crew had recently been, and as he saw the
research installation in its veil of blue light, a memory came
to him unbidden.

It was a memory of something Alan Stern had said to
him one night—Stern the physicist, who might have perished in the trouble last night; Stern, his uncle.

Howard had been sixteen years old, a math prodigy
with a keen interest in high-energy physics, about to be
launched into an academic fast track that both excited and
frightened him. Stern had come to visit for a week that
summer. He was a celebrity: Alan Stern had appeared in
*Time* magazine, "preeminent among a new generation of
American scientists," photographed against a line of radio
telescopes somewhere out west. He had been interviewed
on public television and had published journal articles so
dense with mathematics that they looked like untranslated
Greek papyruses. At sixteen, Howard had worshiped his
uncle without reservation.

Stern had come to the house in Queens, bald and extravagantly bearded, infinitely patient with family gossip, courteous at the dinner table and modest about his career. Howard had learned to cultivate his own patience. Sooner or later, he knew, he would be left alone with his uncle; and the conversation would begin as it always began, Stern smiling his strange conspirator's smile and asking, "So what have you learned about the world?"

They sat on the back porch watching fireflies, a Saturday night in August, and Stern dazed him with starry sweeps of science: the ideas of Hawking, Guth, Linde, himself. Howard liked the way such talk made him feel both small and large—dwarfed by the night sky and at the same time a part of it.

Then, when the talk had begun to lull, his uncle turned to him and said, "Do you ever wonder, Howard, about the questions we can't ask?"

"Can't answer, you mean?"

"No. Can't *ask*."

"I don't understand."

Stern leaned back in his deck chair and folded his hands over his gaunt, ascetic frame. His glasses were opaque in the porch light. The crickets seemed suddenly loud.

"Think about a dog," he said. "Think about *your* dog— what's his name?"

"Albert."

"Yes. Think about Albert. He's a healthy dog, is he not?"

"Yes."

"Intelligent?"

"Sure."

"He functions in every way normally, then, within the parameters of dogness. He's an exemplar of his species. And he has the ability to learn, yes? He can do tricks? Learn from his experience? And he's aware of his surroundings; he can distinguish between you and your mother, for instance? He's not unconscious or impaired?"

"Right."

"But despite all that, there's a limit on his understanding. Obviously so. If we talk about gravitons or Fourier transforms, he can't follow the conversation. We're speaking a language he doesn't know and *cannot* know. The concepts can't be translated; his mental universe simply won't contain them."

"Granted," Howard said. "Am I missing the point?"

"We're sitting here," Stern said, "asking spectacular questions, you and I. About the universe and how it began. About everything that exists. And if we can ask a question, probably, sooner or later, we can answer it. So we assume there's no limit to knowledge. But maybe your dog makes the same mistake! He doesn't know what lies beyond the neighborhood, but if he found himself in a strange place he would approach it with the tools of comprehension available to him, and soon he *would* understand it—dog-fashion, by sight and smell and so on. There are no limits to his comprehension, Howard, except the limits he does not and cannot ever experience. So how different are we? We're mammals within the same broad compass of evolution, after all. Our forebrains are bigger, but the difference amounts to a few ounces. We can ask many, many more questions than your dog. And we can answer them. But if there are real limits on our comprehension, they would be as invisible to us as they are to Albert. So: Is there anything in the universe we simply *cannot know*? Is there a question we can't ask? And would we ever encounter some hint of it, some intimation of the mystery? Or is it permanently beyond our grasp?"

His uncle stood and stretched, peered over the porch railing at the dark street and yawned. "It's a question for philosophers, not physicists. But I confess, it interests me."

It interested Howard, too. It haunted him all that night. He lay in bed pondering the limits of human knowledge, while the stars burned in his window and a slow breeze cooled his forehead.

∞

He never forgot the conversation. Neither did his uncle. Stern mentioned it when he invited Howard to join him at the Two Rivers research facility.

"It's nepotism," Howard said. "Besides—do I *want* this job? Everyone talks about you, you know. Alan Stern, disappeared into some government program, what a waste."

"You want this job," his uncle told him. "Howard, you remember a conversation we once had?"

And he had recalled it, almost word for word.

Howard gave his uncle a long look. "You mean to say you're pursuing this question?"

"More. We've touched it. The Mystery." Stern was grinning—a little wildly, Howard thought. "We've put our hands on it. That's all I can say for now. Think about it. Call me if you're interested."

Fascinated despite himself—and lacking a better offer—Howard had called.

He had been investigated, approved, entered onto the DOD payroll; he had shown up three days ago and toured a part of the facility . . . but no one had explained its essential purpose, the fundamental reason for these endless rooms, computers, concrete bunkers and steel doors. Even his uncle had remained aloof, had smiled distantly: *it will all be clear in time.*

He came over the rise and saw the buildings gilded with blue light; saw the smoke rising from the central bunker. Worse, he saw a fire department ladder truck and chase car inching down the access road, the image fluid and indistinct.

He could not imagine what this veil of light might mean. He knew only that it represented some disaster, some tragedy of a bizarre and peculiar kind. No one was moving in the complex, at least no one out in the open. The facility had its own fire control team, but it wasn't anywhere near the smoldering central bunker—at least, as far as Howard could tell. The blue light made his head swim.

Maybe they were all dead. Including his uncle, he thought. Alan Stern had been at the center of this project, that much had been obvious; Stern had been its lord, its shaman, its guiding presence. If the accident was lethal it would have taken Stern first of all. All this fluorescence suggested some kind of radiation, though nothing Howard could pin down—something powerful enough to kick photons out of the air. He knew there was radioactive material at the facility. He had seen the warning labels on the closed bunkers. They had given him a film badge as soon as he passed the gate.

That was why he'd chased the Two Rivers VFD all the way out here. He didn't think small-town volunteer firemen were trained or equipped to fight radioactive fires. Most likely they weren't even aware of the danger. They might blunder into an event more deadly than they could guess. So Howard had jumped into his car and rushed after, meaning to warn them—still meaning to.

But he saw the trucks hesitate and stop, then reverse, wobble, retreat.

He drove down the hillside to meet them.

Assistant Chief Haldane saw the civilian automobile come over the rise, but he was too dazed to worry about it. He had climbed out of his car, vomited once into the young weeds by the side of the road, then sat on a wedge of natural granite with his head in his hands and his stomach still churning.

He didn't want to see anyone, didn't want to speak to anyone. What mattered was that he was beyond the border of blue light, that he had found his way back into the world of sanity. His relief was immense. He took deep, cleansing gulps of air. Pretty soon he would be back in his sane house in the sane town of Two Rivers and this nightmare would be over. All these buildings could burn to the ground as far as he was concerned—the better if they did.

"Chief?"

He spat on the ground to clear the taste of puke from his mouth. Then he looked up. Standing before him in blue jeans and a pressed cotton shirt was a civilian, presumably the man from the automobile—more like a boy, though, Haldane thought, with his pink skin and his bug-eye glasses. Haldane didn't speak, only waited for this apparition to justify its presence.

"I'm Howard Poole," the civilian said. "I work at the facility. Or I was supposed to—I would be, if this hadn't happened. I came because I thought, if you were fighting the fire, you might not know—there might be some radioactivity in there, some particulate matter in the smoke."

Poole seemed exquisitely uneasy. "Particulate matter," Haldane said. "Well, thank you, Mr. Poole, but I don't believe particulate matter is our problem right now."

"I saw you turn back."

"Yessir," Haldane said. "That we did."

"May I ask why?"

Some of the firefighters had shaken off their queasiness and gathered behind Poole. Chris Shank was there, and Tom Stubbs, both looking demoralized and numb under their helmets and scuffed turnout coats. Haldane said, "You work here, you know more about it than me."

Poole said, "No—I don't understand any of this."

"It's like we crossed a line," Chris Shank volunteered. Good old Chris, Haldane thought, never failed to open his mouth when he could just as well keep it shut. "We were heading down to size up the hazard, and it was weird, you know, with all this light and everything, but then we crossed some kind of line and suddenly it was—I mean, you couldn't tell where you were going or coming from." He shook his head.

"There are *things* in there," Tom Stubbs added.

Haldane frowned. That had been his own perception,

true enough. *Things in there.* But he hadn't wanted to come out and say it. From here, the space between himself and the defense plant looked empty. *Odd,* in some shimmery way, but clearly deserted. So he had seen . . . what? A hallucination?

But Chris Shank was nodding vigorously. "That's it," he said. "I saw . . ."

"Tell the man," Haldane said. If they were going to talk about this, they might as well speak plainly.

Shank lowered his head. Awe and shame played over his face like light and shadow.

"Angels," he said finally. "That's what I saw in there. All kinds of angels."

Haldane stared at him.

Tom Stubbs was shaking his head vigorously. "Not angels! Nossir! Mister, it was Jesus Christ Himself in there!"

Poole glanced between the two men without comprehension, and the Saturday silence seemed louder now. A crow screeched in the still air.

"You're both fucked up," Chief Haldane said.

He looked back into the no-man's-land of the research facility, so thick with light that it seemed as if a piece of the sky had fallen onto it. He knew what he'd seen. It was quite clear in his mind, despite the nausea, the sense of no-direction that had overtaken him. He remembered it. He remembered it vividly. He would remember it forever.

He said, "There's no angels in there, and there sure as hell ain't Jesus Christ. The only thing in there is monsters."

"Monsters?" Poole said.

Haldane spat into the dry earth a second time, weary of all this. "You heard me."

What spread through the town that day was not panic but a deep, abiding unease. Rumors passed from backyard to main street to gatepost. By sunset, everyone had heard about the miraculous barricades of virgin forest north and south on the highway. Several had also heard about Chris Shank's assertion that there were angels flying around the Two Rivers Physical Research Laboratory. Some few even gave credence to Tom Stubbs's claim that it was the Second Coming; that Jesus Christ, two hundred fifty feet tall and dressed in Resurrection white, was about to come striding into town—a point of view condemned Sunday morning at nearly every church service in town. That Sunday, all the churches were full.

The weekend rolled on without electrical power, phone service, or adequate explanation. Most people stayed near their families and told each other it would all come clear soon, that the lights would flicker back and the TV would make sense of things. Food stocks began to run low at the few grocery stores open for business. The big supermarket at the Riverview Mall remained closed, and without power for refrigeration, some said, it was just as well—after two days of warm spring weather it must stink like sin in there.

Saturday night, Dex Graham and Howard Poole exchanged accounts of what they had seen. They were careful at first not to strain each other's credulity; less cautious when they realized they had each witnessed miracles. In the morning they set out to map the perimeters of the town. Dex drove while Howard sat in the passenger seat with a recent survey map, a pencil, and a pair of calipers. Howard marveled at the southern interruption of the highway, then marked it with careful precision on his chart. Similarly the northern limit. Then they followed private roads, logging roads, and the east–west axis of the farm roads. Each ended abruptly in humid pine forest. At the western margin of County Route 5, Howard creased the map with his pencil and said, "We might as well quit."

"It does get a little monotonous."

"More than that." Howard held the map against the dashboard. He had marked every dead end and joined them together: a perfect circle, Dex observed, with the town of Two Rivers in the southeastern quadrant.

Howard used his calipers to mark the center of the circle, but Dex had already seen what it must be: the old Ojibway reserve, the Two Rivers Physical Research Laboratory, where Howard had seen veils of blue light, and where the fire chief had seen monsters.

Sunday, a charter pilot named Calvin Shepperd took off from the air docks at the western end of Lake Merced and flew southeast toward Detroit—or the place on the map where Detroit used to be.

From the air it was easy to see the circle Dex Graham and Howard Poole had mapped. It was as clear as a cartographer's line. Two Rivers—much of Bayard County—had been transplanted (that was the word that occurred to him: like his wife's droopy ficus, *transplanted*) into the kind of white pine forest that must have covered Michigan when Jolliet and La Salle first crossed it. Shepperd, a calm man, understood none of this but refused to be frightened by it; only observed, took note, and filed the information for later reference.

Another troubling piece of information was that his VOR receiver wasn't registering a signal. Which was okay—Shepperd was old-fashioned enough to have calculated his course with a VFR chart and a yardstick, and his dead-reckoning skills were quite intact, thank you very much. He was not one of these modern pilots: RNAV junkies, lost without a computer. But it was peculiar, this radio silence.

He flew south by compass along the coast of the Lower Peninsula, coming within sight of Saginaw Bay. He should have passed Bay City and he adjusted his course to take him over Saginaw, but neither town seemed to exist. He did see a few settlements—farms, mineheads, and some obvious forestry. So there were people here. But not until he was within sight of the Detroit River did Shepperd encounter anything he would call a town.

Detroit was a town. Hell, it was a genuine city. But it

was not Detroit as Shepperd had known it. It was like no
city he had ever seen.

There was air traffic here, large but frail-looking planes
he could not identify, mainly to the south; but no tower
chatter or beacons he could pick up, only hiss in the headphones—which made his presence here a danger. He flew a
broad circle low over the city's outskirts, over long tin-
roofed buildings like warehouses hugging the river's edge.
There were taller buildings of some dark stone, narrow
streets crowded with traffic, vehicles he didn't recognize,
some of them horse-drawn. Afternoon sun stitched the city
with shadows. From Shepperd's vantage point it might have
been a diorama, something in a museum case, not real.
Surely to God, he thought, not *real*.

He had seen enough to make him nervous. He flew
home with the sun at his wingtip, trying not to think about
any of this; it seemed too fragile to bear the weight of
thought. During the long trip back he fretted that he had
made some error in his reckoning, or that Two Rivers might
have vanished in his absence, that he would be forced to
land in the wilderness.

But he knew this terrain, even without its man-made
landmarks, as well as he knew his wife Sarah. The land was
family. It didn't betray him. He was back on the calm surface of Lake Merced before nightfall.

He told no one what he had seen; not even Sarah. She
might have called him crazy, and that would have been
unbearable. He thought about talking to someone in authority—the police chief? The mayor? But even if they believed him, what could they do with this kind of
information? Nothing, he thought. Nothing at all.

He decided to repeat the journey, if only to convince
himself that it had been real. Monday morning, he refueled
at the dock pumps and took off. He charted the same
course to the south. But Two Rivers was barely beyond the
green line of the horizon when Shepperd turned back, his
heart pumping madly and his shirt drenched with sweat.

Something out there had frightened him. Something in the combination of white pine wilderness and dark, angular city had scared him off. He didn't want to see it again. He had seen too much already.


Monday afternoon, a formation of three strange aircraft flew over the town of Two Rivers. The noise drew people into the streets, where they shaded their eyes and stared up into the cloudless June sky. Superficially, the aircraft were conventional enough. Certainly they were old-fashioned: single-engine, propeller-driven, their quilted-metal bodies brilliant in the sunlight. The insignia on their wings were too distant to recognize, but most people assumed the planes were military craft of some kind.

Calvin Shepperd thought they looked like World War II–vintage P-51's, and he wondered what had drawn them here. Maybe it was his fault. Maybe he showed up on some radar screen. No telling what alarm he might have triggered.

But he didn't like that idea, and like most of his ideas since the accident last Saturday, Shepperd kept it to himself.

He watched the three strange aircraft circle once more and then wheel away to the south, pale dots on a pale horizon.


Evelyn Woodward had spent the last of her household money on groceries and a set of fresh batteries for her radio. The batteries were a dangerous luxury—money was scarce, and who knew when the bank might open again?—but she still believed in the radio. It was a lifeline. Once or twice in every long winter a snowstorm would send pine boughs plummeting onto the power lines, and the house would grow cold and dark while the linemen battled the weather. During those times, Evelyn would listen to her radio. The blackout would be announced on WGST; the affected counties would be named. The calm of the announcer was contagious. Listening, you knew the problem was temporary; that there were people out there working on it, mending things in the windy dark.

Despite what Dex and Howard Poole had said, despite the length of the crisis, so peculiar in this lovely June weather, Evelyn still nurtured her hope that the radio would revive. Perhaps WGST was unavailable, but there had been that other station, that curious fragment of it, surely not as sinister as Dex had made it seem.

She replaced the batteries and turned up the volume until the kitchen filled with the spit of static, but no voice came through.

No matter, she thought. Soon.

The radio was a private thing. She turned it off when anyone came into the kitchen, especially Dex or Howard. She was afraid of seeming stupid or naive. It was too easy to see herself as stupid or naive; she didn't need anyone's help. Anyway, time to herself wasn't hard to find. Evenings, Dex and Howard got together in the front room, where Dex had put the old hurricane lamp, and they talked about the emergency—as if, by talking, they could make it sensible, as if they could bury it under the sheer weight of their words. Evelyn went to the kitchen and sat in the gathering dark with her radio: Sunday night, Monday night.

Monday was the day the planes had flown over, an event that had cheered her considerably. Dex, of course, put some paranoid interpretation on it. To Evelyn, the meaning of the planes was much simpler. The problem—whatever the problem *was*—had come to someone's attention. It was being worked on; it was being fixed.

That was the evening the radio began to talk again. When Evelyn heard the voices, faint and laced with static, she smiled to herself. Dex was wrong. Normality was not far off.

She sat at the kitchen table with sunset fading outside

her dusty window and the radio close to her ear. She listened to fifteen minutes of a radio play (there *were* radio plays on this station), about policemen who were religious, or priests who were policemen—she couldn't tell. The actors all had thick accents. Their accents sounded sometimes French, sometimes English, sometimes just unfamiliar; they used curious words from time to time. It must be a European play, Evelyn thought. Something avant-garde. Then there was an ad for Mueller's Stone-Pressed White Flour, "our purity is never questioned," in a similar voice. Then a time check and the news.

According to the news, there had been a naval battle in the Yucatán Channel with tremendous losses on all sides. The *Logos* was damaged and limping back to Galveston, but the Spanish *Narvaez* had sunk with all hands. And the land campaign was meeting stiff resistance in the hills around Cuernavaca.

At home, the announcer went on, Ascension Day had been marked by fireworks and public celebrations from coast to coast. On an unhappy note, incendiary displays in New York Harbor had inadvertently set fire to a pitch and tar warehouse on the Jersey shore and caused the death of three night watchmen.

A pacifist demonstration in Montmagny had been broken up by police. Though it was claimed to be a student demonstration, Proctors said the majority of those arrested were either apostates, trade unionists, or Jews.

More news at the turn of the hour, but first: don't mark another Ascension without a new hat! Millinery to order at Roberge Hats and Yardgoods, a hat for every budget!

Evelyn snapped off the radio, resisting by a hair her urge to throw it across the room.


In the absence of television, Clifford Stockton had spent much of the past three days in the company of his bicycle. The bicycle was more than transportation. It was his

key to the mystery. Clifford was as curious about the events
that had overtaken Two Rivers as any adult—maybe more
so, since there was no explanation he rejected out of hand.
Aliens, monsters, miracles: all fair game as far as Clifford
was concerned. He had no theory of his own. He had heard
his mother laughing out loud (but nervously) at the idea
that angels had been seen flying over the defense plant.
Clifford wasn't keen on the idea of angels himself: he
wouldn't know what to expect from an angel. But he didn't
rule it out. He had tried to get close to the research building
on his bike; but the Two Rivers police had posted a car at
the access road to turn away the curious, so he couldn't
confirm any of this personally.

He didn't really care. The defense plant was a long ride
by bike. There were mysteries closer to home.

For instance, the mystery of Coldwater Road. Coldwater
Road ran for a couple of miles northeast past the cement
factory. It had been zoned for housing, and water and
power lines had been installed—there were fireplugs
planted like tropical shrubs in the raw earth of empty lots.
But no houses had been built. Hardly anyone went out
Coldwater Road (except teenagers at night, he had heard),
and that was fine with Clifford: he had few friends and
quite a few enemies among the kids his age. Clifford was
nearsighted and thin, a reader of books and watcher of
television. He liked his own company. Out on Coldwater
Road he could spend an afternoon in the scrubby fields and
patches of woods without much fear of interruption, and
that was good.

But since Saturday, Coldwater Road had changed. The
grid of vacant lots had been cut in half by what looked to
Clifford like an old, old forest. It was a mystery of enormous proportions.

The forest was deep and cool. Its floor was loamy and it
smelled moist and pungent. It was both inviting and frightening. Clifford didn't venture far into that dimness.

Instead, he was fascinated by its perimeter: a straight

line bisecting the blank lots, maybe curving a little if you stood at the far end of the cleared land and sighted northeast along the treeline—but only maybe.

Not every tree was intact. Where the white pines crossed the border, they were neatly cut. The cut trees were eerie, Clifford thought. The heartwood was pale green and bled a sticky yellow sap. On one side: green branches thick with needles. On the other: nothing.

He tried to imagine some force that could have enclosed Two Rivers, could have drawn it up from the world like the dough in a cookie cutter and deposited it here, wherever *here* was: a wilderness.

He had heard the phrase *pathless wilderness,* and he guessed that was what this was—except, Clifford discovered, it was not *entirely* pathless.

If you turned left where Coldwater Road ended, if you followed the line of woods past the vacant lots, over scrubland and a small hill (from which he could see the cement factory and, far beyond it, the tangle of culs-de-sac that contained his own house), and if you left your bike behind and persisted through berry canes and wildflowers and high weeds, then you came to a trail.

A trail in the new forest, which *approached* Two Rivers but ended there, as all the town's roads ended at the forest.

It was a wide trail where the trees had been cleared and the undergrowth trampled down as if by trucks. A logging road, Clifford would have called it, but maybe it was not that; he made no assumptions.

He walked a few yards down this path, listening to the sway of the pines around him and smelling the moist pungency of moss. It was like stepping into another world. He didn't go far. He worried that the connection between this forest and Two Rivers might close behind him; that he would turn back and not be able to find his bike, his house, the town; only more trees and more of this primitive road, its source or destination.

Monday, riding home along Coldwater Road, he saw

three airplanes pass overhead. Another clue, he thought. He didn't know much about airplanes, but it was obvious to Clifford that these were old-fashioned. They circled, circled, circled, then veered away.

*Somebody's seen us,* he thought. *Somebody knows we're here.*


He spent a day at home with his mother, who was frightened but trying not to show it. They opened cans of Texas-style chili and heated them over wax candles. His mother played the portable radio that night, and for a while there was music, but not anything Clifford or his mother recognized: sad, trilling songs. Then a man's voice that faded into static.

"I don't know this station," his mother said absently. "I don't know where it's from."


In the morning Clifford cycled back to the forest road.

He was there when more planes passed over the town. Bigger planes this time, huge planes, wings bristling with engines. The planes dropped black dots into the June sky: *bombs,* Clifford thought breathlessly, but the dots grew billowing circles: parachutes, men dangling beneath, a rain of them.

And he heard a rumbling from the earth under his feet, and he ducked into the shadow of the trees and watched terrified from the margin of the road as a column of armored vehicles roared past in choking shrouds of dust and diesel smoke, the men at their helms in black uniform bearing rifles with bayonets, none of them aware of Clifford watching as they broke from the forest into scrub waste and daylight and rumbled over sunlit empty lots to the gray ribbon of Coldwater Road.

# CHAPTER 2

Autumn was wet in Boston that year.

The rain began in mid-September and continued for three weeks without surcease—or so it seemed to Linneth Stone, who had spent most of that time cloistered in the humanities wing of Sethian College, correcting page proofs and double-checking footnotes, pausing at odd moments to watch the rain sluice down the high windows and cascade from the rain gutters and over the casements of the library across the square.

*Pagan Cults of Meso-America* was the first tangible fruit of her long struggle for tenure. It both consolidated and justified her career. She was proud of the book. She loved the solid look of the typeset words, invested with an authority the manuscript had lacked. But she had been struggling with the book for half a decade, and what she didn't like to admit was that the work—her life—had begun to border on tedium. Hours of minutiae, days of solitary page-turning, relieved by . . . nothing much. And the rain went on and on.

It was, in its way, not a bad kind of tedium. Her chamber was cosy enough. She was warm against the weather, and there was coffee from the hallway urn, and the periodic clanking of the radiator, like the complaining of some gruff but dependable old friend. The time passed in neat packets of hours and days. But it was repetitious time, and it was often lonely. Few of the senior academics in her department knew what to make of a woman with tenure, especially a relatively young woman: she had turned thirty-four in August. Young, at least, compared to those bearded venerables who had been haunting the stacks and carrels since the Titans walked the earth. They stared at her the way they might stare at a talking dung beetle, or a chimp that had been trained to smoke cigars.

And each night she hurried home to her tiny apartment on Theodotus Street, through the leaf-tumble and autumn air, past rattling motorcarriages and bored dray horses, from warmth to warmth: the warmth of her hot plate and her quilted blankets. *This is success,* she told herself. *This is my career. This is how I mean to spend the rest of my life.*

But each night the memory came of her field expedition three summers ago in the Sierra Mazateca with her guides and two graduate students: a time when she had often been frightened for her life, when she had been dirty, uncomfortable, and too often helpless in the arms of fate. Now she would lie in bed reliving those months. And as terrifying as that time had often been, Linneth thought . . . it had not been *tedious.*

Certainly she didn't want to go back to New Spain. That part of her research was finished. In any case, the entire area was a war zone. But she wondered if the trip had not changed something inside her, had not ignited an unsuspected appetite for—what? Adventure? Surely not. But for *something* to happen. Another milestone. Something that would matter in her life.

Some nights it was almost a prayer. She remembered her mother murmuring prayers at night: ostensibly to Apollo, since Daddy was a paidonomos in that cult, but more likely to the land around their house in rural New York, away from city lights, where the stars were vivid on summer nights and the forest hummed with life. A prayer to the local gods, who went nameless in the New World, at least since the aboriginals had been exterminated or driven west; whose sybils had fallen silent or never spoken from their meadows. "We live in a breathless place," Linneth's mother had once told her. "Without *pneuma*. No inspiration. No wonder the hierarchs are so powerful here."

More powerful than she had guessed, Linneth thought. For her mother, the bad times had come all too soon.

Still, she allowed herself a small heretical prayer. *Deliver me from this lonely sameness,* she thought. *And this damned rain!*

But the gods, her mother would have reminded her, are capricious. Linneth's deliverance came in an abrupt and unpleasant form. And the rain went on for days.


She shook her raincoat off in the chipped tile lobby of her walk-up building, carried it dripping upstairs past two landings decorated with circular framed mirrors, the bane of her life, always giving back reflections at the least flattering hours: dawn or dusk. Her hair was wet despite the rain cap and she looked small in the glare of the incandescent lamps. Small nose, small round face, compressed pale lips reluctant to offer a smile. When she first moved in, she had always smiled at herself in these mirrors. She no longer bothered. "Wet mouse," she whispered. "Linneth, you are a wet mouse."

Her wardrobe was conventionally black, a black blouse and black floorsweeper, buttonhooks tarnished with wear;

underneath she wore a modest bustle and corset that contorted her into the shape of, she supposed, an acceptable female don, though there were not many guiding examples.

Linneth took a longer look at herself in the mirror at the second-floor landing. Women with careers were supposed to be hard. She didn't look hard. Only weary. There were smudges under her eyes. She had stayed up late last night listening to the radio, a program of war songs, lonesome songs about separated lovers. She tried to imagine what it must be like to have a lover at the front—in Cuernavaca, say, where all those lovely white adobe buildings were being shelled. She thought it must be terrible.

She walked down the hallway to her door, which was ajar.

She stopped and looked at it.

Had she left it open? Impossible. She was compulsive about locking her door. There had been robberies in the neighborhood.

Perhaps she had been robbed. The thought of it made her sick with apprehension. She pushed on the door and it glided open. There was a light on inside. She was suddenly aware of the sound of her breathing and the rattle of rain on the frame of this old building. She stepped through the tiny entranceway, past the coat closet and into the sitting room.

There was a man inside. He sat calmly in her large chair with one long leg cocked over the other. He seemed to expect her.

He wore the brown uniform of a senior Proctor. He was a middle-aged man, but trim. His hair was thick and black; his eyes were pale and patient. He smiled at her.

Linneth was numb with fright.

He said, "Come in, Miss Stone. Though you hardly need an invitation into your own home. I know this is unexpected. I apologize."

She didn't want to come in. She wanted to bolt. She wanted to run back out into the rainy dark. But she drew a ragged breath and put her raincoat in the closet and stepped into the light of her floor lamp, a sculptured wooden electric lamp which was the nicest of her meager furnishings, but which she hated now, because this man had touched it.

"Don't be afraid," the Proctor said.

She almost laughed.

He said, "You *are* Linneth Stone—are you not?"

"Yes."

"Then sit down. I haven't come to arrest you."

She sat on the edge of her reading chair, as far from the Proctor as possible. Her racing heart had begun to recover its pace, but her body was on full alert. She felt keenly attentive. The room seemed terribly bright, wholly electric.

"My name is Demarch." She looked at his pips. He added, "Lieutenant," pronouncing it the European way, as Proctors did. "Please relax, Miss Stone. I'm here for a consultation. Your department head said you were the person to speak to."

So the Bureau had already talked to faculty. This was serious. Demarch wasn't here to arrest her, he claimed, but who could believe a Proctor?

She remembered the last time the Proctors had come to her door. Her mother had answered. Linneth had not seen her mother again.

And there were other stories, always new stories, the knock at the door, the disappeared colleague. Academics had been under scrutiny ever since the Alien and Sedition laws were enacted. With her family background, she could hardly be an exception.

Demarch hadn't paid her the courtesy of knocking. He could have come to see her at her office if it was a consultation he wanted. But she supposed a Proctor wouldn't do that. They were too accustomed to intimidation. It was their way of life, so familiar as to be invisible.

She said, "Is this about my book?"

"*Pagan Cults of Middle America?*"

"Meso," she said. "Meso-America. Not 'middle.' "

The Proctor smiled again. "You've spent too much time proofreading. *Meso*-America. I've read the manuscript. Your publishers have been cooperative. It's a fine scholarly work, insofar as I can judge. The Ideological Branch gave it careful attention, of course. Disseminating falsehoods *anti-religio* is still a felony. But we do try to be reasonable. Science is science. You don't strike me as a subversive."

"Thank you. Comparative ethnology isn't advocative. There have been court cases—"

"I know. This isn't about your book, in any case, though the book is what qualifies you. We want you to do some work for the Bureau de la Convenance Religieuse."

"I have my own work."

"Nothing that can't wait. We've arranged a sabbatical— if you choose to take it."

"My book—"

"You must be nearly finished with the proofs."

She didn't deny it. Demarch would know all this. There was a saying: God sees the sparrow fall. The Bureau takes notes.

He said, "We'll need you for six months—possibly as much as a year."

She was aghast. It was too big an idea to swallow: the Bureau wanted her to work for them, to go away for six months, interrupt her life, such as it was. . . . "For *what*?"

"To practice the science of ethnology," Demarch said. "The thing you're good at."

"I don't understand."

"It isn't simple to explain."

"I'm not sure I want an explanation. You said I had a choice? I don't want anything to do with it."

"I understand. I sympathize, Miss Stone, believe it or not. If it were up to me, I would leave it at that. But I don't think the Bureau as a whole would be happy with your decision."

"But if I have a choice—"

"You do. So do my superiors. They have the choice of

putting in a word with your publishers, say, or talking to the chancellor about your academic qualifications in light of your family history." He saw her expression and held up his hands. "I won't say any of this is inevitable. Only that you run a risk if you refuse to cooperate."

She didn't answer, couldn't find words to answer.

He added, "We're not talking about manual labor on some penal farm. This is the work you're trained to do, after all, and only six months out of a long career. It's much less than some people have been asked to give up for their country."

Please, Linneth thought, don't start talking about the war, the noble dead. It would be too much. But Demarch seemed to sense her reaction. He fell silent, his eyes fixed on her.

She said, "What would the Bureau want with an ethnologist?" A woman, at that, she did not add. It seemed out of character.

"Basically, we want you to write an analysis of a foreign village—its mores and taboos, something of its history."

"In six months?"

"A sketch, not a thesis."

"Isn't that the kind of thing you can look up in a book?"

"Not in this case, no."

"I would be working from the field?"

"Yes."

"Where?" It was something to do with the war, she guessed. New Spain, almost certainly.

Demarch said, "You agree to cooperate?"

"Rather than losing tenure? Facing a felony charge or some secret trial?"

"You know better than that."

"Under the circumstances, what can I say?"

Demarch had stopped smiling. "You can say, 'I agree.' "

The words. He actually wanted the words.

Linneth gave him a long, defiant look. Demarch didn't acknowledge it, only gazed passively back. His uniform was

crisp and neat and somehow more intimidating because of
it. Her own rain-wet clothing smelled of damp wool and
defeat.

She lowered her head. "I agree," she whispered.

"Pardon me?" His voice was neutral.

*"I agree."*

"Yes." He reached for his attaché case. "Then let me
show you some extraordinary photographs."


She was allowed three days to finish her corrections to
the page proofs. Linneth paid scrupulous attention to the
work, using it to blot out of her mind the story Lieutenant
Demarch had told her. Even after she had seen the photos
(the strange town so seemingly real, the shopfronts display-
ing impossible goods, the signs in a language only approximately English), she still half-believed that it was a hoax,
some elaborate ruse the Bureau had devised to trick her
into confessing—well, something, *anything;* that she would
end up in prison after all.

In the hallway she passed the department head, Abra-
ham Valcour, who returned her cold stare with an aloof
little smile. There were rumors that Valcour had contacts in
the War Department, that some of his field expeditions had
carried Commissariat spies as part of their luggage. Linneth
had reserved judgment, but not any longer; it was Valcour,
she was certain, who had sent the Proctors to her door. She
imagined the conversation. *Speak to this one. She's intelligent
and malleable, wrote a decent book.* He could be maddeningly
plausible when he wanted to lie. He had never cared for the
idea of a woman in his department, though her academic
bona fides had been inarguable. Certainly he had never
passed up an opportunity to slight her. This was merely the
logical next step, giving her to the Proctors like a choice
bone to a kennel full of dogs. No doubt he hoped she
wouldn't be back. Linneth vowed that she *would* be back, if
only to erase his maddening smile.

Two Rivers, she thought. The name of the town that had appeared in the deep forest of northern Mille Lacs was Two Rivers.

The page proofs went to her publisher bound in brown waxed paper and tied with string.

Home, she packed her heaviest clothes. Autumn came early in the northern Near West. Winters, she had heard, could be very cruel.

She said good-bye to her secretary and to a few graduate students. There was no one else.

# CHAPTER 3

**C**lasses at John F. Kennedy High School started late that year. It was a miracle, Dex thought, that they had started at all. He gave credit to the principal, Bob Hoskins, and a feisty committee of local parents: they had negotiated an agreement with the Proctors, who probably decided it would be safer keeping restless teenagers penned up during the day than to let them run loose.

The problem (well, *one* problem, in a sea of trouble) was texts. Like every library in Two Rivers, the school library had been sacked. "Indexed," the Proctors said. The books had gone out in truckloads last August—not to be burned, it was claimed, but into storage, no doubt into some monkish secret archive, some classified dungeon.

The military consul had even offered new texts, and perhaps that was inevitable, if school went on, but Dex had been appalled by the example he'd been shown: a gilt-edged volume that might have passed for a *McGuffey's Reader* of the 1890s, full of crude cautionary verses about the dangers of syphilis and distilled liquor, and fragments of history that seemed dubious even in the context of this weirdly twisted rabbit hole into which the town had fallen: *Heros and Heresiarchs, Daniel at Ravensbreuck, What Was Won and Lost at the Fields of Flanders.* Handing out such documents to a class raised on Super Mario and the Ninja Turtles was more than Dex liked to imagine.

So he taught his classes informally, as he had always taught them: American history from the Revolution to the First World War. He wrote "chapters" and printed them on an ancient spirit duplicator someone had dragged up from the basement. History, of course, was not what it used to be. Not here. But despite the formidable evidence of the last four months, he could not convince himself that this was meaningless work, that he was communicating to his dwindling classes the folk tales of some lost and impossible dreamland. These events had happened. They were formative, they had consequences: the town of Two Rivers, for instance, and everyone in it.

He was teaching real history. Or so he believed. But his students tended to be listless, and today was no exception; he taught without books, electric lights, a heated classroom, or much enthusiasm; and he was relieved, like everyone else, when the day was over.

He walked home through long shadows. Curfew began at six, but the streets were already deserted. Except for military traffic. Over the last three months Dex had trained himself not to look at the boxy patrol cars. They were always the same, a driver in a black beret and a man with a rifle and fixed bayonet riding next to him, both wearing an expression of bland, bored hostility. It was a kind of face you probably saw a lot of in Honduras or Beijing; it was not a face Dex had ever expected to see in Two Rivers.

But as Dorothy Gale might have observed, he wasn't in Michigan anymore. He had given up trying to guess what

the nature of this place truly was. The only words that
applied were words he had learned from *The Twilight Zone*.
"Another dimension." Whatever that meant.

He climbed the stairs to his apartment. The front room
was as dim and cold as it had been all this autumn. The
military were supposed to be running in a high-voltage line
from the south, but he'd believe that when he saw it. In the
meantime it was cold, and the winter would be much
colder. Deadly, unless arrangements were made.

His sofa bed was open and tangled with blankets—every blanket he owned. In that brief impossible time last
June, between the accident and the military occupation, he
had been clever enough to buy a hurricane lantern and a
supply of lamp oil. The lamp gave him an extra half hour or
so of light each evening. Enough to read by. The Proctors
hadn't confiscated *every* book in town; there were still personal libraries, including his own seven shelves of paperbacks. He was rereading Mark Twain, a bracing exercise
under the circumstances.

He ate cold soup out of the can. The Proctors had distributed "ration coupons" mimeographed on rag paper; you
redeemed them for food at the dispensary in the IGA parking lot. Dex had used up his coupons early in the week but
was sparing with the nonperishable items. Water came from
a truck in front of City Hall: you lined up with your old
milk jug or a camping thermos or whatever container was
handy. The wait was generally about an hour, and the water
tasted of gasoline.

He had not had a hot shower since June. It was possible, Dex had established, to keep himself clean with a cloth
rag and a little soap and a jug of water at room temperature,
but there was no pleasure in it. He had begun to dream
about showers.

He read by the fading daylight until it was too dark,
then put the book aside and watched nightfall through his
narrow window. A rack of cloud had moved in and the
wind was gusting. The street was full of tumbling leaves.

Nobody had raked or burned their leaves this year. The town seemed tatty, seemed gone to seed.

Tonight he didn't light the hurricane lamp. When the room was dark, when the streets were dark, he changed into a black T-shirt, blue jeans, and a navy blue overcoat. He put a can of soup in one pocket, two cans of orange soda in the other. After a moment's thought, he added a bottle of aspirin.

In Dex's experience, everybody obeyed the curfew. There had been a few exceptions. In July, a twenty-seven-year-old man named Seagram had been shot when he tried to cross town after dark to visit his girlfriend. The body had been on display in the City Hall courtyard for three ghastly days.

The patrols had eased somewhat since then, but Dex was still careful stepping out the front door of his building into the windy street.

The wind was an asset. The tossing of the trees, the rattle of all these dry leaves, disguised any sound he was likely to make. There were no streetlights, only the occasional flicker of candlelight from curtained windows; that was good, too. He followed a line of hedges to Beacon Road and took a good long look before jogging across the intersection to the corner of Powell Creek Park. The park was fine cover but hazardous in the cloudy dark. He followed the faint shine of a footpath.

He ducked behind a willow tree as a military patrol rounded the corner from Oak behind the lightless brick primary school, tires crackling on dry leaf. The soldier in the shotgun seat scanned the sidewalks with a high-intensity lamp. Dex crouched motionless, taking shallow breaths until the engine sound and the flickering light faded.

Then he crossed the street to a small wood-frame house, over a lawn grown wild, to the back, down a short span of concrete steps to a basement door. He had memorized the route; in the dark he could see almost nothing. A tree hissed in the black space of the yard. Drops of rain spattered his coat and the air on his lips was cold and moist.

He opened the door without knocking. When it was firmly closed behind him, he struck a match and touched it to the wick of a candle.

This basement room was windowless. The floor was concrete. There were stacks of blankets, food cans (most empty), a few books, a Primus stove.

There was a mattress on the floor; and on the mattress, Howard Poole. His eyes were closed, his forehead beaded with sweat.

Dex sighed and emptied cans from the pockets of his coat. At the sound, Howard turned his head and looked up.

"Just me," Dex said.

The younger man nodded. "Thirsty," he said.

Dex popped a can of soda and pressed two aspirin into Howard's hand. The hand was hot, but maybe not as hot as it had been yesterday.

Howard was suffering from a flu that had been threatening to turn into pneumonia. Dex believed the crisis had passed, but nothing was certain anymore.

Howard turned his wristwatch to catch the candlelight, then sat up in a slow, pained motion. "It's after curfew."

"Uh-huh."

"Kind of risky, coming here."

"I didn't want to be followed."

"You thought you might be?"

"A couple of Proctors came to the door this morning. They know your name, they know you worked at the plant, and they know you were rooming at Evelyn's. They were civilized. No pushing. But a guy followed me to work. I thought it would be better to come here in the dark."

"Jesus." Howard rolled to one side.

"It's not as bad as it sounds. I didn't get the feeling they were hunting you down—just putting some hooks in the water."

Howard sighed. He looked tired of it all, Dex thought: worn out by the sickness, the cold, the hiding.

It was not more than ten days after the tanks rolled into Two Rivers that the military had announced their desire to interview employees of the Two Rivers Physical Research Lab. Howard had refrained from volunteering. Then a lieutenant of the Bureau de la Convenance Religieuse, a man named Symeon Demarch, took over Evelyn's bed-and-breakfast and turned it into his headquarters. And Howard had gone into hiding.

The house they were in was ostensibly empty. It had belonged to Paul Cantwell, a CPA who had been in Florida with his family when the accident happened.

Howard had lifted an expired Michigan driver's license from a desk upstairs and used it to pass as Paul Cantwell at the ration lineups. When he came down with the flu (some variant germ that rode in with the tanks: half the people in town had caught it), Dex used the ID to pick up double rations—a risky business, since hoarding was a punishable offense and ID fraud a capital crime under military law.

Howard said vaguely, "I was having a dream when you came in. Something about Stern. He was in a building, a building all covered with jewels. But I don't remember . . ." The words trailed off.

Stern again, Dex thought. Since the fever set in Howard had often talked about his uncle Alan Stern—who had been the moving force behind the Two Rivers Physical Research Lab; who had died, presumably, in the accident. The fever seemed to have revived him in Howard's mind.

"A woman," Howard said faintly, deliriously. "A woman answered the phone."

Dex opened a can of soup and put a spoon into the younger man's hand. Howard's fingers closed on it in a spasm that was almost reflexive.

"When I phoned him in Two Rivers," Howard was saying. "A woman . . ."

"Is this important?"

The question seemed to clear a shadow. He gave Dex a guilty, odd smile. "I don't know. Maybe." He put the spoon in his mouth. "Cold soup."

"It's good for you. How do you feel, by the way?"

"A little better. I've been awake more often. At least, I think so. It's kind of timeless down here." And he took another spoonful. "Not so many trips to the shitter. I've even been a little bit hungry."

"Good."

He ate in silence for a time. It seemed to Dex that the soup and the aspirin were working a slow transformation in him. It was heartening to see.

They listened as the rain picked up its pace, rattling on a tin awning out back.

Howard put down the empty can and licked the spoon a last time. "I was talking about my uncle. This isn't just raving, Dex. I know I haven't been too coherent. But he was the key to this whole event. Maybe our key to understanding it."

"You think we have a chance of understanding it?"

"I don't know. Yes, maybe."

Maybe Howard could figure out what had happened at the research lab. Dex surely couldn't. He had a hard time understanding the Bohr model of the atom, much less a physical process so catastrophic that it could somehow rewrite history. What had happened here was not Physics 1-A —it wasn't on any curriculum Dex had ever heard of. He shook his head: "You're talking to a humanities major, bucko."

"Maybe we *have* to understand it."

"Do we?"

"I thought about it a lot. You lie here in the dark, you do a lot of thinking. It's our only choice, Dex. We understand it and do something about it, or we just . . . what? Go on like this? Get killed, or imprisoned, or best case, get assimilated?"

Dex had had these thoughts, too, and so, probably, had

most of the citizens of Two Rivers. But no one ever talked about it. It was the great unspoken truce. We will not discuss the future.

Howard had broken the rule.

"You *are* feverish."

"Don't brush me off."

"Okay."

"Don't humor me, either. I'm not that sick."

"I'm sorry. If I knew where to begin—"

"I keep thinking about Stern. I dreamed about him. With the fever—there were times I thought he was here, I mean here in the room. Very real." Howard shook his head and sank back into the mattress. "It all seemed so logical. It made more sense in dreams."


Dex went home after midnight. The weather sheltered him from view and kept military patrols to a minimum, but his clothes were heavy with cold rain and he was shivering helplessly by the time he came within sight of his walkup apartment building. Maybe Howard was right, he thought. Maybe it all made more sense in dreams.

Maybe dreaming was the only way to approach something so incomprehensible. Dex had coped better than most, because his own life had passed into the territory of dreams long ago. He had been sleepwalking since the fire took Abigail and David away from him. His life since then had been a kind of shadowy anticlimax in which even the events of the last few months had been hardly more than a recapitulation, his own bereavement somehow woven into the fabric of the larger world. He supposed Evelyn had sensed this about him, that even the tenderness that had passed between them—and it had been a real tenderness— was nevertheless eclipsed by something darker. He supposed that was why she had elected to stay in the boarding house with the Proctor Demarch. She had been afraid, of course, but not *only* afraid. She had known about Dex: what he had been, what he had lost.

He stood in the darkness under the lintel of the old apartment building and fumbled his wet key into the lock. He thought about Evelyn Woodward and what she had meant to him. For a time she had seemed to be a doorway back into a world from which he had been exiled—not a replacement for Abigail, but a way out of this blind canyon his life had become, into the highlands, the sun-washed places in which he had almost ceased to believe.

She hadn't been equal to that aroused need, and who could be? It was better not to want such things. He had arrived at a sort of *modus vivendi* with his grief, and such deals were best not broken. You wore your grief, and if necessary you ate it and you drank it until it became your substance, until you looked in the mirror one day and there was nothing looking back but grief itself, a man made entirely of sorrow, but still standing, somehow still alive, surviving.

He left his wet clothes hanging over the curtain rod in the shower stall and went to bed, craving these few hours of oblivion before another dawn.


The knock at the door startled him awake.

The knock was peremptory and fierce, a Proctor's knock. He woke blinking at daylight, his heart pounding hard.

He went directly to the door and opened it, apprehensive but not afraid; he was too tired of all this to be afraid.

The only light in the dim hallway was a patch of pale October morning through the east-facing window. Two junior Proctors, pink-cheeked youngsters only just beginning to master the routine arrogance of the professional religious policeman, looked at Dex and past him into the room. Then they moved to opposite sides of the door.

A woman stepped forward.

Bewildered, Dex could only stare.

She was wearing what he supposed his great-grand-mother might have worn in her youth: a black, high-collared, long-sleeved, floor-length dress fixed with buttonhooks over the kind of corset that rendered the female figure as an S-shape, all bosom and buttocks. Definitely not a uniform; there was too much lace at the collar and cuffs. Her dark hair was parted in the middle and swept back to frame her face. She was about as tall as his collarbone.

She looked at Dex with a fierce determination. But she was blushing at the same time, maybe because he'd come to the door in nothing but briefs and a sleeveless T-shirt.

She said, "I'm sorry to disturb you . . . are you Mr. Dexter Graham?"

She spoke with that odd accent he had heard from some of the soldiers. The inflections were European, the vowel sounds almost Irish. She made "Dexter Graham" into something exotic, the name of a North Country highwayman in a Walter Scott epic.

He overcame his speechlessness and said, "Yes, I am."

"My name is Linneth Stone. Lieutenant Demarch sent me to speak to you." She paused. "I can wait, if you need to dress." The blush deepened a little.

"Okay," Dex said. "Thank you." And went to look for his pants.

# CHAPTER 4

Evelyn had been willing to stand in line for water like everyone else.

She had stood in line before. There were special deliveries to the house every Tuesday and Thursday, and the Proctors were generous with it, but she liked having her own ration. It permitted small luxuries: a private cup of coffee, when there was coffee; or tea; or just a quick extra wash on a hot day. The water line was a small nuisance and she didn't begrudge the time she spent there.

Her new dress changed all that.

The dress was a wonderful gift, and she had accepted it in the spirit in which it was given, but not without reservations. It made the growing gulf between herself and the townspeople too obvious.

The dress was of some faintly iridescent, dark green material—bombazine twilled with silk, the lieutenant had said. It came with a complement of underclothing so baroque that she had needed an instruction manual, which the lieutenant also supplied: a tiny hardbound volume called *Appearance, Its Perfection, for Women,* by Mrs. Will. Once Evelyn had deciphered Mrs. Will's peculiar spelling, sorted out a stay from a buttonhook, and understood that in this place a *pin* was called a *pince,* she managed all right.

She even liked, sort of, the way she looked in the dress. The effect was Victorian, of course. Prim. But it did interesting things for her figure. To be so thoroughly covered and at the same time so completely *advertised*—it was odd, and oddly interesting. In Boston and New York, the lieutenant said, all the finer women dressed like this.

But Two Rivers wasn't Boston or New York; it hadn't been even in the old days. And that was the problem. She had already been accused of taking favors from the Proctors who were lodged in her house. Eleanor Camby, the undertaker's wife, had stood behind her in a ration line and whispered the word *quisling* over and over again. Evelyn didn't know the word but understood immediately what it meant. Collaborator. Traitor.

To stand in a similar line wearing green bombazine and lace collars—no, not possible.

She could have just worn her old clothes when she went into the street, but Evelyn sensed that this was precisely what the lieutenant did not want. The purpose of the dress, or one of its purposes, was to make her different, to make her unique.

So when she wanted her water ration she begged a ride from one of the junior officers (Evelyn thought of them all as "baby Proctors"; their ranks were too complex to remember), in this case a young man named Malthus Feliks. Feliks drove her downtown in one of those boxy cars that looked like antique Jeeps.

Feliks wasn't talkative, but he was courteous to her—and that was refreshing. She had learned to expect contempt or at best indifference from the junior officers. They were trained that way, she supposed; too, they must be intimidated by the strangeness of Two Rivers. The town had become a terrifyingly strange place no matter which end of the glass you peered through. Today Feliks drove along the leaf-choked streets at a less than bone-bruising clip, and even smiled once (an acrid Proctor's smile, but genuine) when she commented on the particular blue of the sky. Last night's rain had cleared the air. October skies, Evelyn thought, were the bluest of all.

It was the dress, she thought, that made Feliks more courteous. If not the dress itself, then what it represented. His commanding officer's imprimatur. A mark of possession, if not rank.

*No,* she scolded herself. *No, don't think about it that way. Even if Feliks does.*

She was dismayed to discover that the water truck had been moved. Today it was parked in the lot behind JFK High School. Of all places. She considered telling Feliks to turn around, it wasn't worth the risk of being seen—not *here.* But Feliks might tell the lieutenant, which would leave the wrong impression. And what, fundamentally, was she ashamed of? Nothing. She had nothing to hide.

Water was dispensed to ration card holders between the hours of noon and six; the truck had only just arrived. Feliks exchanged words with the militiamen lounging in the cab of the tanker. The Bureau de la Convenance Religieuse wasn't a branch of the armed forces; Feliks didn't officially outrank these men, but Evelyn had noticed the way the military deferred to the religious police. The powers of the Bureau were vague, hence enormous, the lieutenant had told her. It was easy, he said, perhaps too easy, all things considered, for a Censeur or a senior Proctor to make trouble for an enlisted man. So, naturally, the soldiers were wary of them.

A surly militiaman unlocked the spigot at the back of the truck. Evelyn took her camping thermos from the car. Feliks wouldn't fill it for her and she knew better than to

ask. It was her water, her chore. She stooped to fit the
thermos under the steel faucet and swept her dress out of
the way with one hand. The water gushed out and spattered her shoes. It looked clean but smelled faintly of oil. It
always did.

She filled the thermos to the very top and capped it.

As she walked to the car she risked a glance back at the
school—specifically, at the second-floor room where Dex
taught history to his dwindling classes.

Was there a shadow there?

Was he watching her?

Had he seen the dress?

She turned away and walked with her head high. She
didn't care whether he had seen her. She told herself so.
There was no reason anymore to care what Dex Graham
thought.

The military forces had occupied a Days Inn on the
highway east of town. All the civilian automobiles had been
bulldozed out of the parking lot and replaced with military
machines—tanks, troop carriers, "Jeeps." The flag of the
Consolidated Republic flew from a newly installed wooden
staff, snapping in the brisk October breeze, and Evelyn
gazed at it while Feliks performed his own chore: delivering
a dossier to one of the military commanders.

The flag was blue with white bars and a red star in the
middle. It might have been any country's flag, Evelyn
thought; it was not the American flag but it was not threat-
eningly strange. She had gradually grown accustomed to
the idea that Two Rivers had somehow traveled by standing
still, that it had arrived in a place where things were sub-
stantially foreign. As an idea it was incomprehensible; as a
fact of life—one adjusted. Or at least one ought to.

She had adjusted to other changes. Evelyn had been
married for three years to a man in Traverse City, a notary
public named Patrick Cotter. She had believed *that* would

last forever, too, and it hadn't; her connection to Patrick had been as fragile as the connection between Two Rivers and the United States of America. And her engagement to Dex: that had foundered just as quickly when the lieutenant moved in. The lesson? There was no reliable glue to bind the parts of the world. Nothing was certain except change. The trick was to land on your feet.

Dex had not adjusted; that was his problem. He was still chewing some old bone of self-loathing. It had made him eccentric and stern.

Feliks drove her home. In contrast to the military, the Proctors were relatively few and had chosen a headquarters by the lakeshore. Most of them were bivouacked in the Blue View Motel; civilian employees of the Bureau de la Convenance had a wing to themselves. The highest-ranking Proctors, including the lieutenant and his pions, had lodged at Evelyn's B&B.

She still liked the way the house looked, three stories of Victorian gingerbread with a view of Lake Merced. She had paid for a great deal of restoration when she bought the building and it was still clean despite a summer of neglect. The white paint hadn't faded from the siding, or the robin's egg blue from the trim. She left Feliks to tend his car and hurried inside. It was almost time for lunch. She didn't serve lunch; there was a kitchen at the Blue View with a gasoline-powered generator and provisions shipped in daily. Most noons, she had the house to herself. She opened a ration can, one of the military rations the lieutenant had brought her, contents nameless but not bad if you were hungry enough, and she heated a kettle of her new water over a Coleman stove on the back porch. Tea bags, her last two, went into the china pot. She added hot water and inhaled the earthy fragrance. Would there ever be more tea?

Yes, she thought, there would. Things would be normalized. She would adjust. There was always a reward for adjusting. Small pleasures. Tea.

She took a careful, precious sip and gazed across the

water. Lake Merced was choppy in the autumn wind, empty under a blue sky . . . as empty as Evelyn wished she could be, utterly empty of all thought.


The lieutenant came home at dusk.

She still thought of him as "the lieutenant," though she knew his full name: Symeon Philip Demarch. Born in Columbia, a town on the Chesapeake River, to an English-speaking family with long-standing Bureau connections. Forty-five years old. *Symeon,* Evelyn thought. It sounded almost like *Simon.* Like the flag of the Republic, his name was strange but not completely foreign. She had adjusted to it.

He came to the kitchen and asked her to brew coffee. He gave her a bag of military-issue ground coffee, almost half a pound, Evelyn guessed, and whispered to her, "Save some for later."

He finished business with two of his adjutants and sent them out of the room. The house was dark now and Evelyn began rummaging for lamp oil.

"Don't," the lieutenant said. (*Symeon.*) She put the bottle back on its high shelf and waited for him to explain.

He smiled and went to the dining room table, where there was a military radiotelephone in a scuffed black case. He took up the receiver, cranked the handle, and said a single word: "Now."

"Symeon?" She was bewildered. "What—?"

And then a remarkable thing happened. The lights came on.


Clifford Stockton was in his room when the electricity came back.

He had gone to bed early. He went to bed early most nights. What else was there to do? Under the blankets he was at least warm.

But now the ceiling light winked on—tentatively, at first, as if distant turbines were struggling with the load; then brightly, steadily. And Clifford winced at the sudden glare and wondered whether everything had changed again.

He climbed out of bed and went to the window. Most of the town of Two Rivers was hidden behind the near wall of the Carrasco house next door, but the glow in the sky meant that *all* the lights were on, including the downtown signs and the big spotlights in the mall parking lot, all reflecting from a shelf of low cloud that had rolled in with sunset. The corner of town Clifford was able to see looked like a constellation of new stars, a handful of fire scattered over the earth beyond Powell Creek Park. He had forgotten the way it looked. It looked like Christmas, Clifford thought.

"Cliffy!" That was his mother's voice as she hurried up the stairs, choked with excitement. She opened the door of his room and stared wide-eyed at him. "Cliffy, isn't it *wonderful*?"

She looked feverish, he thought, her eyes too bright, skin flushed red—or maybe it was just the sudden light. She waved her hand and he followed her downstairs. He was wearing his pajamas. He hadn't been downstairs in his pajamas in a long time. It hadn't seemed safe.

She danced through the kitchen, opened the microwave oven to see the light come on, ran a finger along the gleaming white enamel of the refrigerator. "Coffee!" she said. "I think we have some left. Stale, but who cares? Cliffy, I'm making a pot of coffee!"

"Great," he said. "Can I watch TV?"

"TV! Yes! Yes! Turn it on!" Then, a soberer thought: "It probably won't get any stations, though. I don't think we're really back home. I think they just hooked up the electricity."

"We could watch a tape," Clifford said.

"God, yes! Play a tape! Turn it up loud!"

"What should I play?"

"Anything! Anything!"

He took a dusty tape from the top of the stack by the TV, untouched for months. No label. He plugged it in.

It was the last thing his mother had recorded, and it was nothing special, a Friday installment of *The Tonight Show* she had meant to watch Saturday morning, back in June.

The theme music startled him. It sounded amazingly realistic. He was afraid someone outside the house might hear it—but that was stupid. All over town, people must be playing videotapes or records or CDs or whatever noisy thing they felt like.

The colors on TV were supernaturally vivid. Clifford sat mesmerized by the screen. He didn't listen to the talk, just relished the sound of the voices. It was all so boisterous, so carelessly happy.

The sound of the TV was like Christmas in a box, and Clifford didn't understand why it made his mother cry.


Evelyn wore her new dress upstairs and looked at herself in the standing mirror.

She liked the way the new light reflected from the peaks and shadowy valleys of the cloth.

"It looks very well," Symeon said. Not *good* or *nice* but *well*. She liked the way he talked. He was very courteous. Very old-world.

"Thank you." She tried to sound demure, not too brazen. "I feel like I haven't thanked you enough."

"The dress," Symeon said. His smile was enigmatic, his eyes obscure.

She said, "The dress—?"

"Take it off."

"You'll have to help me with the stays."

"Of course."

His hands were large but deft.

# CHAPTER 5

Linneth Stone followed Dex to the high school and sat at the back of his morning classes, flanked by the sullen Proctors in their brown woolen uniforms. (She called them *pions*—according to Dex's French–English dictionary, a "checker" or "pawn," but she used the word respectfully.) For two days Dex discussed the Civil War while this petite woman in Victorian dress took notes and methodically filed them in a calfskin binder. Each day, attention in the class-room migrated away from Dex and toward these apparitions seated at the rear.

Dex had hoped the situation would improve now that electrical power had been restored, but it didn't; the fluorescent ceiling lights only made her presence seem more exotic. Today, at lunch, he told her so.

They sat in the staff cafeteria. There was no hot food, but the artificial light dispelled some of the gloom of the cavernous space. Dex had brought a bag lunch. Linneth, flanked by her guards, sat without eating and listened to his complaints.

"I understand the problem," she said. "I didn't mean to create a distraction."

"You have, though. And that isn't the only problem. It's not clear to me what you're hoping to achieve here. Obviously," a nod at the Proctors, "I can't stop you from sitting in on classes. But I'd like to know what the purpose of it is."

She paused a moment, her expression angelic and distracted, collecting her thoughts. "Only to learn from you. Nothing more sinister. To study Two Rivers and—I don't know what to call it—the place Two Rivers came from. Your Plenum."

"All right, but to what end? If I cooperate, who am I helping?"

"You're helping me. But I see what you mean. Mr. Graham, it's really very simple. I was asked to write a social study of the town—"

"Asked by whom?"

"The Bureau de la Convenance Religieuse. The Proctors. But please remember, I'm a contract employee. I work for the Bureau but I don't *represent* the Bureau, not directly. There are several of us in town, civilian workers I mean, mainly academics. For instance, there is a surveyor, an electrical engineer, a documentary photographer, a medical doctor—"

"Each one writing a report?"

"You pose the question with too much malice. If the circumstances were reversed, Mr. Graham, if one of our villages had appeared in *your* world, wouldn't your government do the same thing? Compile records, try to understand the miracle that had happened?"

"People have died here. In good conscience, I don't know if I can cooperate."

"I can't speak for your conscience. I can only say that my work isn't harmful."

"In your eyes. It's certainly a nuisance to *my* work—we've already established that."

"Lieutenant Demarch sent me to you because he thought a teacher of history would have a broader grasp of cultural issues—"

"Did he? My guess is that he was hoping to piss me off."

She blinked but forged ahead: "I won't attribute motive. The point is that I can go elsewhere if I'm interfering with the school. I really don't care to cause trouble."

Her meekness was maddening. Also deceptive. She was relentless, Dex thought. He looked at her over the trestle table, searching for something in the composition of her features: a glimpse under the porcelain exterior. She came from the world outside Two Rivers, but she wasn't a Proctor or a soldier—and that made her nearly unique, potentially interesting.

Too, her curiosity seemed genuine. She might or might not be a tool of the Bureau, but there were obviously questions she wanted to ask. Fair enough. He had a few questions of his own.

He said, "Maybe we can compromise."

"In what way?"

"Well, first of all—you'd be a lot less conspicuous if you lost your bookends."

"I'm sorry?"

"The gentlemen attached to your elbows."

Both guards gave Dex a stony glare meant to intimidate him. He smiled back. He was tired of the Proctors. They dressed like Boy Scouts and swaggered like hall monitors: *pions,* a good word, he thought.

"I will have to talk to Lieutenant Demarch," she said. "I can't promise anything." But the idea seemed to appeal to her.

"You might consider changing the way you dress, too. It draws attention."

"I have considered that. But I'm new here, Mr. Graham.

I'm not sure what would be appropriate, or appropriately modest."

"You're staying at the Woodward Bed-and-Breakfast?"

"Nearby. The motor hotel."

"You've met Evelyn Woodward?"

"Briefly."

"She's about your size. Maybe she can lend you something. She seems to have a new wardrobe these days."

"Yes. Well, perhaps. Do you have any other requirements?"

"Certainly. A quid pro quo. I want something for my time."

"And what would that be?"

"A map of the world. An atlas, if possible. And a good basic history."

"Your history for mine?"

"Right."

She surprised him by smiling. "I'll see what I can do."


His fever broke the night the lights came back to Two Rivers, and Howard Poole emerged from his sickness feeling fragile but immensely clearheaded. It was as if the disease had starved all confusion from the bone of logic.

He waited a day for Dex to show up, but the schoolteacher didn't come. That was all right, Howard thought. It wasn't always easy for Dex to get away; he might have been followed. It didn't matter. It was time to take some initiative on his own.

At noon, when the ration lines opened and the streets were most crowded, Howard packed some food and bottled water and a camp knife into the ample pockets of a big Navy jacket and stepped out into the biting October air.

Maybe he had been in hiding too long, or maybe it was the autumn weather, but everything he looked at seemed to have been cut from a luminous glass. Sidewalks, windows, the tumbled leaves of the trees, were all thin as ice under a cellophane-blue sky. He wanted to take it all in at once, to hoard these colors against another dark season. He forced himself to walk with his head down. He didn't dare attract attention.

He was carrying identification, actually Paul Cantwell's ID. Lucky Paul, Howard thought, on vacation when the roof of the world fell in. It was good documentation, but there was obviously no photo ID; and the cards, if you looked closely, were all out of date—except for the ration card. He might pass muster if the military questioned him. But he might not. He didn't want to run that risk. It was better not to arouse suspicion.

He crossed the intersection of Oak and Beacon and walked east past lifeless businesses, shop windows shadowy and haunted by ghosts: by cameras, computers, fashionable clothes, big-screen TV sets. No one had stolen these things even in the chaotic first days of the military occupation. Nobody wanted them. They were useless to the natives and frighteningly foreign to the soldiers, the trinkets and ornaments of a lost race.

The town had been in a kind of trance, Howard thought, ever since the tanks rolled down Coldwater Road last June. There had been some gestures of resistance, all futile. A couple of NRA types had taken some ineffectual shots from their upper-story windows. Both men were apprehended and executed publicly and without trial. Two Rivers was a hunting–fishing town, and Howard supposed there were a great many people with their Remingtons still primed and hidden. But what could one rural county do against the weight of a nation? Declare independence?

In a way, they were lucky. As occupations go, this one had not been exceptionally brutal—at least not yet. He remembered reading about Phnom Penh under the Khmer Rouge, where civilians had been shot to death for wearing European eyeglasses, or for no reason at all. There had been no such slaughter here, maybe because the battle had been so one-sided and the prize so peculiar.

So the town had capitulated to its occupation with a dazed shrug. Howard was no exception. He had gone into hiding almost gratefully; hiding was something he was good at. He had grown up fragile and chronically thin. Beaten for his awkwardness, he had learned to take his beatings and go home; he had never complained or even plotted revenge. There had always been the solace of a book.

The name of this behavior, Howard thought, was cowardice. He had stopped denying it long ago, had even acknowledged it as a fundamental component of his character. He knew two essential facts about himself: that he was smart and that he was a coward. It wasn't the worst draw in life's lottery.

A memory came wafting up from his childhood. Often during his illness he had been surprised by these gusts of memory, and maybe he was still sick, because here came another: he was ten years old on the porch of the house in Queens, listening to the rumble of his parents' voices, to one of their winding, pleasantly silly marathons of talk.

"Some people believe," his father had said, "in reincarnation—that we live again and again, and in each life we have a task. A thing to do or a thing to learn." He had reached out absently to ruffle his son's hair. "What about you, Howie? What is it your business to learn this time around?"

Howard had been young enough to take the idea seriously. The question plagued him for days. What *was* he supposed to learn? Something difficult, he guessed, or else why dedicate a life to it? Something he had resisted in all his other lives; some Everest of knowledge or virtue.

Let it be anything, he thought—the names of all the stars, the origin of the universe, the secrets of time and space. . . . Let it be anything but courage.


Past midtown, the streets were mostly empty. It was harder to be inconspicuous here. He shuffled with his hands in his pockets; where possible he took suburban roads, winding his way through the newer and bleaker housing projects that marked the western extremity of Two Rivers. The military patrols would not likely come this way; there was nothing here to draw them. Still, he had to be careful. The soldiers had made a barracks out of a Days Inn on the highway, midway between Two Rivers and the ruins of the Physical Research Laboratory—not far from here.

Howard had pored over a map of the town in the days before the tanks came, and he had a good memory for maps; but these curving roads and culs-de-sac confused him. By the time he found an obscure and plausible way east—following a line of electrical towers where the trees and scrub had been cut back—it was nearly curfew.

He had planned for that. He crossed the highway where it met Boundary Road and followed it a quarter mile north, staying close to the drainage ditch on the left. The shadows were already very long. There were no houses out here, nothing but junk maples and the occasional crumbling gas station. He reached his first objective before dark: a tiny bait and camping gear shop close to the border of the old Ojibway reserve.

He had stopped here with Dex Graham last June. Dex had bought a map and a compass, both long since lost. The store was a tar paper shack with a shingle out front. Uninhabited, as Howard had supposed it would be.

He took a long look up and down the highway. He listened for a time. There was no sound but the rattle of a solitary cricket in the chilly dusk.

A fat, rust-red padlock protected the front door. Howard picked his way through a scatter of bald tires, past the rusting hulk of a '79 Mercury Cougar to the rear door. This door was also padlocked, but one brisk tug separated the latch from the rotting wood of the frame.

A powerful stench wafted out of the dark interior. Howard hesitated, repulsed. Then he thought: The bait. Jesus! There had been two big freezers full of herring roe and dew worms in here. Over the summer the contents must have fermented.

He stepped inside, breathing through his mouth. The only light was the last blue of the sky through a dusty window. Howard moved cautiously down an aisle of bulk goods.

He selected three items: a frame backpack, a double-insulated sleeping bag, and a one-man tent.

He carried them outside and paused to take three cleansing gasps of air.

Then he stuffed the folded tent into the backpack and tied the sleeping roll underneath. He shouldered the pack and adjusted its straps on his shoulders. Then he walked north along the highway until he found a trail into the woods.

The trail was mossy and overgrown but seemed to take him in approximately the right direction. He walked for twenty minutes into the wooded Ojibway land; then it was too dark to go any farther.

He pitched his tent on stony soil and managed to cover it with a nylon fly as the last light faded. Finally he tossed his bedroll inside and climbed in after it.

It would be cold tonight. Maybe cold enough to snow if the clouds thickened. October snow, he thought. He remembered early snowfalls in New York: those brittle, small flakes. Groundwater frozen into crusts of ice, old leaves crisp as dry paper.

He had chosen the sleeping bag blindly, but it was a good one, a winter bag. He was warm inside it. He had walked a long way, and he fell asleep before the last light was gone from the sky.


The dream came as it had come every night for weeks, less a dream than a recurring image that had insinuated itself into his sleep.

It was an image of his uncle, of Alan Stern, but not as

Howard remembered him: this Alan Stern was emaciated and translucent, naked, his back to Howard and his spine cruelly visible under the faint, taut flesh.

In the dream he knew that his uncle was bound or connected to an egg of light larger than himself. Howard thought it looked like a nuclear explosion captured by a still camera as the shock wave began to expand, a static moment between nanoseconds of destruction; and Stern was either held by it or holding it, or, somehow, both.

He turned his head to look at Howard. His thin face seemed unutterably ancient, wizened under a wild rabbinical beard. His expression was a combination of agonizing pain and a fierce preoccupation.

*Stern,* Howard tried to say. *I'm here.*

But no sound came, and nothing registered on his uncle's tortured face.

*Maya,* Stern used to tell him. A Hindu word: it meant the world as illusion, reality as a veil of deception. "You have to look behind the *maya*. That's your duty as a scientist."

It came naturally to Stern. For Howard, it was much more difficult.

One summer on a beach in Atlantic City, family vacation: Stern picked up a stone and gave it to Howard and said, "Look at it."

It was an ancient pebble polished by the sea. Smooth as glass, green as the shadows under water, shot through with veins of rusty red. The pebble was warm where the sun had been on it. Underneath, it was cool in his hand.

"It's pretty," Howard had said, idiotically.

Stern shook his head: "Forget pretty. That's *this* stone. You have to abstract its essence. Learn to hate the *particular,* Howard. Love the general. Don't say 'pretty.' Look harder. Gypsum, calcite, quartz? Those are the questions you have to ask. Pretty is *maya.* 'Pretty' is the stupid man's answer."

Yes. But he didn't have Stern's razor intellect. He put the stone in his pocket. He liked it. Its *particular* color. Its coolness, its warmth.

Howard woke in the deep of the night.

He knew at once it was late—well past midnight, still a long time before morning. He felt breathless and weak in the grip of the sleeping bag. He had slept with his left arm bent under his body and the arm was numb, a useless weight of tissue. But he didn't move.

Something had woken him.

Howard had gone camping once before, a week-long expedition in the Smoky Mountains with his parents. He knew there were noises in the forest and that any odd sound was liable to wake a sleeper in the dark. He told himself there was nothing to be afraid of: the only real danger was from the soldiers, and they were hardly likely to be out in the woods at this hour.

Still, he was afraid of what he might have heard or sensed, the fear like a door that had opened in some deep chamber of his body. He gazed into the darkness of the tent. There was nothing to see. Nothing to hear, either, except the rattle of wind in the trees. Branches groaning in the cold. It was cold outside. The air was cold in his nostrils.

There was nothing out there, Howard told himself, except maybe a raccoon or a skunk wandering through the brush.

He shifted onto his back and let the blood pump into his dead arm. The pain was at least a distraction. He closed his eyes, opened them, closed them again. Sleep was suddenly closer than he would have guessed possible, cutting through his anxiety like a narcotic. He took a deep, shuddering breath that was almost a yawn.

Then he opened his eyes, one last blink of reassurance, and saw the light.

It was a diffuse light that threw the shadows of trees onto the skin of the tent. The light was dim at first, then brighter. The sun, Howard thought dazedly. It must be dawn.

But the light was moving too quickly to be the sun. Tree shadows glided over the fabric above him like marching figures. The light, or its source, was traveling through the forest.

He reached for his eyeglasses and couldn't find them. He was blind without his glasses. He remembered folding them and laying them down somewhere on the floor of the tent—but which side? He had been sleepy; the memory was dim. He swept his hand in panicky circles. Maybe he had rolled over on them; maybe, God help him, his glasses were broken.

The frames, when he touched them, felt as cold and fragile as bone china. He hurried them onto his face.

The light was brighter now.

A lantern, Howard thought. Someone was out in the woods with a lantern. The tent and fly were a vivid orange and impossible to miss. He would be seen, might already have been seen. He tugged the zipper on the sleeping bag all the way down, wanting to be free of it when they came for him—whoever *they* were.

The zipper growled into the silence. Howard shucked off the bag and huddled in the corner of the tent where the flap opened into the cold air outside, ready to bolt.

But the shadows on the tent reached a noon angle and then grew longer; the light dimmed moment by moment until it was gone.

Howard waited for what seemed an eternity but might have been four or five minutes. Now the darkness was absolute once more. He couldn't see his hand in front of his face, glasses or no.

He took a deep breath, opened the tent flap, and crawled outside.

His legs were weak, but he managed to stand.

He was able to see the dim silhouettes of the trees against an overcast sky faintly alight with the dim glow of Two Rivers. There was nothing threatening out here—at least, nothing obvious. No sign of what had passed except a strange, acrid odor, quickly gone. The air was cold and hazy with ground fog.

He staggered ten steps from the tent, suddenly aware of the pressure of his bladder, and relieved himself against a tree. So what the fuck had happened here? What exactly had he seen? A lantern, flashlight, headlights on some car? But there had been no sound. Not even footsteps. Well, he thought, people see weird things in the woods. Swamp gas. Ball lightning. Who could say? The important thing was that it was gone, that he hadn't been seen.

*Probably* hadn't been seen, he amended. But even if he had, there was nothing to do about it. Sleep, he thought, if that was possible, and move on in the morning.

He had reached a state of tentative calm when a second light began to flicker on the pinetops.

He felt marginally less threatened this time. This time he could see what was going on. He crouched in the cover of a young maple and watched the sourceless glimmer rising through a foggy thicket some tens of yards away.

What made it eerie, Howard thought, was its noiselessness: how could something as bright as a spotlight move through these woods without rattling the underbrush? And the smoothness of the motion. A glide. Shadows tall as houses wove among the trees.

Howard squatted in the dark with one hand buried in the loam to brace himself. He felt aloof now, in a state of fine concentration, only a little frightened.

The light moved steadily closer. Now, he thought: now it will come around that hillside and I'll see it. . . .

And it did—and he gasped in spite of himself, cut by a breathless, helpless awe.

The light *had* no source. It was somehow *its own* source. The light was a thing; the light had dimension. The light was a nebulous shape ten or fifteen feet tall, almost too bright to look at, but not quite, not quite. It was not a sphere; it had a shape that was tenuous but seemed to suggest a human form—head, arms, trunk, legs. But the features weren't solid; they twined like smoke, were lost to the air, flickered alive. Veins of color pulsed in the brightness.

It came closer. Closer, it wasn't easier to see. The edges blurred; it was diffuse. It moved like a flame; Howard was suddenly afraid it might come close enough to burn him.

Now it paused a few yards away.

The apparition possessed no visible eyes. Nevertheless, Howard was convinced that it *looked directly at him*—that it regarded him with some complex, chill intelligence that flowed toward him and into him like a slow current.

And then it simply moved on: glided past him and away beyond a scrim of trees.

Howard kept still. There were more lights now, none so close, but all nearby, each casting its own grid of shadows into and around the weaving trees. The woods were *populated* with these things, each one marching on some stately orbit. My God, Howard thought. The urge to pray was powerfully strong. My God, my God.


He watched until each source of this nebulous light had passed and a genuine darkness descended again.

Then—bone by bone, tendons creaking—he lifted himself and stood erect.

The cold wind was brisk but the sky seemed less weighty now. It was ink-blue beyond the eastern margin of the forest. Dawn, Howard thought. That bright star might be Venus.

He stumbled back to the tent bereft of every emotion but a wordless gratitude for the fact of his own survival.

He woke hours later in cool sunlight filtered through orange nylon. His body felt raw and his thoughts were quick and fragile.

Time to start thinking like a scientist, Howard scolded himself. Find the center of this problem.

Or just keep walking: that was the other option. Walk past the ruined research buildings, walk deeper into this forest, south toward Detroit or whatever mutation of Detroit existed here; walk until he found a population to lose himself in, or until he died, whichever came first.

The fundamental question, almost too sweeping to ask, was simply *Why?* So many things had happened to Two Rivers, so many enormous, numbing events. All linked, he supposed; all connected in some causal chain, if only he could begin to unravel it. Obviously the town had moved through an unimaginable latitude of time, but why? Had arrived in a world full of archaic technology and perverse religious wars, but why? Why *here,* of all places? And the night shapes in the forest: what were they?

What single line could possibly connect all these things?

He rolled his tent, fielded his pack, and followed the trail eastward.

Sunlight chased cloud into the hazy east. Howard crossed a brook at its shallowest point, where the water streamed in cool transparency over granite rubble. He wished his thoughts were as lucid. He was out of food; he felt hungry and light-headed.

It seemed appropriate that he was moving toward the heart of the crisis, through the undeveloped lands of the old Ojibway reserve toward the ruined Two Rivers Physical Research Laboratory. Through mystery toward revelation. At least, perhaps. Eventually.

Last night these woods had been haunted. Today, in flickering sunlight, the memory seemed ludicrous. And yet there *was* a presence here, never seen but often felt, a private visitation. He felt his uncle with him as he walked: Stern as a presiding spirit. He guessed that wasn't scientific. But that was how it seemed.

The woods thinned. Howard moved more cautiously here. He came to the logging road that connected the lab with the highway. The road had been widened by military traffic. He waited until a truck rumbled past, its primitive engine loud in the silence. Then he crossed the rutted, wet road and walked parallel to it behind a screen of low pines.

He reached the hill from which, long ago, he had watched Chief Haldane's ladder company move beyond a border of blue light. Another trail crossed the road here. It seemed to lead to higher ground along this ridge, and Howard followed it through berry thickets and white pine, sweating under his Navy coat. It was afternoon now and the sunlight was warm.

He came to the peak of the ridge. The Two Rivers Physical Research Laboratory lay in the flatland beyond. Howard felt conspicuous in this elevated place. He shrugged off his pack and left it under a tree. The ridge sloped steeply here and Howard lay on his belly at the edge of it, looking down an incline of rock and wild grasses.

The ruined buildings were still enclosed in their dome of iridescent light. They looked much the way Howard remembered them looking in the spring. The central bunker had stopped smoking, but nothing else had changed—the grounds were embalmed in this glaze of illumination. The single elm outside the staff housing had kept all its leaves. There was a breeze, at least here on this escarpment, but the tree was not moving.

Human activity was restricted to the outside of this perimeter. Obviously, the military had taken an interest in the Two Rivers Physical Research Laboratory. It would have been easy enough to deduce that the lab was at the center of what had happened at Two Rivers, and this persistent skein of light would have captured anyone's attention. The soldiers had put up a wire fence around the circumference of the property. Tents and a pair of tin sheds had been erected. The contrast was striking, Howard thought. Inside the dome, everything was pristine. Outside, the grass had been trampled into mud, ditches had been turned into latrines, garbage had been heaped in enormous mounds.

His attention was focused so closely on the lab that he didn't hear the footsteps behind him until they were too close. He rolled onto his back and sat up, ready to bolt for the trees.

Clifford Stockton regarded him through magnifying-lens eyeglasses. The boy blinked twice. Then he held out a wrinkled paper bag.

"My lunch," he said. "You can have some if you want."

Howard said, "How did you know I wasn't a soldier?"

They sat in the shade some yards away from the edge of the escarpment.

"You don't look like a soldier," the boy said.

"How can you tell?"

"The way you're dressed."

"I might be out of uniform. I might be in disguise."

The boy inspected him more closely. He shook his head: "It's not just your clothes."

"Okay. Still—you should be careful."

Clifford nodded.

The boy had left his bicycle inclined against a tree. He offered Howard half a sandwich wrapped in brown paper and a drink from a thermos of cold water. Howard had brought his own water on this expedition, two Coke bottles tucked into the deep pockets of his jacket, but most of that was gone. He drank from the thermos and said, "Thanks."

"My name is Clifford."

"Thank you, Clifford. I'm Howard."

The boy offered his hand and Howard shook it.

Then, briefly, they worked at the food. It wasn't much of a sandwich, Howard thought, but it was better than most of what he'd been eating lately. Some kind of coarse-ground bread, some meat, probably military rations, not bad if you were hungry. He discovered he was very hungry indeed.

He finished the sandwich and licked the pale grease from his fingers. "Have you been here before, Clifford?"

"A few times."

"Long ride out from town, isn't it?"

"Yes."

Howard felt at ease with the boy. Maybe it was his obvious myopia or his solemn style, but he felt an echo of his own childhood here. One look at Clifford and you knew he was the kind of kid who kept a collection of coins or bugs or comics; that he watched too much TV, read too many books.

His eyes were pinched and cautious, but Howard supposed that was natural; everyone was cautious nowadays.

He said, "How safe is it up here?"

"It's a long hike up from the valley. I've never seen a soldier here. Mostly they stay near the trucks."

"How often do you come here?"

"Maybe once a week or so. Like you said—it's a long ride."

"So why come at all?"

"Find out what's happening." The boy gave Howard a thoughtful stare. "Why are *you* here?"

"Same reason."

"You walked from town?"

Howard nodded.

"Long walk."

"Yup."

"First time?"

"Yes," Howard said. "At least, since the tanks came."

"It's quiet today."

"Isn't it always?"

"No," the boy said. "Sometimes there are more soldiers or more Proctors."

Howard was instantly curious, but he didn't want to intimidate the boy. He ordered his thoughts. "Clifford, can you tell me what they do here? This might be important."

Clifford frowned. He balled up his sandwich wrapper and tossed it into the dark of the woods. "It's hard to tell. You can't see much without binoculars. Sometimes they take pictures. A couple of times I saw them sending soldiers in."

"What—into the lab?"

"Into one of the buildings."

"Show me which one."

They crept to the edge of the escarpment. The boy pointed to a tall structure at the near perimeter of the parking lot: the administration building.

Howard remembered Chief Haldane and his firefighters on the first Saturday after the transition. They had ventured a few yards into that radius and had come out babbling about monsters and angels . . . and sick, Howard remembered, perhaps sicker than they knew. Haldane had died this September, of symptoms that sounded like a runaway leukemia. "I'm surprised they can go in there."

"They wore special clothes," Clifford said, "like diving suits, with helmets. They went in and they came out."

"Carrying anything?"

"Boxes, filing cabinets. Books. Sometimes bodies."

Bodies, Howard thought. The installation wasn't as empty as it seemed. Of course not. People had died here . . . died in their beds, most of them, neatly out of sight.

"They're really well preserved," the boy added.

"What?"

"The bodies."

"Clifford—from this distance, how can you tell?"

The boy was silent for a time. Some nerve had been touched, some delicate truth. The boy avoided Howard's eyes when he finally spoke: "My mom has a friend. A soldier. Who comes over. That's how we get bread for sandwiches. Chocolate bars sometimes." Clifford shrugged uncomfortably. "He's not a bad guy."

"I see." Howard kept his voice carefully neutral. "But he talks sometimes?"

The boy nodded. "At breakfast mostly. He brags."

"He's been here?"

"He was on duty when they brought out a body. He said it was like it only just died. It hadn't decomposed." Another shrug. "If he's telling the truth."

"Clifford, this could be the most important part yet. Do you remember anything else he said? Anything about what they're looking for here, or what they found?"

The boy settled on a granite shelf away from the lip of the escarpment. "He didn't say too much. I don't think he's supposed to. He said people come out of there, even the ones in suits, talking about the weird things they've seen. They can't stay inside too long or go too far. It makes them sick. Some of the first people who went in, died."

Howard thought again of Chief Haldane's leukemia.

"And at night," the boy continued, "everybody leaves. Nobody stays out here at night. It gets strange."

"Strange how?"

The boy shrugged. "That's all I remember. Luke doesn't really talk that much. Mostly he complains about the Proctors. He hates them. Most of the soldiers do. It's the Proctors who keep bringing people out here; the soldiers just follow orders. Luke says the soldiers have to take all these risks because the Proctors decided this place is important." The boy paused, seemed to hold the thought a moment. "But it is important, isn't it? That's why you're here."

"Yes," Howard said. "That's why I'm here."

The boy turned away. He looked small against the blue sweep of the sky. A wind came up the escarpment.

The boy said, "So much has happened. No one knows where we really are—where the whole town is. It just seems like such a long way back home." He turned to Howard, frowning fiercely. "I don't know what happened out here, but it's hard to believe anybody could fix something like that."

Howard looked at the forest beyond the ruined buildings, at the Ojibway land blending seamlessly into ancient white pine wilderness. The hills rolled to a horizon lost in autumn haze. It would be so easy to walk into that vastness. Die or find a new life. Leave.

"Maybe it can be fixed," he said. "I mean to try."

He learned what he could from Clifford, and when the boy took his bike and cycled away Howard sketched a crude map of the compound, estimating distances and the rough circumference of the dome of light.

He crossed the highway before dark and spent another night in the woods nearer to town; nothing disturbed his sleep.

He left his camping gear wrapped in the tent fly and buried under a mound of leaves—he might find his way back here someday—and hiked home through town. He stank of his own sweat and he was desperately thirsty, but he made it back to his basement before curfew without arousing suspicion.

Howard had brought very few possessions into this new world. They were all contained in his single canvas shoulder bag, stashed behind the water heater in the Cantwell house. He brought the bag out and opened it. There was not much inside. Some notebooks, journal extracts he had planned to read, his birth certificate, his lab credentials . . . and this.

Howard took it out of the bag and examined it under a light.

A single sheet of canary-yellow paper torn from a note pad.

On the paper was written, *Stern.*

And a telephone number.

# CHAPTER 6

Milos Fabrikant was the eldest of the battalion of scientists assigned to the work of constructing a nucleic bomb.

Each day, weather permitting, he bicycled from his home—a dreary bunker full of dreary male physicists—to his place of work, an office in one of five enormous buildings occupying a bleak, flat hinterland of northern Laurentia.

Each day, he was drawn to the same observation: everything here was too large. The landscape, the sky, the works of man. Indeed, here was the largest structure the human race had ever created, a huge box-shaped building full of air-evacuated calutrons—he cycled past it on a plain of smooth, black asphalt, under a sky threatening rain.

In the year since the work began in earnest, Fabrikant had ceased to be impressed by this hubris of man and nature. He would be seventy years old before the next Ascension Day, and what pleased him—one of his few private pleasures—was something much simpler: his continuing ability to make this daily two-mile bicycle trip. Riding, he felt like an athlete. He had colleagues as young as forty (that pig Moberly, the materials engineer, for instance) who would be exhausted by half the journey. Rattling through a grim dream of war on his old blue bicycle, Fabrikant felt as if he might live forever.

He was a physicist, but the great physicists, the legend went, do all their best work in their twenties. Maybe so, Fabrikant thought. His real work here was in administration, not theory. He was an administrator, nevertheless, who understood the project in every detail, who grasped the work in all its splendid, terrible beauty.

He had been involved in nucleic science for years. He remembered the primitive laboratories at the Université de Terrebonne, before the war made everything urgent, where he and the physicist Pariseau had packed an aluminum sphere with powdered uranium metal and heavy water and lowered it into a swimming pool—the pool at the old gymnasium; a new one had lately been built to replace it. What they had created was a primitive nucleic pile: neutron multiplication above unity for the first time in a laboratory. But the aluminum sphere had leaked, and when the pool was drained the uranium caught fire. There was an explosion— chemical, thank God, not nucleic. The old gymnasium burned to the ground. Fabrikant had feared he would lose his tenure; but the paper he wrote won him a scholastic prize, and the university collected handsomely, he was told, from the insurance.

But such fruitful imprecision was no longer allowed. Now Fabrikant spent his days negotiating with the war economy, balancing its amazing largesse against its even more amazing stinginess. For instance: ten thousand pounds of copper for the calutrons. No problem. But paper clips had been on back order for six months.

Purified silver, but no toilet paper.

And the endless requisitions were all routed through Fabrikant's office, which also conducted goodwill tours for military procurement officers and endless informal accountings to Bureau officials skeptical of any expenditure on "mere" science, even a weapons project.

He left his bicycle in a broom closet, climbed two floors and said good morning to Cile, his secretary. She smiled without conviction. Fabrikant's office faced west, where much of the view was occluded by the separation buildings, vast gray strongboxes streaked with rain. Beyond them, tundra. Chimneys vented steam into the foggy air.

He looked at the schedule Cile had prepared. All morning was devoted to a single meeting with a Proctor who had flown in from the capital: a Censeur named Bisonette. Subject of meeting, not stated. Another command performance, Fabrikant thought wearily. A fit agenda for a bleak morning: parading some hobble-footed bald monolingual bureaucrat past the diffusion chambers. He sighed and began to rehearse his own dubious French. *Le réacteur atomique. Une bombe nucléaire. Une plus grande bombe.*

Was it evil, Fabrikant sometimes wondered, even to consider constructing such a weapon?

The military misunderstood the project. One told them, so-and-so thousand tons of TNT. And they would think, *Ah, a big bomb.*

But it was not that. Fabrikant had glimpsed the potential, saw it perhaps more clearly than his colleagues. To liberate the energy locked into matter was to tamper with nature at the most fundamental level. Nucleic division was the prerogative of the stars, after all, and what were the stars but the provinces of God?

"If he flees westward, he finds the fire. If he turns southward, he finds the fire. If he turns northward, the seething fire meets him again. Nor does he find a way to the east to be saved, for he did not find it in his days of incarnation, nor will he find it in the day of judgment." The Book of Thomas the Contender—Thomas the Humorless, Fabrikant had thought when he was forced to memorize the verses in secondary school. Doom at every compass point. Fabrikant wondered if he had become the hands of Thomas, manufacturing the vehicle of that ultimate flame.

But the Spaniards were pressing at the western border, and the news was not as rosy as the radio made it seem, and the Republic was worth preserving—for all its faults, Fabrikant thought, it was at least a place where the two races, the French and the English, had achieved a *modus vivendi*; it was more liberal than the European monarchies, with their nationalist heresies or Romish paganisms. So yes, a bigger bomb, a seething fire, to devastate Seville, perhaps, or some military port such as Málaga or Cartagena. And then the war would be over.

He looked up from these musings and a cold cup of coffee as Cile introduced the Censeur, M. Bisonette. Tall, a stubble of white hair, eyes sheathed in wrinkled flesh. Long-fingered hands: *aristocratic,* Fabrikant thought. Damn the French. At Consolidation, there had been no official decision that the English would control the civilian government and the French would dominate the religious hierarchy—but that was how it had turned out, a permanent standoff rendered as constitutional tradition. Miraculously, for 150 years, the truce had held. *"Bonjour,"* Fabrikant said. *"Bonjour, Monsieur Bisonette. Qu'y a-t-il pour votre service?"*

"My English is adequate," the Censeur said.

Implying: *Better than your French.* Well, that was true enough. Fabrikant was secretly relieved. "More than adequate, obviously. I apologize, Censeur. Please, sit down and tell me what I can do for you this morning."

The Censeur, who carried a leather case, directed at Fabrikant a smile that provoked his deep suspicion.

"Oh, many things," the Censeur said.

Cile brought more coffee.

"Your work here is the separation of uranium," M. Bisonette said, consulting a sheaf of papers he had drawn from his case. "Specifically, the isolation of the isotope, uranium 235, from the raw ore."

"Exactly," Fabrikant said. Cile's coffee was hot and thick, almost Turkish. Tonic against the northern chill. Taken in excess, it gave him palpitations. "What we ultimately hope to achieve is a cascading nucleic division of the atom through the release of neutrons. To accomplish this—" He looked at Bisonette and faltered. The Censeur was regarding him with a bored contempt. "I'm sorry. Please go on."

This might be serious.

"You're pursuing three routes to purification," Bisonette intoned. "Gaseous diffusion, separation by electromagnetism, and centrifugation."

"That's what these buildings are for, Censeur. If you would like to see the work—"

"The electromagnetic and centrifugal projects are to be discontinued and abandoned. The diffusion will be pursued with certain refinements. You'll be sent blueprints and instructions."

Fabrikant was aghast. He could not speak.

Bisonette said mildly, "Do you have any objections?"

"My God! *Objections?* Whose decision is this?"

"The Office of Military Affairs. With the consent and approval of the Bureau de la Convenance."

Fabrikant couldn't disguise his outrage. "I should have been consulted! Censeur, I don't mean to offend, but this is absurd! The purpose of running three processes simultaneously is to determine which is most effective or efficient. We don't know that yet! Diffusion is promising, I admit, but there are still problems—*enormous* problems! The diffusion barriers, to take an obvious example. We've looked at nickel mesh, but the difficulty—"

"The barrier tubes are already in production. You

should have them by December. The details are explained in the documents."

Fabrikant opened his mouth and closed it. Already in production! Where could such knowledge have come from?

Then it struck him: the obvious implication. "There's another project. That's it, isn't it? They're ahead of us. They've achieved a usable enrichment."

"Something like that," M. Bisonette said. "But we need your cooperation."

Of course. The Bureau must have sponsored its own research program, the hypocrites. Wartime redundancy. My God, Fabrikant thought, the waste!

And—admit it—he was ashamed that he had been beaten to the finish line; that somewhere else, all his problems had been solved.

He looked at his coffee cup, all appetite fled.

"The bomb itself," Bisonette was saying. "You have a preliminary design?"

Fabrikant worked to recover his composure. Why was it the Proctors must always strip a man of his dignity? "A sort of nucleic gun," he told Bisonette, "although this is premature, but in essence, a conventional explosive to compact the purified uranium—"

"Look here," Bisonette said, and handed him a technical cutaway drawing of what Fabrikant mistook, at first, for a soccer ball.

"The casing contains these cells of explosives. The core is a hollow sphere of plutonium. I'm not a theorist, Monsieur Fabrikant, but the documents will explain it."

Fabrikant gazed at the drawing. "The tolerances—"

"Will have to be precise."

"To say the least! You can achieve that?"

"No. *You* can."

"This is untested!"

"It will work," Bisonette said.

"How can you know that?"

The Censeur displayed once more his secretive, sly smile. "Assume that we do," he said.

Fabrikant believed him.

He sat alone in his office after the Censeur left. He felt stunned, immobilized.

He had been rendered useless in the space of—what had it been? An hour?

Worse, it all seemed too real to him now. These blue-prints were evidence that the project would go ahead; the Censeur's certainty was undeniable. The atom would be divided; the fire would seethe.

Fabrikant, who was not conventionally religious, never-theless shivered at the thought.

They would sunder the heart of matter, he thought, and the result would necessarily be destruction. Theologians spoke of the *mysterium coniunctionis*, the mystery of union: in Sophia Achamoth, of man and woman, perfect androg-yny; in nature, of particle and wave, the uncollapsed wave function; the balance of forces in the atom. A balance which Fabrikant, like some noxious demiurge, was about to dis-turb. And cities would be destroyed, if not worlds.

He felt like Adam, imprisoned by the Archons in a mor-tal body. And here, on this desk, was his Tree.

*Its branches are the shadow of death; its sap is the unction of evil and its fruit is the wish for death.*

His last question to the Censeur had been, "How far has this gone? Has the bomb itself been tested?"

"There is no bomb until you build it," Bisonette told him. "The testing you may leave to us."

# CHAPTER 7

Until the spring," Censeur Bisonette said. "Pacify the town until the spring. Can we trust you to do that?"

There was an insult lurking in the question. Symeon Demarch looked at the telephone with a sour expression.

It was Evelyn Woodward's telephone, finally connected to the external world through some sort of impedance transformer the military engineers had installed: no more radiotelephones. But the handset, pink and lightweight and obscenely curved, felt peculiar in his hand. It was made of a substance like Bakelite, but less substantial; an oil-based synthetic, the engineers said.

"The town is already pacified," Demarch said. "The town has been pacified for months. I don't anticipate a problem as long as the militia cooperates."

"It will," said Bisonette's distant, metallic voice. "Corporal Trebach is not in a position to argue with the Bureau."

"He seems disposed to."

"He'll be tamed. The weight of the Bureau is about to fall on his shoulders. The corporal has not led an impeccable life."

"If you threaten him, he'll blame me. I'm the one on the scene."

"No doubt. But we'll also tell him you've been ordered to report any obstruction. That should rein him in. He doesn't have to *like* you, Lieutenant."

"All right. What about the Ideological Branch? I've had complaints from the Ordinal attaché."

"Delafleur? A pompous idiot. *Une puce.* Pay no attention."

"The Ideological Branch—"

"The Ideological Branch is under control," the Censeur said. "I'm giving them what they want."

"What Delafleur wants is to destroy the town."

"He can't. Not now."

"Not until spring?"

"Precisely."

"Is there a schedule?"

"Do you need to know more? There should be a packet from the Oversight Committee in a week or two. All I want is your guarantee that the situation is stable for a few more months."

"It is," Demarch said, understanding that his head had just been inserted in a noose: if anything went wrong now, the blame would fall on him. But he was trapped in his own momentum. He heard himself say, "I guarantee it."

"That's all, then." The Censeur broke the connection.

Demarch hung up the telephone and sighed. Then he turned and saw Evelyn Woodward standing in the doorway.

How much had she heard? It was impossible to know. Or to guess what she would make of it. Briefly, he reran the conversation in his mind, sorting his own words from the Censeur's: how much could she guess?

She seemed to look at him oddly, but that could have been his imagination. She was an alien, after all. Mistakes were easy to make with these people, especially in matters of body language.

She said, "I came to see if you wanted coffee."

"Yes, please, Evelyn. I would like a cup of coffee." He gestured at the desk, which had once been her desk, in a room in which she had once kept accounts for her auberge. "A little more work to do tonight."

"I see. Well, I'll be back in a minute."

She closed the door behind her.

Demarch picked up the most immediate paper on the desk. It was the first of Linneth Stone's reports, essentially her working notes. He had intended to read it tonight, but he wasn't enthusiastic at the prospect. Linneth Stone was a career academic and wrote like one, tedious pensées in the passive voice.

*On the evidence of Subject's accounts and numerous contemporary published Works (cf.* Time *magazine,* Newsweek, *etc.), the Institution of Marriage in the United States was undergoing a process of rapid Change, from predominantly traditional, religiously sanctioned Monogamie (with a minority of exceptions) to a commonplace of Divorce and Re-Marriage and unorthodox Arrangements including unmarried Parenting and even a certain sanctioning of like-gender Relations.*

Venery, bastardy, and sodomy, in other words. Demarch thought of his own wife and child in the capital. Dorothea had been instrumental in his rise through the ranks of the Bureau: she was a Francophone of good family, an essential career asset for someone like Demarch, born an Anglophone in a rural town. The Bureau de la Convenance was a vast, incestuous bureaucracy—a labyrinth of old families. Demarch's connection had been tenuous, through his mother Célestine, who was cousin to a retired supérieur ancien named Foucault; that and his university degree had been enough to get him in the door of the Académie at Belle Ile. Dorothea opened doors more arcane and significant. Her father, a Censeur, had shepherded Demarch through a long stint as an Ideological Branch operative. He had earned his bona fides there, had put in years and fought for promotion. Still, even today, aging Censeurs like Bisonette spoke to him with the disdain of a pureblood for a half-breed.

Dorothea had been essential to him and he could not imagine leaving her. Divorce was not altogether uncommon among Valentinians in the upper echelons of the civil service, but Demarch disapproved. According to Linneth, American literature spoke often of love. Well, so did every popular literature. But the educated classes were supposed to know better. Marriage had very little to do with love. It was an institution, like the Bureau or the Federal Bank. You don't cease banking simply because you no longer "love" the bank.

Love fades; wasn't that inevitable? And the demands of the body were fickle. One made arrangements to deal with the physical aspect. One did not, Demarch thought, indulge in melodrama or attempt to rewrite history.

Or maybe that was only the voice of his own buried conscience. His father had been a Sethian of the Order of Luther, a deacon of the Church and a moral pacifist. Hedrick Michael Demarch: the fierce Saxon consonants always made him think of the sound of a dog gnawing a bone. The name still echoed in the lieutenant's mind, though his father had died ten years ago; sometimes, too, the voice itself, the tides and swells of its disapproval.

He thought of Bisonette's nucleic bomb project, dramatically hastened by documents the Bureau had culled from the libraries of Two Rivers. Apparently there was enough in the generally distributed literature to advance the research by months. Once the Censeurs had given this strange documentation their imprimatur of authenticity, it had gone to the engineers and scientists, who had turned it into blue-prints.

This was work Demarch had helped along; it had been his idea to archive the libraries first of all. Theologians in the Ideological Branch had still been debating the meta-physical status of Two Rivers while Demarch was shipping east its books. That was something else his father had taught him: the value of a book.

But what kind of a world had he hastened into being? His son Christof was eight years old. Now Christof would grow up under the shadow of this transcendent weapon, just as the inhabitants of Two Rivers had. Maybe it was the bomb that would unleash the other horrors: the anarchy, the drug addiction, the rampant immodesty.

An October wind rattled the window. Demarch looked up from his thoughts. Evelyn had come back with coffee on a wooden tray; she stood at the doorway waiting to be noticed. He waved her into the room.

She glanced at the window and shivered. "Cold out there. All the leaves are off the trees. It could be a cold winter ahead."

He stood and drew the blinds. "Winters are often cold here. But you must know that." Reminding himself of the fact. "We shared the weather, if nothing else."

He had seen Evelyn's map of the United States, and the contours of the landscape were identical: the fingers of the Great Lakes, the coastlines and the rivers. Her map had been more crowded with roads and cities, and all the names had been ludicrously strange, but he supposed the weather in the Near West must have been the same. "Snow before too long," she said. "Will that complicate everything? I mean, supplies and so forth?"

"The road from Fort LeDuc has been reinforced. We have mechanical ploughs."

"I see."

She seemed to want to linger. Maybe it was the sound of the wind in the eaves. The house was empty but for the two of them; it had become Demarch's private headquarters. It was comfortable but large enough to be lonely.

He glanced back at the desk, at Linneth Stone's typed pages.

*Subject maintains that American Morality has always been a Battle-ground between contending Ideas of Liberty and Virtue. In the last Century—*

But the last century could wait until morning. He was tired. He turned off the desk lamp.

"Come to bed," Evelyn said.


Evelyn was passive in bed. Demarch preferred it that way. He was not a passionate or athletic lover. He never lost sight of the fundamental incongruity of the act—one of the several jokes God had played on Man. Evelyn's motion under his weight was as delicate as a breath, and she sighed at the climax.

He was as fond of her as he had been of any of his occasional women. He liked her silences as much as her words. She knew when not to speak. She was quiet now, looking at him with sleepy eyes.

He kissed her and drew away. He had worn a fish-skin —what Evelyn called a condom, a singularly ugly word. He peeled it off and took it to the bathroom and flushed it away and came back to bed chilled by a tide of cool air. Evelyn was already asleep, or seemed to be. He adjusted the blanket over her shoulders and admired the terrain it made of waist and hips, so unlike Dorothea's. He closed his eyes. The north-country wind rattled the window. She had been right about the snow. Snow soon, he thought.

His mind drifted back to Bisonette's telephone call and Linneth Stone's ethnological notes. He thought of the town of Two Rivers, dropped from the sky by an unknown magic; itemized, dissected, cataloged, ultimately to be destroyed. The Ideological Branch, an avant-garde of Christian probity, could not abide the prolonged existence of the town. It

posed too many questions; it argued for a world even
stranger and more complex than their celestial troupeau of
angels and Archons. They hated especially the town's mu-
tant Christianity, a Christianity almost Judaic in its insis-
tence on one Creator, one risen Christ, one Book.

And yet here was Evelyn, a heretic by anyone's standard, though she claimed she had never taken religion "too
seriously"; she was human, spoke English, was clothed in
flesh not different from his flesh. He had felt her heart
beating under the bump of her ribs. She was not a criminal
or a succubus; merely a bystander.

One could not offer such arguments to the IB. They
were more fascinated, more frightened, by the dome of blue
light in the woodlands. It partook of the miraculous and
was therefore, they reasoned, their property. Give credit
where due, Demarch thought: some of the IB men were
brave; some of them had walked into that light and walked
out sickened or insane. Some had died, of what the doctors
eventually called an irradiation disease. But the metaphysical puzzle was finally too much to endure. The town and all
its inhabitants were *malum in se* and must be erased from
the earth.

And how better than with Bisonette's nucleic bomb?
Which, in any case, would need to be tested.

But Evelyn. Evelyn was human. Evelyn would have to
be taken care of.

He would have to look into that.


He had scheduled an interview the next day with Linneth Stone's "Subject," the history teacher, Dexter Graham.

The sitting room of Evelyn's hostel made an odd reception for a lieutenant of the Bureau. Leafless tree branches
tapped the high windows; the furniture was large and padded. A Persian carpet decorated the floor and a mantel
clock ticked into the afternoon silence. A moat of stagnant
time.

Graham arrived between two pions in blue winter vestons, escorted in from a cloudy cold day. There was frost on the schoolteacher's shoes. He wore a gray windbreaker tattered at the seams and was more gaunt than Demarch remembered. He looked at Demarch without visible emotion.

The lieutenant waved at a chair. "Sit down."

Graham sat. The pions left. The clock ticked.

Demarch poured coffee from a carafe. He had interviewed dozens of the town's preeminent men in this room: the mayor, the city councillors, the police chief, clergymen. Their eyes always widened at the sight of a hot cup of coffee. Demarch was always scrupulously polite. But there was never a cup for the guest. Of such humble stones, the fortress of authority was built. He said, "I gather your work with Linneth Stone is going well?"

"It's her work," Dexter Graham said. "I work at the school."

The insolence was amazing. Refreshing, in a way. The lieutenant had grown accustomed to the automatic deference of civilians, to the uniform as much as to himself. Dexter Graham, like many of the citizens of Two Rivers, had never learned the reflex.

Since the executions last June, many had acquired it. But not this one.

"Miss Stone arranged some liberties through my offices. She won't be escorted by guards, for instance. Are you cognizant of the fact that this is a considerable generosity on my part?"

"I'm aware that it's a little out of character."

"I don't want you to trespass on that generosity."

"I don't intend to."

"In the course of the last several months we've had notable cooperation from the town's responsible leaders, Mr. Graham—everyone from the mayor to your principal, Bob Hoskins." Which was all true. Only the churchmen had been truly problematic, and Demarch had promised them they would be allowed to carry on their odd species of worship. Clement Delafleur had protested all the way to the capital. But it was only a temporary arrangement, after all. "You're something of a pillar of this community yourself, Mr. Graham. I need your cooperation, too."

"I'm not a pillar of anything."

"Don't be modest. Though I admit the record tends to support you there. Transferred five times in fifteen years for violations of school board protocol? Maybe you chose the wrong profession."

"Maybe I did."

"You admit it?"

Dexter Graham shrugged.

Demarch said, "There is an aphorism. One of our writers defined a scoundrel as a brave man without loyalty to his prince."

"There aren't any princes here."

"I was speaking figuratively."

"So was I."

The clock rationed a few more seconds into the still air.

"We've done a great deal for the village," Demarch said. "We've restored water. We've laid electrical lines all the way from Fort LeDuc fifty miles south. Those weren't easy decisions. They were opposed. No one understands what happened in this patch of woods, Mr. Graham; it's very strange and very frightening. Good will has been shown."

Graham was silent.

Demarch said, "Acknowledge that."

"The water is running. The lights are on."

"But despite that generosity we still have reports of curfew violations. A man about your size and age was seen crossing Beacon Street after dark."

"It's a common size and age."

"The curfew isn't a joke. You've seen what happens to criminals."

"I saw Billy Seagram's body on a cart outside City Hall. His niece walked past the body on the way to school. She cried for three hours in the classroom. I saw that." He leaned over to tie a ragged shoelace, and Demarch was fascinated in spite of himself by the casual gesture. "Is that why you brought me here? To put the fear of God into me?"

Demarch had never heard the expression. He blinked. "I don't think that's in my power, Mr. Graham. But it sounds like a prudent fear."

He was insolent, but was he dangerous?

Demarch pondered the question after Graham was dismissed. He pondered it that night as he climbed into bed with Evelyn.

She had been nervous about the interview. Demarch supposed she thought he was petty enough to hate Graham because Graham had been her lover. "Don't get angry with him," she said. Imagining that *anger* had anything to do with it.

Demarch said, "I only want to understand him."

"He's not dangerous."

"You're defending him. That's a noble impulse, but it's misplaced. I don't want to kill him, Evelyn. My job is to keep the peace."

"If he breaks the law? If he violates the curfew?"

"That's what I mean to prevent."

"You can't frighten him."

"Are you saying he's stupid?"

She turned out the light. The temperature outside had dropped and there were fingers of frost on the windowpane. Dim radiance from a streetlight traced a filigree of shadow on the opposite wall.

"He's not that kind of man," Evelyn ventured. "He told me a story once. . . ."

"About himself?"

"Yes. But he told it like a story about someone else. He said, suppose there was a man, and this man had a wife and a son. And suppose he was always careful about what he said or did, because he might lose his job or something bad might happen to his family, and he cared about his family more than anything. And then suppose the man was out of town, and there was a fire, and his house burned down with his wife and child in it."

"He lost his wife and son in a fire?"

"Yes. But that's not the point. He said it was the worst thing that could happen to this man—a complete loss of everything at the center of his life. And he survived it somehow, he went on living. And then, Dex said, the man noticed a strange thing. He noticed that there was nothing left to hurt him. What could be worse than *this*? Death? He would have *welcomed* death. Losing a job? Trivial. So he stopped hiding his opinions. He told the truth. He got in trouble, but there was no threat that meant anything to him. No more terrors. For instance, he used to hate riding in airplanes, he was a white-knuckle flier—but not anymore. If the plane fell out of the sky and he was killed . . . well, that was territory his wife and child had already visited. Maybe he'd find them there, waiting for him." She shivered. "You understand? He was brave almost by accident. It got to be a habit."

"Is this a true story? Is that how he seemed to you?"

"Some of the edges have worn off. This was all a long while ago. But yes, that's how Dex seemed."

Brave, Demarch thought, but probably not dangerous. A man with nothing to lose has nothing to defend.


Later, on the verge of sleep, Evelyn said: "There are more soldiers around town. Another truckful came past today."

Demarch nodded, not far from sleep himself. He was thinking of Dorothea. He was thinking of Christof's small face, his eyes bright as porcelain china.

"Symeon? Is something bad going to happen to the town? When you were talking on the phone—"

"Hush. It was nothing."

"I don't want anything bad to happen."

"Nothing bad will happen to you," the lieutenant said. "I promise. Now sleep."


In the morning there was half an inch of snow on the ground. Demarch's boots crunched on the frozen paving stones as he walked to his car; wet snow tumbled from the branches of the trees as he drove to the heart of the town, where the dismantling of Two Rivers had already begun.

# CHAPTER 8

The last of autumn was an unsettled time in Two Rivers.

Mornings were often achingly cold; afternoon skies were cloudy or a stark, brittle blue. Woodsmoke drifted through the commons. Women in the food lines wore down jackets or bulky cloth coats; men shuffled forward with parka hoods drawn or caps pulled over their ears. No one lingered in the streets.

Things were changing, people whispered.

For instance: every day now, between the hours of seven and eight in the morning, two or three militia trucks would come into town popping blue smoke from rust-caked tailpipes. The trucks were drab green and always manned by six or eight soldiers. A truck would park outside a building—most often a store or warehouse—and the soldiers would stretch and climb shivering down from the tailgate and file inside. Inside, they would box items and tag them and stack them for loading into the truck.

They took not everything, but each of a kind: one toaster, one television set, one of every variety of home and office computer. Nothing was spared this inventory of the town, not chairs or shoe polish or window shades; but special attention was devoted to technical devices, especially anything with a microchip or a memory.

It seemed to Calvin Shepperd, ex-charter pilot and watchful citizen—who made the trip to the food depot every three days because Sarah refused to suffer the indignity —that the soldiers must be taking all these objects to some gargantuan museum . . . a museum of notions and appliances, a kind of Noah's ark of dry goods.

It was systematic looting, he thought, and it would take a while to complete, but eventually this work would be finished, the town would be cataloged and all its treasures itemized and locked away, and then . . . well, he couldn't guess. He didn't know what would happen then; he knew only that the idea of it filled him with dread.


On a cold morning late in the year, Linneth Stone gave Dex Graham a map packed in a cardboard tube.

He unrolled the document across the chipped Formica top of a table at Tucker's. Tucker's Restaurant had reopened in mid-October with the permission of the Bureau. The menu was limited to eggs, cheese, bread, coffee, milk reconstituted from powder, and a kind of chopped steak everyone had learned to avoid. Still, the opening had been a morale booster. Dex supposed it was meant to be.

Last night's wet snow kept the breakfast trade at home. Dex and Linneth were alone in the diner. Linneth had disguised herself in a casual blouse and modest skirt, but she still looked odd here, Dex thought, misplaced in a vinyl booth. He tried to imagine what her natural setting would be. Someplace more dignified. Someplace with a carpet, not this peeling linoleum. Tablecloths, not Formica.

He used the salt, pepper, and sugar dispensers to peg down three corners of the map. Then he drew a breath and took his first comprehensive look at the new world.

The map shocked him, although he had anticipated much of what he saw. The shock came not from the novelty but the blunt declaration of it. The miraculous, in blue ink and fine print.

Linneth was patient while he stared. She said, "Tell me what strikes you."

He put together his impressions. "The East is more crowded than the West."

She nodded. "The East was settled first, of course. English and French colonies. All the old cities: Boston, Montmagny, Montreal, Manhattan. During the War of Brittany, the colonies declared their independence. The Republic was a consolidation of the fifteen eastern provinces. It expanded west as the aboriginals were killed or resettled. Obviously, a great deal of the Far West is still virgin land."

He traced the blue snake of the Mississippi River from the province of Mille Lacs to the city of New Orleans. To the west was a grid of prairie and mountain provinces: Athabasca, Beausejour, Sioux, Colorado; Nahanni, Kootenay, Platte, Sierra Blanca, from the Beaufort Sea to the border of New Spain. New Spain was approximately Mexico, with a panhandle up the western coast as far as what would have been southern Oregon. There was no Canada. The Republic ruled everything north of the fortieth parallel.

"The Spanish lands are disputed, of course. The war."

"The whole map is less crowded." Cities were sparse even as far east as the Great Lakes. "What's the population of the world?"

She frowned. "I remember reading the estimate. Two billion?"

"Where I come from, it was nearer six."

"Oh? I wonder why?"

"I don't know. The two histories must be fairly similar. We speak the same language, more or less, and I recognize some of these names. If our histories are like a tree—one branched left, one branched right—it might be useful to know where they divided."

Linneth seemed to concentrate on the idea. It was new to her, Dex supposed. She hadn't been raised on *Star Trek,* the "parallel world" as a place where Mr. Spock wears a beard.

"If the histories 'branched,' as you say, it must have happened a long time ago. The religions are different."

"But there are still parallels. We both have a prominent Christianity, even though they're different in detail."

"Considerably. Before Calvary, then?"

"Or not long after. First century, second century, say. Before the Romans adopted Christianity. Before Constantine."

Linneth blinked. "But they didn't. The Romans, I mean. There *were* no Christian emperors."

Charlie Tucker brought two plates of bread and cheese, for which Dex exchanged a handful of food coupons. Charlie gave Linneth a long look. He had heard her accent. He looked worried.

She nibbled a wedge of cheese and waited for Charlie to wander back behind the cash desk. "Some of the Apologia are addressed to the Antonine emperors. Ecumenicists are always pointing to Clement, who gives a good impression of an erudite pagan. But no Roman emperor explicitly embraced the Cross. It's an odd idea. So perhaps that's the point of division—your Christian emperors."

"Maybe." Dex thought about it. And then he reminded himself why she was here. "Is this for your dossier?"

"History isn't my subject. In any case, the Proctors emptied your libraries. They can ferret this out for themselves." She added, "I would hardly dare counsel them on religious matters. This would all be very blasphemous if it weren't a matter of record."

"I'm sorry," he said. "I'm still not sure when I'm talking to you and when I'm talking to the Bureau."

"Perhaps I should wear two hats. One when I'm myself, and one when I'm an agent of the state."

"Which one are you wearing now?"

"Oh, my own. My own particular hat."

"In either hat, you have me at a disadvantage. You know my history—"

"Very little, to be truthful. Only what I've learned from you or the public material. The books were all locked away months ago."

"Still, you know more about my history than I know about yours."

She opened her calfskin case. "I brought this for you. I borrowed it from one of the militiamen. He said it was for his daughter, but he was reading it himself. A children's book, I'm afraid, but it was the only history I was able to locate on brief notice."

The book was a tattered duodecimo in hard covers, the title etched in gold leaf:

*THE EVENTS OF HISTORY,*
*FROM CREATION TO THE PRESENT DAY,*
*WITH ILLUSTRATIONS.*

It gave off a pungent reek of wet canvas. Dex took it from her.

"You can form an approximate notion," Linneth said, "though I do not vouch for the details."

He looked at her again. He wondered what the book represented—was it a promise kept, a strategic offering, simple kindness? Her face was unclouded, in some ways as perfect a face as Dex had ever seen, round and generous and serene. But reserved. For every ounce given, an ounce was withheld. And maybe that was not surprising, under the circumstances, but still . . .

She said, "I would like a book in return."

"Which book?"

"One of yours. I peeked into your room, when the Proctors brought me to your door the first time. You own books. You're a reader. But not history. Something literary. Something you like. I think that would be instructive."

"For which hat?"

Briefly, she looked offended. "My hat."

He had been carrying the dog-eared paperback of *Huckleberry Finn* in his jacket pocket for a month, and he was reluctant to part with it. He took it out and handed it to her. "The text is more than a century old. But I think you'll get the drift."

"The drift?"

"The essence. The meaning."

"I see. And the book is a favorite of yours?"

"You could say that."

She accepted it reverently. "Thank you, Mr. Graham."

"Call me Dex."

"Yes. Thank you."

"Tell me what you think of it."

"I will."

He rolled up the map and volunteered to walk her back to the civilian housing at the Blue View Motel. Outside, she frowned at the weather—sunny today, but cold enough that an early snow hadn't melted from the road. In her white jacket she might have been anyone, Dex thought. Any good-looking woman on a windy sidewalk. The wind reddened her cheeks and earlobes and carried away her breath in foggy wisps.

He wondered when he would see her again. But he couldn't think of a plausible reason to ask.

She stopped and faced him at the corner of Beacon and Oak. "Thank you for escorting me."

"You're welcome."

She hesitated. "Probably I shouldn't say this. But I've heard rumors. Rumors about curfew violations. The Proctors are looking into it. Dex—"

He shook his head. "I've already had this warning. Demarch threatened me personally."

Her voice was nearly a whisper. "I'm sure he did. That is, he *would*. It's in his nature. But I don't mean to threaten you. All I mean to say is, be careful."

She turned and hurried away, and he stood on the windy sidewalk looking after her.


The *Two Rivers Crier,* a weekly newspaper, had not seen an issue since the crisis in June. That autumn, it published a new edition.

The *Crier* had been edited from an office on Grange Street, but the presses were in Kirkland, sixty miles away; since June, much farther than that. Where the town of Kirkland had been, today there was pine forest and an icy creek.

The new *Crier,* a single folded sheet of rag pulp, was a collaboration between a past editor and a committee of Bureau surveillants. The text consisted of announcements from the military and the Proctors. Power failures in the east end were sporadic and would be repaired before the end of the month; a new food depot had been opened at the corner of Pritchard and Knight. There was also a ringing editorial in which the reappearance of the paper was said to augur better times for Two Rivers, "carried as if by stormy gusts into a strange ocean and sailing under the calm winds of cooperation toward safe harbor."

Prominent on the back page was a column announcing a program under which single men between the ages of seventeen and thirty-five were permitted to request relocation and job training elsewhere in the Republic, a living wage to be paid until such time as the men were established in their new lives. It was open to "White Men, Jews, Apostates, Negros, Mulattos, and Others—All Welcome." It attracted considerable attention in town.

There were only a few volunteers. Many were transients

who had been passing through when the accident happened and saw no reason to stay. Some were young men chafing at the friction of martial law. All were accepted for relocation.

The first convoy left town November 3 with a cargo of twenty-five civilians.

Some had families. Some waved at sisters or parents as the transport truck banged south from the A & P parking lot in a gusty, cold rain.

Some were smiling. Some were weeping. All of them promised to write. No letters were ever received.


Clifford Stockton often thought about his father, especially when the soldier was visiting his mom.

His father was a commodities broker living in Chicago (or who *had* lived in Chicago, before everything changed), and he never visited. "A good thing, too," his mother used to say when Clifford pressed her on the subject. "He has his own family there. His own children."

He never visited and he never wrote. But twice a year—at Christmas and on his birthday—Clifford would get a package in the mail.

There was always a card with Clifford's name on it and the appropriate sentiment: Merry Christmas. Happy Birthday. Nothing unusual there.

But the *present*—the *present itself*—was always great.

One year his father sent him a Nintendo game machine and an armload of cartridges. Another time, UPS delivered a radio-controlled scale model P-51 Mustang. The least exciting gift had been a fully equipped chemistry set, confiscated after two weeks when Clifford dropped a test tube and stained the living room shag beyond repair. The most exciting present had come last May: a two-hundred-channel programmable scanner that could eavesdrop on police, fire, and emergency frequencies—as well as on cellular telephones, though hardly anyone in Two Rivers had possessed one.

Clifford had not thought much about the scanner since June. Since the invasion, there had been no power to plug it into; it languished in the closet in his room, on the shelf above the coat hangers . . . ignored, but not entirely forgotten.

Tonight Luke was visiting. Which meant Clifford was confined to his room after nine o'clock. Which left him with not much to do.

He could read. The library was closed permanently, a fact Clifford still had trouble grasping, but the cashier at the Silverwood Mall Brentano's, a friend of his mother, had gone to the store with her key last summer and "borrowed" a bag full of science fiction paperbacks for him. Clifford was working his way through *Dune,* and he spent an hour or so on the intrigues of that desert planet.

But he wasn't in a reading mood, and when the downstairs television fell silent (his mother had been showing Luke her videotape of *On Golden Pond*), Clifford rummaged in the closet for his Game Boy. He found it; but the AC adapter was lost and the batteries, he discovered, were long dead.

The scanner, neglected on the upper shelf, caught his eye. Clifford decided he ought to brush the dust off, if nothing else. He stood on a chair and lifted the metal case down.

He put it on his desk. He liked the way it looked there, the liquid crystal display glittering in the lamplight. He extended the antenna and plugged the cord into the wall.

He hit the scan button and let the internal logic search the airwaves. He didn't expect much. One of the Two Rivers Police Department patrol cars was still allowed to roam around town, so there might be a little police chatter; or something from the fire department, under new management since Chief Haldane died. But both channels were silent.

Idly, he tuned to what should have been the marine band—and suddenly the room was full of voices.

Voices announcing street corners, voices acknowledging the announcements. Clifford was instantly fascinated. It had to be the militia, he thought. Patrol cars making their rounds, calling out checkpoints. *Oak and Beacon, all silent. Camden and Pine, all quiet here.* Clifford punched the monitor button and settled down to listen.

The talk went on. Mostly, the militiamen sounded bored. Periodically, they complained about the cold.

*Checkpoint, Third and Duke. We're almost frozen out here.*

*Noted. Beware ice, James. The streets are slick in Babylon tonight.*

Babylon was what the soldiers called Two Rivers. Luke had told him that.

*No signs of life along the highway. Nico, is it true they're serving pot roast in the commissary tomorrow night?*

*That's the rumor. Supply truck hasn't been in today, though.*

*Samael's pants. I was looking forward to a hot meal.*

*You'll be looking forward to an obscenity demerit if you're not careful. Philip? Your callout is late.*

But now his mother's voice came down the hallway and through the door of his room: "Cliffy? Have you got the TV on?"

"*Shit,*" Clifford said, startling himself a little. He reached for the volume control on the scanner. In his panic, he jerked it the wrong way.

The speaker screamed, "FOURTH AND MAIN! FOURTH AND MAIN! ALL QUIET AT FOURTH AND MAIN!"

Clifford hit the off switch and yanked the power cord out of the wall socket. The scanner was important. He understood that without thinking about it. The scanner was important and he had to hide it, or it would be taken away from him.

He heard his mother's bedroom door swing open.

*"Cliffy!"*

He looked at the high shelf of his closet. Too far away. He lifted the scanner and bent to slip the heavy case into the dusty darkness under his bed. It fit, but only just. The cord trailed behind. He kicked it under the hem of the bedspread.

The door to his room sprang open. His mother stood in the doorway clutching a pink nightgown at her neck and frowning hugely.

"Cliffy, what the *hell* is all that noise?"

"Playing with the Game Boy," he said—lamely, but his mother wouldn't understand the limitations of a hand-held game machine. She had a name for every electronic device Clifford owned: they were all "Fucking Noisy Boxes."

"Yeah?" She glanced at the bed, suspiciously. The Game Boy was lying there. The battery cover was off and the battery well was empty, but his mother wouldn't notice, Clifford thought. Probably. "Well . . . keep it down, okay? You could have woke up the whole neighborhood!"

He said, "I'm sorry. It was an accident."

"It's after ten. Spare a thought for somebody else for once in your life."

"Okay. All right."

She turned away.

Luke was behind her. He wore his uniform. The shirt was unbuttoned to the waist. His chest was a mass of dark, curly hair; his eyes were bright and curious.

He took a step inside Clifford's room and said, "Who is the Game Boy?"

"It's not a who. It's an it. A machine. A game machine."

"Like Nintendo?"

"Yeah, like Nintendo." *Please,* Clifford thought, *don't ask to see it.*

"Cliffy," Luke said. "You must show it to me sometime."

"Sure."

"It sounds like a radio, you know."

Clifford shrugged.

The soldier looked hard at him. "You're not playing tricks on me, are you?"

"No."

"*Est-que vous êtes un petit criminel? Un terroriste?* Eh, Cliffy?"

"I don't understand," Clifford said, quite truthfully.

"See that you don't."

"Luke!" His mother, from down the hall. "Come on!"

The soldier winked at Clifford and left the room.


Since September, classes at John F. Kennedy had been reduced to two days a week. Dex supposed the futility of it had become obvious: nobody at JFK High would be going to Harvard or MIT, not this year or next year or ever. The only thing he was giving these kids was an illusion of normalcy, and maybe that wasn't a good or useful commodity anymore . . . maybe it was even dangerous.

His afternoons were free. He had spent the last two afternoons reading Linneth's history book and today he decided to discuss the contents with Howard Poole. The pressure on Howard had relented over the last few weeks; the Proctors seemed suddenly less anxious to pursue the mystery of the research lab. A daylight visit was possible. Still, Dex took precautions on his way to the Cantwell house. He walked past Oak Street to Powell Creek Park, then doubled back and approached the house from the south.

Howard had been bolder about his Cantwell identity lately. The neighbors seemed to accept the masquerade, or at least none of them had reported him to the militia. But the neighbors were aware of him: they watched, Howard said. People living on the military dole, confined to their houses by fear and bewilderment, had little to do but stare out the window. Dex felt their eyes as he crossed the brown front yard between scabs of ice. He walked quickly between the hedge and the side wall to the back door. He knocked and waited, shivering under the bulk of his jacket. The day had started cold and never warmed up. The last thing this town needed, he thought, was a hard winter. But it felt like a hard one rolling in.

Howard opened the door. Howard wore a threadbare blue sweater, the tail of a white shirt peeking out under the hem. His blue jeans were grimy and he wore gloves on his hands. He waved Dex in and led him to the kitchen. The Cantwell house had been equipped for oil heat, of which there was none, but Howard kept the interior doors closed and the electric oven running, so the kitchen, at least, was passably warm.

Howard offered coffee. "You can get coffee on the ration card now. But I'm still using up what was in the cupboard. It's a little stale but there's plenty of sugar."

Dex nodded and sat at the small table while Howard measured water into a carafe and fed it into the coffee machine. Now that the power was back everyone had these toys to use: coffeemakers, blenders, microwave ovens. The appliances seemed newly frivolous—almost sinful, after months of privation.

"I think he might still be alive," Howard said. "I've been thinking it over, and I believe that's a real possibility."

"Slow down. *Who's* alive?"

"My uncle," Howard said impatiently. "Stern."

And Dex sighed. Every time he came here Howard talked about his uncle. His uncle, the *genius loci* of the Two Rivers Physical Research Lab, the mysterious Alan Stern, and who the hell knows, Dex thought, maybe the guy *was* an important part of what had happened out there. But it had begun to look like an obsession, and Howard himself, gaunt and long-haired, had begun to look obsessed.

Last week he had told Dex about his trip to the Ojibway reserve. There had been apparitions in the woods, Howard said. Which was far from impossible. Dex had ceased passing judgment on the operating rules of the universe. Plainly, the universe was a stranger place than he had imagined. He could accept the possibility of luminous beings out in that scrubby old pine forest. But it seemed equally plausible that Howard had hallucinated the whole episode. Howard had been through a lot, hiding from the Proctors in a basement all summer, enduring a long bout with fever. Maybe Howard's window on reality had clouded a little, and if so, who could blame him?

Howard said something about a telephone. Dex, impatient, took the history book out of the pocket of his coat and dropped it on the kitchen table. Howard stopped talking and stared at it. "What's that?"

And Dex explained.

"All right," Howard said. "Okay, that could be important. Have you read it?"

"Uh-huh."

"Learned anything?"

"Well, it's not exactly the *Oxford History of the World.* You want a summary? It starts with the Garden of Eden. Adam gets a human body from the Archons—"

"The which?"

"Archons. Minor gods. Adam is psyche and Eve is spirit and the serpent isn't necessarily the bad guy, but after that it's fairly straight Genesis all the way to Moses and the pharaohs. Egypt, Greece, and Rome are presented as fairy tales—Romulus and Remus and the genius of Plato and so on, but at least it's recognizable." He accepted a cup of coffee. Howard sat opposite him, wide-eyed, listening intently. "It starts to go wrong around the second century. Valentinus is the Great Christian; Irenaeus is the persecutor of the faithful. The conversion of Constantine never happened. Rome was a seat of classical paganism until at least the 800s, and there are hints that Hellenic paganism is a vital religion even today—at least, in certain unenlightened foreign countries. Christianity didn't dominate Europe until the Age of the Heresiarchs, approximately the thirteenth century, when a number of hostile churches were unified after Europe was conquered by a Gallic king. By this time, of course, it's not what you or I would call Christianity. It's wildly syncretic and it has a huge library of apocryphal books, all Holy Writ, more or less."

Howard took the volume from the table and leafed through it. "Still, the similarities are so broad. . . ."

"The movements of peoples, the evolution of language. It's as if history wants to flow in certain channels. Broad ethnic groupings persist, and there are roughly analogous wars, at least up until the tenth or eleventh century. There are plagues, though they follow different patterns. The Black Death depopulated Europe and Asia no less than five times. The colonization of the New World was delayed. Technologically, they're maybe fifty or sixty years behind us. In terms of population, a century or even two."

"Talk about the religion," Howard said.

"There's nothing very explicit in the book, but it hints at some very strange things."

"You said 'Archons' . . ."

"Uh-huh. And somebody called Sophia Achamoth, and the serpent as a kind of benevolent teacher smuggling out secrets from Heaven—"

"It sounds like Christian Gnosticism."

"I don't know a lot about that."

Howard took his cup in both hands and rocked back on the legs of his chair. "Before Christianity was unified in the Hellenic world there were various schools of Christian doctrine, all kinds of books claiming to be narratives of the life of Jesus or secret keys to Genesis. The New Testament—*our* New Testament—is what was left after orthodox bishops like Irenaeus purged the texts they disapproved of. Some of these Christian mystery cults were pretty strange, from our point of view. They believed in scripture as a kind of coded message; you were enlightened when you penetrated the mystery. So they were called Gnostics—the ones who know. Valentinus was a major Gnostic figure." He sipped the coffee, made a face, spooned in more sugar. "I suppose, in this world, the Gnostic churches were never suppressed. They became the dominant strain of Christianity."

"Okay." Dex stared across the table. "So how does a graduate physics student know so much about Gnosticism?"

"From Stern," Howard said. "He talked about Gnosticism all the time. He was obsessed with it."

And they were silent for a while.


They drank Howard's thick, stale coffee until curfew was less than an hour away. Daylight began to fade from the window; the sky was a gray turmoil. Despite the oven, the kitchen grew colder.

At last Dex pushed his cup away and said, "We have to stop dicking around, Howard. Four, five months, we've all been in a walking daze. Begging for scraps of water and electricity. It's time to wake up. This isn't a good place we've come to. The town isn't safe, and every day the fences get higher and trucks take away some more people. We need a way out."

Howard shook his head. "We need a way *home*."

"You know how unlikely that is."

"We don't know anything, Dex. Not until we understand what happened at the lab."

"Is it really important? Even if we do figure it out, is that a reprieve? I'm not a physicist, but I'd bet what happened at the defense plant was a kind of explosion. Some kind of really weird explosion that blew half of Bayard County into the next universe, but still, an explosion—and even if you *understand* an explosion, you can't put it back in the bottle. Some things are irreversible. I would guess this is one."

"It may be. But what's the alternative? The fences are already up, Dex. The best fence is the forest and the weather. There's only the one road out, from what I've heard, and it leads straight to Fort LeDuc, which is a military town. Sixty miles away. It's not practical to hike that far."

"It could be done," Dex said.

"Maybe, with the right gear and supplies. Then you have the problem of arriving without money or ID or useful skills. And evading the Proctors while you're at it. And who are we talking about here? You, me, a few able-bodied men? It would still leave most of Two Rivers under martial law."

"I know. I'm not happy about it. If you have a better idea, tell me."

"We find Stern."

"Jesus, Howard." Dex sighed. "What makes you think he's alive?"

"His telephone number. He gave me a private number where I could reach him. Mostly evenings, he said. I wrote it down."

"I don't see—"

"No, listen. The thing is, *it's a four-one-six exchange*. Everything at the lab, including the dorms, was a seven-oh-six number. Here in town, most numbers are four-one-five, four-one-six, four-one-seven. The one time I called his private line, a woman answered. Not a switchboard. Just, 'Hello? Yes?' So the obvious implication is that he had a town residence, an apartment or a room or maybe a woman he was seeing. He might have been there when the accident happened."

"More likely he wasn't. If something was going on at the lab, wouldn't he have been involved?"

"Well, I don't know. Not necessarily."

"But you don't have any real evidence he's alive. You haven't seen him."

"No—"

"It's a small town, Howard."

"He would be hiding. Like me. Maybe somebody picking up rations for him, so he doesn't have to go out in the street. But no, I have no direct evidence. Just . . ."

"What?"

"A feeling."

"Pardon me, but that's not too scientific."

"A hunch. No, it's not scientific. But, Dex, doesn't it

seem like there's something happening here? I won't say 'supernatural,' that's a stupid word, but something out of the ordinary?"

"That's a safe bet!"

"Not just the obvious. I mean, subtler things. Dreams. My dreams are different now. Visions. Maybe what I saw in the woods was a vision. I never believed in so-called psychic phenomena. But since the accident at the lab . . ." He shrugged. "I don't know what I believe. Maybe a hunch is not something to ignore."

That was logical, Dex thought, but it was a suspicious kind of logic. He pinched the bridge of his nose. "All you have is the number?"

"No address. Stern didn't like people knowing too much about him—even a favorite nephew."

"The Proctors hooked up their own phone lines, but they haven't fixed the exchanges. I don't know what the hell good a number is."

"Well, it might be in the phone book."

"What, under *Stern*?"

"Obviously not. But I keep thinking about the woman who answered. The *way* she answered. Her tone of voice. Casual. Proprietary—it was *her* phone. Probably the number is in the book, but under another name."

"Great. There must be twenty-five thousand names in the Bayard County phone book. What do you do, leaf through it a page at a time?"

"No. Nor is there any way to get the information from the phone company, or whoever used to be the phone company. That stumped me for a long time. But the man who owned this house, Paul Cantwell, he was a CPA. You know what he has in the bedroom upstairs? A PC with every kind of accounting and data-basing software known to man. Quite capable of sorting the phone book for a number."

"You can't type in the text of the phone book. Or does he have that on disk, too?"

"No, but look: we don't *have* to type it in. You know what an optical reader is?"

"Takes text from a printed page."

"Right. So we can scan the phone book. Feed it to the computer a page at a time."

Howard was dangerously enthusiastic about this, Dex thought. "You have an optical reader in the house, too?"

"No. That's the tricky part. We need to get one. There's a store on Beacon—"

"Howard, all those stores are roped off. The Proctors are shipping out the contents."

Howard leaned forward, rattling his empty cup. "I walk down Beacon every time I go to the food depot. There's a store called Desktop Solutions on Beacon between Oak and Grace. The Bureau inventory is working south from Oak and west from the lakeshore. They haven't been there yet."

"Still, it's behind a rope."

"I can cross a rope."

"There are militiamen on every corner."

"They're sparser at night," Howard said.

"Oh," Dex said. "Oh, no. They're on a hair trigger out there, Howard. They shoot people."

"Out the back gate of this house there's an alleyway that runs to Oak. Across Oak there's a similar alley in back of the Beacon Street shops. The alleys aren't well lit and they aren't patrolled like the main streets."

"Purely insane. And what are you taking this risk for? A telephone number?"

"To find out what happened!" Howard was visibly trembling. "To *know*, Dex! Even if we can't go home. And anyway—Christ, it's my uncle!" He looked down. "I don't know anybody in this town except you. I never really lived here. My family was all in New York State. Except Stern."

"Howard . . . no matter what, the odds are he's dead."

"I can't leave it at that."

The light in the window had faded. The clouds were

heavy. Dex looked at his watch. It was past curfew. He was stuck here for the night.

He looked at Howard: painfully young, a kid in duct-taped glasses. A damn fool.

"Maybe you ought to make some more coffee," Dex said. "We can't leave until the moon is down."

# CHAPTER 9

Even at the raw end of autumn, even in the brittle hour after midnight, Two Rivers owned a tenuous warmth.

From its highest point, the hill above Powell Creek Park, the town fell in dark terraces of wood-frame houses, small lawns, and neat brick storefronts to the hidden shore of Lake Merced. Streetlights cut irregular circles into the windy night.

The town faded to black at its border. It was isolated in the hilly northern peninsula of the province of Mille Lacs, a territory of trading posts, lumber towns, iron mines, copper mines. Here, the darkness had a weight.

There were wolves in the forest, and periodically that autumn they had come loping into the outskirts of town, their curiosity aroused by the powerful and unfamiliar mixture of human scents. But the wolves, after a cautious investigation, almost always chose to avoid the paved streets. There was something in this mingled air they didn't like.

Beyond the westernmost arc of the lake, on what had once been Ojibway treaty land, the ruins of the Two Rivers Physical Research Laboratory cast a delicate light across the belly of a cloud. Other lights moved unseen among the trees.

In the town itself, along the gridwork of empty streets, the only moving lights were the headlights of the patrol cars; the only sound was the sound of their motors, of their tires gritting on the frost-white asphalt.

Luke was not visiting tonight, and Clifford's mother had gone to bed at ten o'clock. When she didn't have company she went to bed early and slept almost till noon. Which was okay with Clifford.

He stayed up much later. He was allowed to sleep in as long as he wanted, and he had learned that when his mother went to bed—braced by stiff doses of the unlabeled distilled whiskey Luke brought her on a weekly basis—the house became his own.

He owned it. From the cavernous, cluttered living room to the dark and scary basement, it was his domain. On nights like this the house seemed immensely large. It was a kingdom, vast and a little eerie, and he was its uneasy ruler.

Tonight Clifford chose to stay in his room with the radio scanner. Since last week he had been spending most of his nights listening to the military radio traffic, the scanner's speaker disconnected and his Walkman headphones plugged in so his mother wouldn't hear. He was careful to keep the scanner a private business. He had learned a lot from it.

He had borrowed the folding map of Two Rivers from the kitchen drawer and tacked it up on his bulletin board. (He took it down—a precaution—when Luke was visiting.) For three consecutive nights he had used it to track the military patrol routes through town. He gave each car (there were ten in all) a letter of the alphabet, and he wrote down the time whenever an intersection was called out. He had needed to stay up until four in the morning, with the help of some coffee brewed without permission, but the final product of this systematic eavesdropping was a complete schedule of the nightly curfew patrol: where the cars would be and when.

The last few nights, Clifford had been double-checking his results. They seemed accurate. A car might be late at a checkpoint or call in early, but never by more than a few minutes. There might be a few rogues, visitors like Luke who had made acquaintances among the townspeople, but even Luke was usually careful to observe the curfew; it was a barracks deal involving more of that white corn liquor that allowed him to stay out all night on Friday or Saturday. Clifford had overheard this explanation and took it to be true.

Armed with his notes, Clifford had drawn his own amendment to the map: a pencil-line route connecting his house to Powell Creek Park. Given the right timing, this was the way a person on a bicycle could travel to the park and back without crossing the path of a patrol car.

The idea of a nighttime bicycle jaunt had come to him last week. The scanner made it a practical possibility, but the idea was intrinsically appealing. Curfew had made the night a forbidden zone, but Clifford had always liked the night. He liked summer evenings with their hush and warmth and the lingering smell of trimmed lawns and hot supper; he liked winter nights, so cold the snow squealed under the pressure of his boots. But above all he had liked autumn evenings, smoky and mysterious; and most of this autumn was already gone—had been stolen from him, he thought.

Too, he liked the idea of exercising the secret knowledge the scanner had given him, using it to his own advantage.

He was afraid, of course, but he was powerfully tempted. On a windy night like this the temptation was especially strong. He sat for a time in his room in the dark, listening to the headphones and resting his elbows on the windowsill. The window glass was cold. Wind turned the branches of a leafless oak in the yard next door, and when the high clouds opened, there were stars. It was well after midnight now. All the patrols were on schedule.

He looked at his watch and made a mental calculation. The decision he came to was sudden and wordless. He didn't even think about it, just moved. He padded downstairs, turned on the hallway light, and found his sneakers; he laced them high and tight.

He put on his padded blue winter jacket and locked the door behind him when he left.

His bike was leaning against the wall of the garage. The handlebars were shockingly cold, and Clifford wondered whether he ought to have worn gloves. But there was no time to go back. He was on the clock now—and the schedule was tight.

The wind tugged his hair as he rolled down the empty street. Every house was dark. The bicycle's bearings ticked into silence, and the clouds lifted like a curtain on a great show of stars.


What made this dangerous, Dex Graham told himself, was the peculiarity of the empty town. It was too easy to feel alone. Hence safe. Hence careless.

He wanted to say this to Howard, but they had resolved not to talk unless it was absolutely necessary. The sound of their voices might wake someone, and there ought to be no witnesses to this expedition.

The alley behind the Cantwell house passed between tar paper garages and the brittle remains of vegetable gardens. The paving was ancient and frost-cracked. Set back on each side, wood-frame houses slept behind wooden siding, screen doors, peeling shingles. Lights were sparse. Dex carried a crowbar in his right hand and resisted a juvenile impulse to bang it against these fence slats.

Howard stalked ahead in long, nervous strides. He wants this over with, Dex thought. But caution: caution was vital.

They walked downhill in the deepest shadows and stopped where the alleyway opened onto Oak Street.

Crossing Oak was going to be the hard part, the big question mark. Oak Street divided the town from east to west and had once carried most of the traffic to the cement plant and the quarries. It had been widened last year and lamp standards had been planted every ten yards. The light was surgically bright. Worse, the road intersected every commercial street including Beacon; a car might turn any corner for four blocks in either direction without warning. The road was an asphalt desert, much too wide and as hospitable as a guillotine. The wind came down that avenue in frigid torrents.

"We should cross one at a time," Howard whispered. "From the other side you can see more of the intersection," pointing to Beacon a block away where a traffic light rattled in a cold gust. "Then, if it seems safe, wave the second man across."

"I'll go," Dex said.

"No. I should be the one."

The declaration was brave. Dex felt a little of what this trip meant to Howard. Howard never talked much about himself but Dex had learned a few things about him, in the same wordless way he came to understand the kids who filed into his classroom every September: by gesture and posture, by what was said and what wasn't. Howard took no delight in defying authority. Dex pictured him as the bright, quiet kid who always picks a desk at the back of the room, the one who doesn't smoke on school grounds or liberate bags of M&M's from the corner grocery. The one who follows the rules and takes a certain pride in doing so.

Not much like me, Dex thought. A middle-aged man with no possession but himself and too careless even with that. He said, "No, I'll go."

Howard seemed to be working up an objection, but Dex made it moot by vaulting out onto the windy space of Oak Street.

He sprinted toward the opposite side. He felt a little giddy, actually, out here on the empty pavement. Once, when he was seventeen and living with his parents in Phoenix, he had gotten drunk at someone's party and ended up walking home at four in the morning. On an impulse he had stepped into the middle of what in daylight was a busy suburban street, and he had sat down cross-legged on the white line. King of creation. There had been no other pedestrians that night, no traffic, only dry air and a patient, starry sky. He had stayed in that sublime lotus for almost five minutes, until he saw a distant wink of headlights; then he got up, yawned, and sauntered home to bed. It amounted to nothing. But the feeling still lingered in his memory.

He was tempted to sit down in the middle of *this* street. A dumb and reckless notion. It was a familiar impulse, though, the urge to wave some flag of defiance in the face of the universe, and he supposed one day it would get him hurt or killed—probably sooner than later, given the state of things. But at times like this he felt both genuinely alive and somehow closer to Abigail and David, who had perished in the fire fifteen years ago. Maybe they were around one of these dark corners. Maybe, if he tempted fate, fate would deliver him to his lost wife and son.

But he crossed Oak without incident and stopped, a little breathless, in the shadows on the opposite side.

The silence seemed larger here. He paid attention to it, sorting through wind-sounds for the rumble of a motor. There was nothing. He braced himself against a brick wall and leaned into the street. He looked hard east and west and saw only streetlights, traffic signals, and the icy white sidewalks.

He located Howard's silhouette in the alleyway and waved an all-clear.

Howard jogged toward the meridian of Oak in gawky, birdlike strides. He wore a khaki hunting jacket that came nearly to his knees and a black watch cap too low over his eyes. His duct-taped eyeglasses winked in the artificial light. He looked like a cartoon terrorist, Dex thought, and why the hell didn't he get a move on? He was a target out there.

Howard had only just crossed the white line when Dex saw headlights probing the corner of Oak and Beacon.

He took a half step out of the alley and waved frantically at Howard, trying to hurry him in. Howard saw him and did exactly the wrong thing: froze in place, confused and frightened.

Dex heard the sound of an approaching motor, probably headed south on Beacon. We are seconds away from being seen, he thought. Shouting was a risk, but unavoidable now. He cupped his hands. "Howard! Get the fuck over here! RUN, YOU DUMB SON OF A BITCH!"

Howard looked left and saw the headlights reflected in window glass. It seemed to untangle his legs. He began to sprint, and Dex admired the speed with which the physicist covered those final yards of blacktop.

But the car, a black patrol car, had turned the corner, and there was no way of knowing what the men inside might have seen.

"Get down," Dex said. "Down behind the Dumpster. Back against the wall. Draw your knees up." And he did the same.

The patrol car had turned and was coming their way along Oak; he could tell by the sound of its engine.

It growled a lower note. They've seen us, Dex thought. He tried to imagine an escape route. South down this alley and maybe out some fire lane to Beacon or one of the suburban streets: get lost in tree shadows or crouch under a porch . . .

There was a sudden light. Dex watched it sweep the alley. He pictured the patrol car, the driver, the militiaman in the passenger seat with a hand-held spot. He was aware of the sound of Howard's tortured breathing. "Run," he whispered. "Run if you have to. You cut left, I'll cut right."

But the alley was suddenly dark again. The engine coughed and tires crunched on cold asphalt.

Dex heard the sound fade down Oak.

Howard let out a shuddering breath.

"Must be they only caught a glimpse," Dex said, "or they'd be down here after us. Christ, that was a near call." He stood and helped Howard up. "I vote we get the hell back across Oak and head for home while we can. Pardon me, Howard, but this whole thing was a stupid idea."

Howard pulled away and shook his head. "We didn't get what we came for. We're not finished. At least, I'm not. You can go home if you want."

Dex regarded his friend. "Well, hell," he said finally. "Look who's Rambo."

Clifford Stockton sat at the top of the high hill at the center of Powell Creek Park with his bicycle beside him and the cold night wind plucking his hair.

There had already been flurries of snow this season, and it felt like there might soon be more, although the sky tonight had grown crisply, vividly clear. But the cold didn't bother him. It was exhilarating. He felt completely alive and completely himself, far from the world of his mother and the soldiers and school.

The town lay at his feet. From this high place it resembled the map he had pinned to his bulletin board back home. It was completely static, a grid of stationary lights, except for the patrol cars performing their slow waltz. The cars moved like a glittering clockwork, pausing a beat at each intersection.

"Go to hell," Clifford told them. This was a whisper. A delicious heresy. The wind carried it away. But there was nobody around to hear him. Giddy, Clifford stood up and shouted it. "GO TO HELL!"

The patrol cars wheeled on, as implacable as the motion of the stars. Clifford laughed but felt near tears.

It was almost time to go home. He had proved he could do this; all that remained was to prove he could get back safely. He was excited, but the cold air began to seem colder and he thought about his room, his bed, with a first pang of longing.

He picked up his bike. Down the brick path to Cleveland Avenue and west toward home. That should be easy enough.

But something caught his eye.

The hilly part of Powell Creek Park overlooked the business district. Clifford enjoyed an unobstructed view down to the intersection of Oak and Beacon. He saw the twin red taillights of a patrol car as it reached the corner—on schedule.

But the car turned west on Oak . . . and shouldn't it have gone *east*?

And now the car slowed, and that was strange, too. Its spotlight probed an alleyway behind Beacon Street. Clifford crouched on the grass, watching. He felt suddenly vulnerable, too obvious. He wished he had his scanner; maybe he could listen in.

The spotlight winked out and the patrol car moved on along Oak and turned a corner. It disappeared from Clifford's view behind the stores on Knight, but he was able to track the glow of its headlights. Down Knight to Promontory, farther from the park. Then east again. Then, mysteriously, back onto Beacon.

*Circling,* Clifford thought.

And now slowing, now stopping.

The headlights winked off.

Something was happening, Clifford thought. Something was happening or was about to happen on Beacon Street.

Far off along Commercial Street he saw a second car coming fast, probably summoned by the first. A call must have gone out by radio. All the patrol cars were converging on Beacon.

Which meant the schedule was messed up. . . .

Which meant he wasn't safe here.

He ran for his bike.

Dex Graham worked the point of the crowbar between the frame and the rear door of Desktop Solutions and leaned on it. The lock came away from the wood with a sound like a gunshot. Howard winced.

The door sprang open. Dex said, "Be my guest."

Howard pulled a long watchman's flashlight out of the deeps of his jacket and entered the store.

Dex stayed outside, watching the alley. He calculated that this trip from the Cantwell house to the computer store had taken no more than twenty minutes, though it seemed like much longer. Thank God, the deed was nearly done. Here we are, he thought, two of the least likely break-and-enter artists ever to jimmy a lock in the town of Two Rivers. And the least competent.

Now that the adrenaline rush had faded, he was cold. He rubbed his hands together and warmed them with a breath. Alone here, he was uncomfortably aware of the perilous distance between himself and safety. Until the close call with the patrol car there had been an edge of excitement to this trip; that was gone, replaced by a sour anxiety.

The wind rattled a loose doorway down the alley. Winter at the heels of a wind like that, Dex thought. When he came here five years ago he had been startled by the severity of the northern Michigan winter. He wondered how much of Two Rivers would survive the season and what would be left of it by spring. The question was unanswerable but the possibilities were mainly bleak.

He heard a percussive rattle and whirled to face it, but the culprit was only a dog, a hound nosing a trash barrel overturned by the wind. The dog looked at Dex with an expression of rheumy indifference and shivered from the neck down. I know how you feel, Dex thought.

He looked at his watch, then peered into the dim interior of the store. "Hey, Howard, how you doing in there?"

No answer. But Dex could see the beam of Howard's flashlight poking around—a little too vigorously, Dex thought. He took a step inside. "Howard?"

Nothing.

"Howard, it's cold out here! Bag your loot and let's get going, all right?"

He felt something touch his leg. Overcome by a sudden sense of unreality, Dex looked down. Here was Howard: crouched behind the cash counter with sweat beading on his pale forehead. Howard had grabbed Dex's ankle and was waving some panicked, indecipherable signal.

Dex guessed this ought to be frightening, but for a long moment it was only confusing. He said out loud, "What the hell?"

And the flashlight beam continued to probe the darkness—but not Howard's flashlight.

Another presence loomed in this dark arcade of shelves and desks, suddenly visible as Dex's eyesight adjusted to the dark. He turned to face the rear door just as the beam of light pinned his shadow to the wall. He saw his shadow ride up toward the ceiling, as loose-jointed and comical as a marionette. Then there was a flash and a deafening bang, a pressure and a pain that knocked him off his feet.

He heard Howard shouting something: it might have been *Don't shoot!* or *God damn!* And he felt his left arm twitch in a useless, distant fashion, and the wet warmth of blood.

And then footsteps.

And then a sudden, second light—the brightest yet.


Clifford decided to ride home by way of Powell Road, which crossed Beacon north and uphill from the business district.

It was a short ride down the park path and out the gate onto Powell. Home from the park was a gravity-assist all the way. The bicycle bearings shrilled into the dark and Clifford felt the wind on his face like a barrage of needles. The big houses near the park blurred past on each side of him, fading behind him like an elegant dream.

He leaned on the hand brakes at the corner of Beacon and came to a stop beside a tall privet hedge.

Curiosity and prudence had begun a pitched battle in the pit of Clifford's stomach. Curiosity had the advantage. He peered around the hedge, downhill toward the shops south of Oak.

There was not much to see from this distance; only a distant light, a headlight, which winked out when he looked at it: another patrol car.

Would it be dangerous to try to get closer? Well, obviously it would. No doubt about that. He had seen the bodies on that wooden cart outside City Hall last June, and the memory put a jog into his heartbeat. People had been killed for what he was doing right now.

But it was night and he was agile and he could always hide or run . . . and anyway, it wasn't him they were after.

He wheeled down Beacon almost all the way to Oak, keeping close to the trees and hedges of these big lawns, most of which had grown high and weedy over the summer.

At Oak, Clifford pulled up next to a dark automobile parked at the curb and noticed with a sudden shock of fear that it was a *military patrol car* and that he had come abreast of it with the idiotic boldness of a four-year-old. He dropped his bike and was about to run for the cover of a leafless willow tree when he saw the car was unoccupied; both soldiers must have crossed Oak and gone down Beacon, where he could dimly see a motion, a commando-style jog from storefront to storefront, and the dance of several flashlight beams.

He had come too far and was too exposed. He lay in the grass considering his options. He didn't think he was in danger, at least not yet. He was fascinated, almost hypnotized, by his proximity to something potentially important, something somber and hidden.

Then Clifford heard a bang like a firecracker and saw a simultaneous flash of light. Someone had fired a gun, he thought, and the implication of that simple event seemed to wake him from a daze. The soldiers were shooting at someone—the soldiers were quite possibly *killing* someone.

And maybe it should have scared him . . . but mostly it made him angry.

He thought again of the dead bodies outside City Hall. That had angered him, too, though it had been too awful to absorb all at once; the anger was subtle, it lingered, it had no outlet. This was more immediate, and Clifford's anger focused to a fine point. The soldiers had no business here, no business telling people what to do and certainly no business shooting them.

He wanted to do something about it, take some retaliation, and he looked around helplessly—and saw the patrol car parked a few feet away.

The canvas roof was closed against the weather but the door might not be locked. Clifford crossed the sidewalk and grasped the unfamiliar handle. It opened easily. He leaned inside, distantly amazed at his own audacity. The interior of the car smelled of worn leather and cigarette smoke. The air was stale and still warm. He leaned across the bench seat wondering what sabotage he might be able to perform. His eyes fixed on the knobbed lever projecting from the floor. A gear shift, he guessed. He remembered his mother explaining the gears on her Honda. Experimentally, Clifford grasped the handle and twisted it. Left and down. Left and down.

He didn't know what kind of gear mechanism this automobile might have; there was no reason to expect it to work like the cars he was accustomed to. But it did possess a neutral gear and Clifford knew at once when he found it. The car inched forward, its tires crackling on the cold street.

He sat up in alarm. The patrol car was rolling at an angle across Beacon, which was useless; it would only fetch up undamaged in the drainage ditch. He needed to get out . . . but first he twisted the oddly shaped steering wheel until the car was pointed more or less directly down the slope of Beacon, a steep enough incline to get some real momentum going.

Which happened more quickly than he expected. Clifford scrambled back across the bench to the open door and found the pavement scrolling past at a surprising speed. He closed his eyes and jumped, an awkward leap; he hit the sidewalk with feet, hips, shoulders. He tore his shirt and scraped his palms bloody. He would have to explain this to his mother, come the morning. If he ever reached home.

He hurried back to the shadow of the tree to watch the empty car, which had already rolled a considerable distance. Its motion was stately at first, then alarming. Its speed increased until it seemed to Clifford as if the car had been launched from some enormous slingshot. It rattled over every bump in the road, took small but perilous leaps; now, well across Oak and down the empty avenue of Beacon, it tilted perilously on two wheels and then righted itself. The slope of the street declined past Oak but the runaway car seemed to take no notice.

He tried to figure out where it would impact. The hardware store, he thought, or, no, it was veering right; the barber shop, the bookstore—the gas station.

Clifford gasped and held his breath.

He felt a sudden awe at the enormity of the events he had triggered. He understood that there was going to be more damage than he'd imagined—damage on a huge scale, damage that made his knees weak with anticipation.

He couldn't guess at the speed of the patrol car as it left the road, but he thought it might be going faster than any car had ever gone on Beacon Street. The tires came up over the lip of the curb and the whole car seemed to levitate above the air-and-water dispenser at the Gulf station. It rotated as it moved, the back end rising as the nose dipped, and when Clifford realized it was going to collide with the self-serve gas pumps he instinctively covered his ears.

A grinding crash echoed up the empty road. Clifford watched through eyes squeezed nearly shut. He saw the patrol car sheer off a pump unit before it came to a full stop. There was a last rattle, a fading hiss, then silence, and Clifford dared to take a breath.

Then the patrol car's damaged battery shorted itself into a spreading pool of gasoline, and it looked as if the sun itself had risen over the rooftops of Beacon Street.


Nicodemus Bourgoint, a line soldier of the Fifth Atha-basca Infantry, had been due for shipment to the Mexican front when he was diagnosed with a peptic ulcer and trans-ferred to domestic duty in the otherworldly town of Two Rivers. Given a choice, he would have preferred the front.

There, the dangers were predictable. War didn't frighten him. Getting shot or blown up, that was a human thing. It was a fate anyone might come to.

But Two Rivers frightened him. It had frightened him from the beginning. The soldiers detailed to Two Rivers had been offered no explanation of the existence of the place, barring some aphorisms from a Bureau attaché about the bountiful mysteries of God. The Genetrix Mundi was end-lessly fecund, Nico supposed, and there might well be an

occasional wrinkle in the Pleroma, but that was small consolation when one was condemned to endlessly patrolling
the vacant streets of this terrifyingly strange place. Not only
that, but the accommodations were crowded, the duties
were tedious and repetitive, and the food was bad. The
mess sergeant had been promising roast beef since August;
it never arrived.

He longed for home. He had been raised on a cattle
ranch in the northern province of Athabasca and he felt
confined by these wooded hills, these leafless trees, the
alien village. Never more so than tonight. He had been
assigned night patrol with Filo Mueller, who liked to tor-
ture him with campfire stories about headless corpses and
one-legged ghosts, and as much as Nico tried to conceal the
uneasiness this caused in him, some evidence of it always
showed on his face—much to Mueller's amusement. Such
things simply weren't funny, Nico thought. Not in *this*
place.

Of course, when they turned the corner of Oak and
Beacon and saw the figure disappearing down the alleyway,
all frivolity ceased. Nico wanted to stop and give chase; but
Mueller, a devious sort, argued for calling in reinforcements
and circling the block. "Let our trespasser think we gave
up. If we chase him, we'll lose him. You're not a hunter, are
you, Nico?"

"My uncles hunt buck in the mountains," Nico said
defensively.

"But you never went with them. You're not the type."

They circled the block. Mueller radioed for another car,
and Nico was all in favor of waiting for it to arrive. But
Mueller spotted the glint of someone's flashlight in a store
window and fixed his serpentine stare on Nico. "You go in,"
he said.

Mueller was Nico's superior by a degree of rank and
technically entitled to give the order, but Nico assumed he
was joking. It was the look on Mueller's face that convinced
him otherwise.

The son of Samael was *grinning*.

"Take your pistol out of its pouch for once," Mueller said. "Demonstrate some testicles, Nico."

"I'm not afraid."

"Good for you. Go on."

But he *was* afraid. He hated these shops, with their windows full of incomprehensible goods. One of the stupider infantrymen, a huge man named Seth, was forever proclaiming his idea that Two Rivers was actually a settlement on the outskirts of Hell; that these truncated roads had once run straight to the Temple of the Lord of the Hebdomad, the Father of Grief.

The idea was childish but sometimes annoyingly plausible. For instance, tonight. Nico, moving as slowly as his pride permitted, approached the door of a building called Desktop Solutions. The sign, in its odd graceless English script, was confounding. Like so many of the inscriptions on these stores, it made no sense; the words had no comprehensible connection to one another. Just like Unisex Hair or Circuit City, it seemed to promise the impossible or the absurd. The shapes in the window were only gray boxes, small items like miniature television sets, plain and uninviting.

He drew his pistol. A sense of unreality overtook him as he pushed open the door—thank God, it wasn't locked—and braced himself in a shooter's stance, pistol in his right hand, flashlight in his left. This might be a dream, he thought. He might be in the barracks sleeping. He hoped he was.

He saw a gaunt figure duck behind a desk, and his attention focused instantly. He stepped closer, wishing someone had come with him, even Mueller, but surely Mueller and his reinforcements would be here soon; he came close enough to see the man huddled on the floor without a weapon, and he was about to order the man to stand when a second figure approached from the rear with a crowbar in his hand. Nico aimed his flashlight at this new apparition. The man blinked and turned.

Nico's finger tightened on the pistol and it bucked in his hand—he wasn't even certain he had meant to fire; only that it happened almost without his volition, an event to which he was an accessory but not the main cause. The man was wounded. The man fell. Nico took another bewildered step forward. The shot man was unconscious and his friend huddled over him, eyes wide on Nico.

"Don't move," Nico said.

"Don't shoot," the other man pleaded. Nico held the pistol trembling but level and wondered where Mueller was. Surely he had heard the shot? What was keeping him?

Then there was a thunderous crash from *behind* him, and a light so bright it seemed to drain the color out of everything. And the window glass came hurtling inward in a thousand fragments.

Nico Bourgoint felt the glass cut his back and arm. He turned, and dropped his pistol in astonishment at what he saw: the Lord of the Hebdomad rising in a pillar of flame from the opposite side of the street.


Dex did not begin to make sense of events until he was in the alley, his good arm over Howard Poole's shoulder and his feet moving by some logic of their own.

He looked at Howard, who was breathless and bleeding from what looked like a hundred small cuts. "What," he said. It was meant to be, *What are we doing?* But the words evaded his grasp.

Howard gave him a brief look. "Run. If you can run, just do it."

They jogged together. Each step triggered new fireworks from his shoulder and arm, no longer numb, alas. He didn't look at the wound. He had never been keen on the sight of blood, his own or anyone else's, and he couldn't afford another spell of light-headedness.

He did risk a glance behind him. He saw what appeared to be a large-scale hallucination.

Above the pebbled roofs of the Beacon Street shops, above the rain gutters and the tangled telephone wires, a column of fire had risen into the cloudless night sky. The flames as they ascended became a luminous shade of blue, and in that coruscating substance, it seemed to Dex, there were faces, immense and endlessly shifting.

"God's sake," Howard rasped, "don't *stop!*"

They crossed Oak and were some yards uphill along the crowded lane when Dex said, "Wait."

Howard regarded him with a desperate impatience.

"We're leaving a trail," Dex said. "Look."

Bright drops of blood had speckled the asphalt. Connect the dots, Dex thought. They'll find us by morning.

Lights had winked on in all these houses, but there were deep shadows among the alleyside sheds and fences, and all attention must be focused on the fire. They crouched in a tangle of darkness.

"It's mostly me. Howard, you have to bind this wound. Or apply a tourniquet."

"I don't know if I can do that."

"I'll tell you how. Put down that box, first of all." Dex squinted at it. The optical reader. "You stole the damn thing after all, didn't you? In spite of all this?"

"I had it in my hands when the soldier came in. It's what we went for."

"You're a single-minded son of a bitch, Howard."

"You learn that in grad school." He took a breath. "It's hard to tell, but it looks like the wound is in the fleshy part of your arm. Clear through. It's bleeding a lot but it's not, uh, gushing. What do I tie it with?"

"Use your belt for a tourniquet. Tight above the injury. Any kind of cloth to soak up what leaks."

Howard worked while Dex sat on the cold ground and fixed his attention on the board fence next to him. It had once been painted, but the paint had all peeled away except for a few flakes clinging to the grain. The fence had once been white. Tonight it was gray, mottled by the light of the distant fire.

The pain was enormous and his grip on consciousness a little uncertain. He said, "Howard?"

"Uh?"

"What the hell happened back there?"

"I don't know. Something blew up. Lucky for us."

"A coincidence?"

"I suppose so. Synchronicity, at least. I'm about to tighten this."

Dex counted silently to ten. His vision blurred somewhere around seven. Make words, he instructed himself.

"What happened back there . . . it was strange."

"Uh-huh."

"Not natural."

"I guess not."

"Basically, it was weird."

"You could say so. *There*." A final tug. "Can you stand up?"

"Yeah." But he was unsteady.

"Can you walk?"

"Oh, yeah. I'd better walk. It's pretty much walk or die, don't you think?"

Howard didn't answer.


Clifford turned and ran when he saw the pillar of blue fire. He was halfway up the block when he remembered his bike. He screwed up his courage and went back, grabbed the bike and straddled it, and cut west on Oak because it was the quickest, if not the least conspicuous, way home.

His view of the events on Beacon Street had been comprehensive, and he understood everything up until the moment of the explosion. It unrolled inside him like a movie, like a videotape spliced into a maddening loop. His anger. The empty patrol car. Working the gear lever. His rising dread when he understood what the consequences would be. And the explosion at the gas pumps, and then—

But that part made no sense. In his tape-loop memory, it looked like this: the gas pumps detonated in a ball of fire . . . and then *something*, something like a vast ethereal blue spark, had come down from the sky to touch the fireball; and the spark had coalesced into a cobalt-colored snake about as wide as the Gulf station and twisting up into the night sky as far as the eye could reach. It seemed to Clifford that the column had curved a little to the west, but he wasn't sure. He hadn't been looking at it with scientific detachment. With panic, if anything. In that terrible moment it had occurred to him that he might somehow have caused *the end of the world itself,* because the blue light had not been merely light; it had been full of faces and forms— *human* faces and forms. One in particular. A grim, bearded face. God or the devil, Clifford thought.

His bike flew through the November darkness like a wild bullet. His legs pumped in a ceaseless fury that would have startled him if he had been aware of it. His only thought was of home; his house, his room, his bed.

He slowed when he reached the suburban part of town. He had to; his breathing was so labored it hurt his lungs, and he had a painful stitch in his side. He let the bike drift to a stop and put one leg down to steady himself. Reluctantly, fearfully, he turned and looked back at Two Rivers.

The pillar of blue flame was gone, to Clifford's immense relief. Maybe he had only imagined it. He must have. But the ordinary fire burned on; he could see the glow of it reflected from houses on the high ground near Powell Creek Park. What pained him now was the knowledge that *none of this could be taken back,* not ever—for the rest of his life he would be responsible for blowing up the Gulf station (and please God, Clifford thought, let no one have been *inside it*). . . . The memory was part of his permanent luggage, and worse, it would have to remain a secret. This was something he could never be caught at or confess to, not in

Two Rivers under the rule of the soldiers. There was no juvenile court in Two Rivers anymore; there was only the executioner.

He pedaled the rest of the way home unaware of the tears on his face. Home, he parked his bike out of sight; he unlocked the door, stepped inside, locked it behind him; unlaced his sneakers and put them in the hall closet; padded upstairs to his room. The sight of the bed made him instantly, staggeringly tired. But there was work yet to do.

He stripped his torn and dirty clothes and took them to the bathroom. He wedged them into the dirty-clothes hamper, down toward the bottom; his mother was lax about the wash these days and she probably wouldn't notice anything out of the ordinary—his clothes were often dirty and many of them had been torn since June.

Then he turned on the taps, hoping the sound of running water wouldn't wake his mother. He stood in the tub and used a washcloth to soak the dirt off his face and sponge the clotted blood from his hands and elbows. When he seemed clean, front and back, he wiped down the tub, then rinsed the cloth and stuffed it into the hamper with everything else.

He turned off the water and the light and tiptoed back to his room. He put on pajamas: his old ones, a little too tight nowadays, flannel with blue and white stripes. Then, only then, he allowed himself the bed.

The sheets were as cool and welcoming as absolution and the blanket contained him like a prayer. He meant to plan his excuses if anyone questioned him tomorrow, but his thoughts quickly turned to nonsense and a tide of sleep carried him far away.

Tom Stubbs was asleep at the fire hall when he heard the Gulf station blow. He sounded the alarm and made sure his crew was out of their cots, but the truth was he couldn't do much until the telephone rang.

Mr. Demarch had made it quite clear last July. The Two Rivers Volunteer Fire Department performed a valuable service, and they would be supplied and maintained—but if they left the station after curfew and before this newly installed radiotelephone rang, they'd be shot like any civilian.

Two pumpers and the ladder company were waiting when the call finally came. Tom acknowledged it hastily and ran to the lead truck, which rolled at once.

He knew as soon as they turned onto the slope of Beacon Street that this was no ordinary fire. The Gulf station was indeed burning; the underground tank had recently been filled with that leaded diesel the military cars ran on, and it looked like one of the topside pumps had not only caught fire but gone gusher. But that wasn't all. Like the fire at the defense plant so many months ago, this fire had a frightening aspect. A tower of blue light rose from the flames to the sky . . . and maybe arched a little, Tom thought, as if its rainbow trajectory might bring it down somewhere over Ojibway land. But it faded before that. It was a vein of light with, if you looked long enough, *faces* in it—and that was terrifying.

The fire at the defense plant had been terrifying too, but that had not stopped Chief Haldane from attempting to fight it, and the chief remained an idol in Tom's eyes even after his untimely death this past summer. With that in mind, Tom drove as close as he could to the Gulf station, supervised his men as they connected at the mains, and did his level best to end the conflagration.

The column of strange light faded to nothing in the steam, and that was fine with Tom. It made him nervous to work with the Devil looking on.


Dex Graham left Howard at the Cantwell house and made his own way home, over the younger man's protests. "Makes sense," he told Howard. "Right now there's chaos.

In the morning there'll be soldiers everywhere, and they might be curious about a wounded man."

"You can make it?"

"Yes."

At least he thought he could. He took it street by street. Pain, and the dizziness that rode with it, came in tidal movements of ebb and flood. He was only dimly aware of the sound of sirens, the distant flicker of firelight.

He reached his apartment after an eternity of footsteps. The stairs seemed at a steeper angle than he remembered; he whispered small encouragements to himself as he climbed.

He locked his apartment door behind him and left the lights off. Now you can rest, he thought, and reached for the bed as darkness took him.


Among those who had witnessed the strange phenomenon above the burning Gulf station, reports were mixed.

Soldiers reported seeing what they described variously as Ialdaboath, Samael, a Demiurge, or the Father of Grief.

Civilian witnesses in the neighboring houses claimed they had seen God or, like Tom Stubbs, the Devil.

Only Howard Poole connected that visitation in the sky with Alan Stern, and Howard didn't file a report.


By morning, everything east of Oak stank of smoke and diesel fuel.

# CHAPTER 10

Dex woke with the sun in his eyes and the knowledge that time had passed—too little or too much time, he wasn't sure which. The events of the night had been large and significant and he dreaded the returning memory. He tried to roll onto his side but a starburst of pain prevented him. He tried again, more slowly, and discovered he was stuck to the bed.

He peeled away the bloody sheet from the shirttail bandage Howard had wound for him and managed to sit up. He didn't remember loosening the tourniquet, but he must have done so. That instinct had saved him a close encounter with gangrene, he thought—at least, so far. He was thirsty, feverish, and appallingly weak.

He went to the sink in a drunkard's stumble. He poured a glass of water. Sip it, he thought. From the medicine cupboard, four aspirin. One two three four.

He was scheduled to hold classes between ten and twelve and it seemed to Dex he really ought to try to be there, as impossible as it might seem at the moment. The soldiers or the Bureau could be keeping an eye on his movements; he didn't want to draw attention to himself by staying home. The Proctors might be looking for a wounded man. Better not to appear wounded. The trick would be to avoid collapsing in the street.

He examined himself in the bathroom mirror. When the storefront window blew in he had been turned away from it; his face wasn't cut, though his back, when he worked his shirt loose, seemed to have been flayed nearly skinless. The cuts weren't as bad as they looked, fortunately; only a lacework of shallow lacerations after he sponged the scabbed blood away. But not pleasant.

His arm . . .

Well, he was able to move it, though the effort cost him dearly. Wait until the aspirin takes hold, he told himself. The aspirin would help, at least a little . . . though a mere four Bayers, under the circumstances, might be a spit in the wind. As for the wound itself, he didn't want to risk disturbing the makeshift bandage. He didn't want to bleed again. Of course, it would have to be changed; it might already be infected. But later. This afternoon, say. When he could faint at leisure.

He put on plausible work clothes a cautious step at a time. The bandage bulked conspicuously under a clean shirt, but the sport coat disguised it.

Could he walk the five blocks to JFK High? He guessed so. He felt disoriented, but it was probably no worse than the disorientation of a bad case of the flu. The aspirin might at least take the fever down. Two classes: he could handle that.

The walk passed in a series of curiously static tableaux. Here was the front door of the apartment block, open on a cold November morning. Here was the sidewalk arrayed before him like a flickering alabaster river.

Here, the soldier on the corner with his high-collared black uniform and expressionless face, eyes tracking Dex as he passed.

Here, much later, the school. Ancient brick Victoriana. Small high windows. The big door.

The corridors were dirty and smelled of sour milk. They were abandoned nowadays except for a few stalwarts, student and faculty. Dex felt more lucid here, soothed by the bleak familiarity of the building. The aspirin had not done much for the pain or the fever but seemed to allow him to rise a distance above these things. He nodded at Emmy Jackson, who was still manning the reception desk. The principal, Bob Hoskins, hailed him as he approached his classroom.

"Damn cold," Hoskins said. "The power's off again. As you no doubt noticed. Some idiot blew up the Gulf station last night and the Proctors are so PO'd they cut the electricity. For a full week, somebody said. If you can imagine anything so petty."

Dex said, "Have they caught anyone?"

"No. Which is precisely what's bothering them, in my opinion. If they had some poor soul to hang I'm sure they'd be delighted." He squinted at Dex. "Are you all right?"

"Flu."

"Well, there's plenty of it going around. You sure you can manage? You look awfully pale."

"I'll be okay."

"Well. Knock off early if you have to." Hoskins sighed. "I don't know how much longer we'll be here anyway. It's like minding an empty store. Sad but true."

The classroom was as cold as the rest of the building. Dex had left his notes at home and doubted his ability to lecture coherently for forty minutes. When his first students shuffled in, wrapped in shabby winter coats, he declared a study session and assigned them a chapter to read—three hectographed pages on America in World

War I. "When you're done you can talk among yourselves."

The time passed. He sat at the big desk and pretended to grade assignments. The assignments were real, and he kept them in front of him and remembered to turn a page now and again, but the words were unintelligible. The printed or handwritten letters had developed lives of their own; they bobbled over the paper like loose balloons.

The urge to put his head down and sleep was powerfully strong, and by the end of his second class he was afraid he would simply nod off—his head was inclining when the bell rang. Students shuffled out, some looking at him oddly. Shelda Burmeister, a studious girl in high-powered corrective lenses and a torn turquoise sweater, paused at his desk until the others were gone. "Mr. Graham?"

"Yes?" He swiveled the weighty beam of his attention toward her. "What is it, Shelda?"

"I think you cut yourself." She nodded at the desktop.

He looked down. Blood had traveled down his left arm and pooled just beyond the cuff of his coat. About a tablespoon, he thought.

"I guess I did," he said. "I mean, cut myself. Thank you, Shelda."

"Will you be all right?"

"Yes. Go on. I'm fine."

She left. He stood up. More blood trickled down the wounded arm. Now he was conscious of the distasteful warmth of it. He held the cuff closed and moved to the door. Maybe he could clean up in the staff men's room, change the bandage. . . .

The door opened before he reached it and Linneth Stone stepped into the classroom. She was fresh and impossibly radiant in a white blouse, gray skirt. He looked at her with some confusion.

"Dex? I know we didn't have an appointment. But the afternoon was free and I thought—Dex? My God, what happened?"

She caught him as he fell and lowered him to the floor. There was blood on the blouse. He meant to apologize. I'm sorry, he wanted to say. But Linneth, the classroom, the school, all vanished into a sudden night.

# Mysterium Tremendae

## PART TWO

The past gives birth to the present.

According to the laws of thermodynamics, nothing dies; only form changes. We reenact our evolution in the womb. As a species, our history is engraved in every cell.

But evolution can only operate under the dicta of natural law—the evolution of the universe as much as the evolution of life. In the first nanosecond of the primordial singularity, everything that now exists became an implication needing only time to achieve embodiment. The early universe contained human consciousness the way an acorn contains an oak.

The Gnostics speak of the Protennoia: Mind as the original substance of the world; a Protennoia derived from an Uncreated God, aggenetos (ungenerated) and androgynous.

Humanity as a fractal subset of Mind in an imperfect Pleroma. Our divine spark, our apospasma theion, an ember of the Big Bang. Consciousness = the quantum mechanics of the *archaic universe erupting into cold matter through the medium of humanity.*

*I think we are the lever by which something unspeakably ancient moves the world.*

—from the secret journal of Alan Stern

# CHAPTER 11

Coming back to the capital, even for a week, was a restorative for Symeon Demarch. No matter what happened here —and he expected nothing good from his scheduled meeting with Bisonette—he would have time to draw at least a few unfettered breaths.

He rode a truck to Fort LeDuc, where a ponderous air transport waited on the military runway. The airplane had been outfitted with a padded wooden bench along its steel inner wall, an instant nuisance to Demarch's spine, and the four smoky engines with their immense blades rattled the fuselage and deafened the passengers. The most reliable air transportation had gone to the western front months ago. But Demarch forgot his discomfort as soon as the vehicle lifted above a plain of cloud and wheeled away from the setting sun. He was going home.

He let his attention focus on the circular window opposite him and his thoughts drift away. Except when the plane banked into a turn there was only the sky to see, a winter blue turning to ink at the apex. The electrical heating labored and Demarch turned up the collar of his veston.

It was altogether dark when the aircraft circled down to the capital. The city was invisible except for its lights, but Demarch's spirits were buoyed by the sight. All that grid of electricity was familiar territory. Parts of it he knew by heart. He picked out the stone pavilions of the Bureau Centrality as the plane lost altitude, a few windows shining in the hierarchs' buildings and watch lanterns burning in the courtyards. Then a landing field rose to meet the wheels.

He shuffled out of the aircraft with the other passengers, a few enlisted men who watched him guardedly as he crossed the tarmac to a waiting car. The Bureau had sent him a vehicle and driver. The driver spoke no English and his French was deeply accented. A Haitian, Demarch supposed. A number of Haitians had lately been imported to fill menial jobs emptied by conscription.

"*Neige*," the driver said. "*Bientôt, je pense.*" Snow soon. No doubt, Demarch told him, and let the conversation languish. He was happy with his own musing as the miles spooled past. There was not much traffic even in the narrow streets where the sacral brothels were. But it was late, and of course there was the gasoline rationing. One saw more horse-drawn vehicles these days than before the war. Dorothea had written him about a sugar shortage, too. Everything was rationed. But the fundamental nature of the countryside hadn't changed, especially here beyond the city center. Telegraph poles lined the cobbled road, and the smell of burning sod was pungent in the cold air.

He was surprised at the upwelling of pleasure he felt when the car came abreast of the house. It was a small house compared to the rambling compounds of the Censeurs farther west, but spacious enough and respectably old. It had belonged to an uncle of Dorothea's and still did not properly belong to Demarch; it was an extended loan from the Saussère family during his posting to the capital. But he had lived here for ten years. It was as much a home as any place had ever been. More so.

He thanked the driver and walked briskly up the stone steps to the door. The door opened before he touched it. Dorothea stood in a halo of lamplight, perfect and beckoning. Light twinkled from the silver crucifix pinned to her bodice. He embraced her and she offered her powdered cheek for a kiss.

Christof peeked at him from behind a banister, frowning. Well, Christof had always been shy at reunions. It was hard for him to have a father so often absent. But that was what it meant to be born into a Bureau family.

Dorothea whispered, "Father is here." And Demarch saw the wheelchair rolling from the study, Armand Saussère seeming to smile but as inscrutable as ever behind his vastly old face.

Demarch closed the door on the night air. The smell of home surrounded him. "Christof, come here," he said. But Christof kept his wary distance.

The same driver arrived in the morning to take him to town. The temperature had dropped but the sky was cloudless. *"Pas de neige,"* the driver said. No snow. Not yet.

Demarch let familiar sights lull him until the car passed under the eagle gates of the Bureau Centrality. The Centrality was a town of its own, with its good and bad neighborhoods, its loved and hated citizens. The Censeurs in their black hats and soutanes moved across the courtyard between the Ordinage and Propaganda wings like stalking birds. Demarch felt compromised in his simple lieutenant's uniform. When he worked here he had seldom crossed the invisible line separating staff officers from the hierarchs' quarters . . . unless he was summoned, always a frightening episode. Well, today he had been summoned, too.

He left the Haitian driver and crossed the pebbled yard

to the Département Administratif. The halls inside were marbled and high and supported by half-columns set into the walls. This was the heart of the Centrality, part temple, part government. It was a more powerful government, within its sphere, than the Praesidium a mile away. Clerks and pages called it "the capital's capital."

Censeur Bisonette waited in a conference room, a tall room with a mosaic floor and a long oaken table. Bisonette was at ease in a high-backed chair, his angular face composed. He didn't stand when Demarch entered. Demarch stepped forward and bowed. His footsteps echoed from the high ceiling. Everything here was designed to intimidate. Everything did.

"Sit," Bisonette croaked. They would speak English. It was a concession, or an insult, or both. "I want you to know our thoughts on the investigation."

*Our thoughts:* the Bureau's new doctrine. *The investigation:* Two Rivers. Among the hierarchs it was always *the investigation*, a nebulous enquiry whose object must never be named or defined. Demarch had learned the protocol in those first mad months.

Bisonette said, "The inventory and warehousing should be speeded up. Another military detail has been assigned— they'll be there when you get back. I want you to report to me on their progress."

"I will."

"The technical and academic assessments can proceed apace. How is that going, by the way?"

"A great deal has been written. Ultimately, I don't know how valuable it will be. Copies have gone to the Ideological Branch, but I can have them forwarded directly to the Département if you'd prefer."

"No, never mind. Let the archivists deal with it. There was an explosion, I understand . . ."

"A fire at a gasoline depot."

"Accidental or sabotage?"

"Well, we aren't sure. It seems now as if a militiaman

might have neglected to set his hand brake. There was a robbery, but the fire may be coincidental."

"May be?"

"It's impossible to know, at this stage."

"Delafleur insists it was sabotage."

Wasn't it Bisonette himself who had called Delafleur "a pompous idiot"? Demarch sensed Bureau politics at work here, a turn of the wheel, probably not to his advantage. "Of course it could have been, but there's no way to prove it."

"Personally speaking, though, you have a suspicion?"

"A simple robbery and a careless soldier. But again, I can't present evidence."

"Yes, I do understand that. Your bets are covered, Lieutenant Demarch."

He felt himself blushing.

The Censeur said, "We don't want to see any more episodes of the kind. But in the end it doesn't matter, because we've advanced our schedule."

It took a moment for the significance of that to sink in. When it did, Demarch felt faintly dizzy. "The weapon," he said.

Bisonette nodded, watching him closely. "Progress has been faster than we expected. We've already dispatched engineers to erect a test gantry. The prototype should be available within a matter of weeks."

"I thought—you said the spring."

"That's changed. Do you object, Lieutenant Demarch?"

How could he? "No. Although I wonder if it gives us time to extract everything we can from the, ah, enquiry."

"Oh, I think we've extracted a considerable amount. We'll be mining the archival material for decades, you know, from what I understand. I think that's enough. We can't really let the situation stand as it is, Lieutenant. None of us knows what happened in that place and I doubt that any of us ever will—it's beyond comprehension, which is to say it's in the nature of a miracle. If we wait to *understand* it, we'll be waiting until the end of time. In the meantime there's a real risk of contagion, both figuratively and literally. You might look at their medical arcana some time. These people may be carrying diseases, and that poses an immediate risk. They're certainly carrying *ideological* diseases." He shook his head. "The site has to be burned, and if I had my choice I would sow the ground with salt—though if this weapon operates as promised, that won't be necessary."

Demarch tried to rein in his thoughts. Be practical, he instructed himself. "It might take time to make arrangements. People will be suspicious if we start shipping out soldiers en masse."

"I'm sure they would. But most of the soldiers won't be shipped out."

"I don't understand."

Bisonette shrugged as if to dismiss an annoying triviality. "The town was manned by second-rate troops. They've seen more than we want them talking about. They're disease vectors, at least in the figurative sense. But don't worry. We'll extract the people we trust."

After he left Bisonette he made an unscheduled stop at the small peripheral building marked *ENQUÊTES,* where he had once held a desk job. He kept his collar up and walked briskly to the office of Guy Marris, an old friend.

Friendship was important in the Centrality. Friendship governed what gossip you heard, the pivot on which a career might turn. Guy had been a *wine friend,* in Bureau jargon: someone you trusted enough to get drunk with.

Guy's office was a small room—a closet, compared to Bisonette's conference chamber. Guy, a bespectacled man with more gray hair than Demarch remembered, looked up from a stack of requisition forms. "Symeon!"

Demarch nodded and they talked for a time, the usual what-are-you-doing-back-in-town and what-about-the-family. But this wasn't entirely a social visit, and Demarch began to drop hints to that effect, until Guy said, "You want a document—is that it?"

"I need a set of identification papers. Really just the basics. Enough for someone to show at checkpoints or to an employer."

Guy studied his face for a long moment and then said, "Come with me."

They walked to the courtyard, a standard maneuver if you wanted privacy. Demarch wondered why, after all these years, the hierarchs had never found a way to eavesdrop on this windy common. Or maybe they had. Or maybe they knew about it and still permitted a sliver of secrecy: no machine runs efficiently without a little grease.

Guy Marris shivered at the frigid air. He took a Victoire cigarette from the package in his breast pocket and lit it with a match. "I think this is unofficial work you're talking about."

"Yes," Demarch admitted.

"Well . . . tell me the essentials. I don't promise anything."

"A woman. Mid-thirties. Make her thirty-five. Dark hair. Height, five foot eight. Weight, say ten stone."

"She sounds intriguing."

"You still write documents, I hope." There were times when Bureau operatives needed manufactured identification, and Enquêtes was the department they came to—at least, that was how it was done when Demarch worked here.

"Oh, we do documents," Guy said, "that hasn't changed, but an unauthorized requisition . . ." He shook his head. "I suppose I could attribute it to someone else. But everything is signed for, Symeon. My name ends up on the paperwork one way or another. Mind you, if it reaches the file room, it's as good as lost." He smiled. "Have you *seen* Records? We call it the Library of Babel. But in the meantime, if anyone asks questions . . ."

Demarch nodded. He already felt guilty about asking. About jeopardizing a friend.

"Forgive me," Guy said, "but you never struck me as the type. A liaison is a liaison, but you never let it get between you and the Bureau. Is this a special woman?"

"I don't mean to bring her home to Dorothea. Only to save her life."

Which was true. His feeling about Evelyn Woodward was that she didn't deserve to die. It didn't go deeper than that, because he wouldn't allow it to.

His father-in-law had once warned him to beware of women. *They're dangerous,* he had said, grinning lewdly. *They make your soft parts hard. And your hard parts soft.*

Briefly, Demarch wondered what hardness inside him Evelyn Woodward had somehow managed to thaw.

The wind was cold and Guy was beginning to seem nervous. The tip of his Victoire flared as he drew on it, and the tobacco crackled in the chill air. "How long can you wait?"

"A week."

"That's not much."

"I know."

Guy Marris took a last draw on the cigarette and crushed it under the heel of a dress shoe. "Come see me before you leave."

"Thank you," Demarch said.

"No, don't thank me yet."


He gave Christof a toy he had brought from Two Rivers: it was called a Rubik's Cube, Evelyn had said, and Christof was delighted with the unexpected way it turned and twisted in his hands. He insisted on taking it to bed. Dorothea led him upstairs, and Demarch sipped an evening brandy with his *beau-père,* his father-in-law Armand. They sat in the library under the eye of more than five hundred books, property of the Saussère family—mainly bound collections of sermons, some of them older than Armand himself. Demarch had never liked this room.

Armand sat brooding in his wheelchair. Five years ago he had suffered a stroke that paralyzed his right leg and removed him from active Bureau duty. His mind was unaffected, the doctors said, but since the stroke he had seemed more withdrawn, less apt to share himself.

Tonight the brandy seemed to loosen him. He turned his head slowly and fixed Demarch with a birdlike one-eyed gaze. "Symeon . . . this hasn't been an easy posting for you, has it?"

"You mean the enquiry?"

"Yes. The 'enquiry.' We're so shy of words. Plain words are dangerous. But make allowances for me. I'm short of wind. Tempted to brevity. It must be difficult for you."

"Well, I think I've done a respectable job."

"Hard for a man to preside over such strangeness."

You don't know the half of it, Demarch thought. But Armand still cultivated his Bureau contacts: he obviously knew more than Demarch would have guessed. He said, "Of course. . . ."

"And so many deaths."

"Actually, there haven't been many."

"But there will be. And you know it."

"Yes." He shrugged. "I don't think about it."

"But you do, you know. One always thinks about it. And if you *don't* think about it, you dream about it." Armand lowered his voice until it was a rumble from the deep barrel of his chest. Demarch leaned forward to listen. "I was at the Mandan River," Armand said, "after the Lakota rebellion. They don't tell you about that in the Académie, do they? No, nor in any other sort of school, except to say that a menace was disposed of. Careful words. Discreet. They don't tell you what the camps looked like with their watchtowers overlooking the prairie sloughs. How the grass goes on for miles and miles. They don't tell you how muddy it was that spring. Or how the smell from the furnaces lingered when the bodies were burned. The bodies of men and women and children—I know one isn't supposed to call them that, but that's what they were, or seemed to be, whatever the condition of their souls. I suppose their souls went up with the smoke. A body is some ounces lighter when it dies . . . I read that somewhere." His eyes seemed to glaze. "Everything is a test, Symeon, in our line of work."

"Am I being tested?"

"We're always being tested." Armand sipped his brandy. "We're all subordinated, not just the ones we kill. There are no victims. You have to remember that. We're all in the service of something larger than ourselves, and the difference between us and those corpses is that we are its *willing* servants. That's all. That's all. We're spared because we put our bodies on the altar every day, and not just our bodies, but our minds and our wills. Remember the vow you took when you joined the Bureau. *Incipit vita nova.* A new life begins. You leave your priggish little intellect behind."

The brandy made him reckless. He said, "And our conscience?"

"That was never yours," Armand said. "Don't be absurd."


He turned out the lights after Armand wheeled himself away. The fire had burned down to embers. He finished his brandy in the dark and then moved upstairs.

The old man's words seemed to follow him in stuttering echoes through the chilly house. *We put our bodies on the altar every day.* But for what? *Something larger than ourselves.* The Bureau, the Church, the Protennoia? Something more, surely. Some idea or vision of the good, a republic of permissible relations, a step up from the barbarism of the Lakota and all the countless other slaughtered aboriginals.

But the corpses pile higher every day, and need to be burned.

Dorothea was asleep when he joined her in bed. Her

long hair lay across the pillow like a black wing. She reminded him of a temple, serene and pale even in sleep.

He stood a moment watching the snow that had begun to fall beyond the double panes of the bedroom window. He thought about Christof. Christof still acted like a stranger. *The way he looks at me,* Demarch thought. *As if he's seeing something alien, something that makes him afraid.*

Bisonette telephoned after five days. "We think you should go back tomorrow," the Censeur said. "I'm sorry to cut short your time with your family, but the arrangements have already been made."

"What's wrong? Has something happened?"

"Only Clement Delafleur getting a little overzealous in your absence. I'm given to understand he's hanging children in the public square."

He kissed Dorothea good-bye. Christof was presented for a kiss and consented to it. Probably he had been coached.

He told the Haitian driver to stop at the Bureau Centrality on the way to the airport.

Guy Marris was in his office. Demarch said he was stopping to say good-bye; he had been summoned back to duty.

His friend wished him luck and shook his hand. At the door, he tucked a sheaf of papers into the pocket of Demarch's veston. Neither man spoke of it.

It had snowed a little, the Haitian driver said, but it would snow much more before long.

# CHAPTER 12

Linneth arranged with the school's principal to take Dexter Graham back to his apartment, as inconspicuously as possible, in the principal's automobile, which he still drove from time to time although his hoard of gasoline was almost exhausted. Mr. Hoskins was wary of her intentions but understood the urgency of the situation. She was aware of the way he watched her in the rear-view mirror. The distrust was mutual, but there was nothing to be done about that.

Fresh snow had fallen, and the rear tires slipped each time they turned a corner. No one spoke during the drive. When the car stopped, Linneth helped Dex out of the rear seat. His blood, she saw, had stained the upholstery. The principal pulled away quickly and left them alone in the twining veils of snow.

Linneth guided Dex up the steps to his apartment. He

was lucid enough to use his door key but he passed out again when he reached the blood-stained bed.

Linneth had learned emergency aid during her three years with the Christian Renunciates. She stripped his shirt and unwound the sodden, dirty bandage from his arm. Dex moaned but didn't wake. The injury under the bandage leaked blood and suppuration in lazy pulses. Linneth cleaned it with water and a cloth, as gently as possible, but the pain was unavoidable; Dex screamed and twisted away.

"I'm sorry," she said. "But this has to be done."

"Get me something. The aspirin."

"The what?"

"In the bottle on the kitchen counter."

She fetched the small tubule of pills and peered at its label. The fragmented English defied interpretation. "Is it a narcotic?"

"A painkiller. And it'll bring the fever down."

She shook out four tablets at his instruction and he swallowed them with water. She said, "Do you have a disinfectant, too?"

"No. Uh, wait, there's some Bactine in the medicine cabinet. . . ."

"For cleaning wounds?" She didn't like the way his eyes wandered. He might not be coherent.

"For cuts," he said. "You spray it on cuts."

She found the Bactine and experimented until she understood the operation of the aerosol bottle. When she came back to the bed Dex had closed his eyes again. He didn't rouse until she bathed his injury with the disinfectant; then he screamed until she gave him a wadded pillow-case to bite on.

The wound was patently a bullet wound. The missile had passed through the fleshy part of his upper arm. She would have liked to close the injury with stitches, but there was no needle or thread at hand. He did have sterile cotton in a bag in the bathroom medicine cabinet, and she used

some of that to pack the wound and a clean linen bandage
to wrap it. But his fever was very high.

She pulled a kitchen chair near to the bed and watched
him. Within an hour the fever had subsided, at least to her
touch, and he seemed to be sleeping peacefully. That was
the effect of the antipyretics, Linneth supposed. Still, she
didn't like the way his wound had looked—or smelled.

The light from the window was thin and gray. The
snowy afternoon had begun to wane. She called his name
until he opened his eyes.

"Dex, I have to go. I'll be back. If possible, before curfew. You'll stay here, won't you?"

He squinted as if to bring her into focus. "Where the
hell would I go?"

"Out to make more trouble, I don't doubt."

She put a second blanket on him. The room was cold
and he owned no fireplace or gas jets.


She hurried through torrents of dry, granular snow to
the town's medical clinic.

The town of Two Rivers lacked a hospital. This building
was the nearest thing: a cube of consulting rooms with
windows of tinted glass and a wide tiled lobby. Dr. Eichorn
would be here today, if her luck held. She identified herself
to the soldier at the door and asked where she could find
him. "First office left off the lobby," he said, "last time I saw
him, Miss."

Dr. Eichorn was the medical archivist who had been
called in, like Linneth, by the Proctors. He was a tall, hair-
less, patrician Southerner, a teaching physician with a degree in natural history. She found him at a desk in a
consulting room. He was wrapped in two woolen sweaters
and a scarf, frowning over the pages of a medical journal,
eyeglasses thick as jeweler's loupes riding the end of his
nose. She tapped the open door. He looked up and his eyes
narrowed in some combination of suspicion and annoy-

ance. "Miss, is it, Stone? We met in the commissary—didn't we?"

"Yes. . . ." Now that she was here, she didn't know how to begin.

"Is there something I can help you with?"

"Yes, there is." Forge ahead, she thought. "Dr. Eichorn, I need a course of sulfa drugs."

"You mean, you're sick?"

"No. It's for a friend."

He was like a muddy pond. It took time for things to sink in. Eichorn pushed the journal aside and leaned back in his chair. "You're that woman anthropologist from Boston."

"I am."

"I didn't know you were also a medical prodigy."

"Sir, I'm not. But I was trained by the Christian Renunciates and I know how to administer drugs."

"And how to prescribe them?"

"The object is to ward off infection in a wound."

"A *wound*, you say."

"Yes."

"One of your anthropological subjects?"

The question was awkward, but Linneth nodded.

"I see. Well, maybe the best thing would be if the patient came to me directly."

"That would be difficult."

"Or if you took me to the patient."

"It isn't necessary." She worked to keep any hint of desperation out of her voice. "I know your time is valuable. I'm asking this favor as a colleague, Dr. Eichorn."

"As a *colleague*? Am I the *colleague* of a woman who studies savages?" He shook his bald head ponderously. "Sulfanilamide. Well, that's problematic. There was trouble last night—you may have heard of it."

"Only rumors."

"Shooting in the main street."

"I see."

"A fire."

"If you say so."

Eichorn studied her from his turgid depths. Linneth waited for his verdict. She counted silently to ten and was careful not to lower her gaze.

"In this building," Eichorn said, "there are antibiotics the like of which I've never seen. I don't know where this town came from or where it may be going, but there were some clever people here. We'll be reaping the rewards for decades. We owe someone a debt, Miss Stone. I don't know who." He rubbed his scalp with a bony hand. "No one will miss a bottle of pills. But let's keep this between us, yes?"

Linneth knew that something inside her had changed, but the change had been gradual and she couldn't be sure of its nature or degree. It was as if she had opened a familiar door and found a strange new landscape beyond it.

Maybe the change had begun when the Proctor Symeon Demarch invaded her home in Boston, or when she arrived in this impossible town. But the axis and emblem of that change was surely Dexter Graham—not only the man but the qualities she had espied in him: skepticism, courage, defiance.

She thought at first his virtues might be common American virtues, but the evidence for that was scant. Linneth had sampled the magazines and newspapers of his world and found them brash but often vulgar and concerned above all else with fashion: fashions in politics as much as fashions in dress; and fashion, Linneth thought, was only that drab whore Conformity in gaudier paint. Dexter Graham defied convention. He seemed to weigh everything— everything she said to him, her words, her *presence*—on an invisible scale. He had the bearing of a judge, but there was nothing imperious or awful in it. He did not exempt himself from judgment. She sensed that he had long ago passed some verdict on himself, and the verdict was far from favorable.

Obviously, she should have turned him over to the soldiers as soon as she saw his wound. But when she thought about it she remembered a passage in the book he had given her, *Huckleberry Finn,* by Mr. Mark Twain. Much of the book had been hard to decipher, but there was a pivotal moment when Huck debated whether he ought to turn over his friend, the Negro Jim, to authorities. By the standards of his time, giving up Jim was the right thing to do. Huckleberry Finn had been told he would go to Hell and suffer unspeakable torment if he abetted an escaped slave. Nevertheless, Huck helped his friend. If it meant going to Hell, then he'd go to Hell.

*I'll go to Hell, then,* Linneth thought.

The sulfa pills rattled in her coat pocket as she paced through snowy gloom. Because the electricity had been turned off to punish the townspeople, there would be no streetlights tonight. The military patrols had been redoubled but the snow would slow them down.

She was allowed to come and go as she wished from the civilians' wing of the Blue View Motel. She ate dinner at the commissary in order not to arouse suspicion. The dinner was a stew of beef in watery broth and slices of dense bread buttered with suet. She told the pions who patrolled the hallway that she would be working on a paper tonight and didn't want to be disturbed. She left a lamp burning in her room and pulled the curtains. When the pions adjourned to the lobby to smoke their noxious pipes, she went out a side door into the windy dark. She fell twice, hurrying along the empty streets. The church bell was tolling curfew when she reached Dexter Graham's apartment.

She fed him sulfanilamide and aspirin and sat with him through the night. When Dex slept, she slept on the sofa across the room. When he woke, often raving or thrashing, she bathed his forehead with a damp cloth.

She was aware of the danger of being here and of the danger Dex was in. The Proctors were like poisonous insects—harmless enough if allowed to toil undisturbed in their nests; lethal if aroused. She remembered the day the Proctors came to arrest her mother, before she was sent to the Renunciates, and that ancient fear rose like flood water from the culverts of memory.

While she cooled his forehead she admired Dexter Graham's face. He was handsome. She seldom thought of the men she knew as handsome or unhandsome; they were threats or opportunities, seldom friends or lovers. The word *lover* sounded lewd even when she pronounced it in the privacy of her thoughts. Her last "lover," if he could be called that, was the boy Campo. That was in the old days when she was very young and before the idolatry laws were enacted. Her father had taken the family to the annual civic service in Rome, where the Temple of Apollo was festooned with garlands and the Bishop of Rome himself rendered the oracles of the Prophetess in Latin hexameter. Linneth was bored by the ritual and sickened by the sacrifice of the animals. She avoided services and stayed in the paradeisos where foreign visitors lodged—or at least, she promised to. In fact she escaped each morning and taught herself to ride the buses and elevated trains; and she met Campo, an Egyptian boy who had come to the shrines with his family as Linneth had come with hers. They spent their meager allowances together on the trams, at the zoo, in the cafés. He told her about Alexandria. She told him about New York. In secret, in his small room in the paradeisos, they undressed one another. Her first and last lover, Campo. On the great passenger steamer *Sardinia,* bound for New York Harbor after the rites were finished, Linneth's mother interpreted her silences and frowns. "Sometimes we meet Pan in unexpected places," she said, smiling obliquely. "Linneth, weren't the fountains lovely?" She supposed so. "And the choirs in the shrine?" Oh yes. "And the flowers, and the perfume, and the priestess on the axon?" Yes. "And that African boy we saw you with?" Linneth supposed he was lovely too.

She remembered the sunny days on the steamship with the Atlantic Ocean churning behind. She had seen distant mountains of ice, blue as summer air, floating off the Grand Banks. At night, constellations turned like mill wheels in the sky.

After that her life had changed. The Proctors took her to finish her schooling with the Christian Renunciates at their gray stone retraite in snowy Utica (New York, not Greece). She had worn gray dresses that swept the floor and she had learned the Christian panoply of gods, Archons, Demiurges, and dour apostles. And there had not been a lover since Campo, whose skin had smelled wonderfully of cinnamon and cedar.

When she was little her mother told her, "The god who lives in the forest lives in your belly and in your heart." She wondered if her fierce scholasticism, her invasion of the masculine strongholds of library and carrel, had really been a search for that outcast god: in whose myths, villages, meadows, sacred places? Campo and Pan and the Golden Bough, she thought; everything we worshiped or should have worshiped or neglected to worship.

She tended Dexter Graham through his fever as the snow fell from the dark sky.

After a day he woke and was able to drink a bowl of soup, which Linneth heated over a wax candle. He was thin under the many blankets (she bathed him with a sponge and changed his bandage often), and she saw that the wound and the fever had drawn heavily on his stores of life and strength.

She thought he might have lost some of his distrust of her, and that was good, although his eyes still followed her

—if not suspiciously, at least curiously—as she moved about the room.

She was away often enough to establish her presence in the civilians' compound. In the evenings she came back. When Dex was awake, she talked to him. She asked him questions about the book, *Huckleberry Finn*.

The decision Huck Finn makes about Jim, she explained, represents a well-known heresy. To say *Well, then, I'll go to Hell* . . . to imply that there exists some moral standard higher than Church and Law, and that this standard is accessible even to an ignorant peasant boy . . . that Huck Finn might have a firmer grasp of good and evil than, for instance, a Proctor of the Bureau . . . well, people had burned for less.

Dex said, "Do *you* think it's a heresy?"

"Of course it is. Do you mean, do I think it's true?" She lowered her voice and eyes. "Of course it's true. That's why I'm here."


A week passed. The snow mounted on the sill of the window and the talk between Linneth and Dex gathered a similar weight. She brought a paraffin heater to make his small rooms bearably warm, though she still had to wrap herself in sweaters and Dex in blankets. And she brought food: pails of stew, or bread with crumbling wedges of cheese.

Linneth talked about herself as the snow sifted against the window glass with a sound that made her think of feathers and diamonds. She told him about her childhood, when the forests near the family's stone house had seemed enchanted during the icebound winter days; about mugs of mulled wine, devotions in mysterious Latin, storybooks wrapped in red paper and imported from the pagan states of southern Europe and Byzantium. Her father was bearded, devout, aloof, and learned. Her mother told secrets. *Something lives in everything,* her mother said, *if only you look for it.*

When the idolatry laws were passed and the Proctors came to take her father away, he went wordlessly. A month later they came back for Linneth's mother, who screamed all the way down the drive to the boxy black truck. The Proctors took Linneth, too, and sent her to the Renunciates, until a Christian aunt in Boston bought her free and arranged for her education, the best education money could buy.

Dex Graham talked about a wholly different childhood: suburban, fast-paced, suffused by the glow of television. It was a freer existence than Linneth could imagine; but narrow, too, in its way. Where Dex came from, no one talked much about life or death or good or evil—except, Linneth pointed out, Mr. Mark Twain; but he was of an older tradition. Was it possible, she wondered, to suffocate in triviality? In Dex's world one could spend one's entire life in a blaze of the most florid triviality. *It blinds you,* he said, *but it doesn't keep you warm.*

She asked if he had been married. He said yes, his wife had been Abigail and his son had been David. They were dead. They died in a fire. Their house had burned down.

"Were you there when it happened?"

Dex looked at the ceiling. After a long time he said, "No."

Then: "No, that's a lie. I was there. I was in the house when it caught fire." She had to lean closer to hear him. "I used to drink. Sometimes I drank to excess. So one night I came home late. I went to sleep on the sofa because I didn't want to disturb Abby. When I woke up a couple of hours later the air was full of smoke. There were flames running up the stairs. Abby and David were up there. I tried to go after them but I couldn't get through. Burned the hair off my face. The fire was too hot. Or I was too scared of it. Neighbors called the fire department and a guy with an oxygen mask dragged me out of the house. But the question is—in the end, nobody could say what started the fire. The insurance people investigated but it was inconclusive. So I keep thinking, did I knock over a lamp? Leave a cigarette burning? The kind of thing a drunk does." He shook his head. "I still don't know whether I killed them."

He looked at her as if he regretted saying it, or feared what she might say; so she didn't speak, only took his hand and touched a cooling cloth to his forehead.


She came to the apartment every day, even when his recovery made it obvious she wasn't needed. She liked being here.

The room Dex Graham occupied was sparsely furnished but oddly pleasant, especially now that the punitive week had passed and the lights were back on. It was a cloistered space, a bubble of warmth in the snow that seemed never to stop falling. Dex tolerated her presence and even appeared to welcome it, though he was often subdued, often quiet. There was a dimple of pink flesh where the bullet had entered his arm.

The wound still hurt him. He favored the arm. She had to mind the injury when she came into bed with him.

This was a sin, she reckoned, by some lights; but not a sin of the forest or the belly or the heart. The Renunciates would call it a sin. So would that Bureau ideologue, Delafleur. Let them, Linneth thought. It doesn't matter. Let them call it what they want. I'll go to Hell.

# CHAPTER 13

On the first night of that cold week, when the windows grew opaque with ice and the street was crowded with soldiers, Clifford tore up his maps and notes and flushed them down the toilet. The maps were evidence of his guilt. They might not prove anything, but they would surely get him into trouble if Luke, for instance, found them.

He couldn't dispose of the radio scanner as easily. He buried it under a stack of encyclopedias of science at the back of his bedroom closet—but only until he could think of a more permanent solution.

His mood alternated between boredom and panic. In those first days after the fire, wild rumors circulated. Clifford's mother passed them on, absentmindedly but in meticulous detail, over the meager dinners she made him sit down to. (She kept perishables in the snow on the back step since the refrigerator wasn't working. Mostly there was bread and cheese on the table, and not much of that.)

People had seen peculiar things, his mother said. Some people claimed they saw God that night, or maybe it was the Devil—though what either one of them would want with the Beacon Street filling station was beyond her. According to Mrs. Fraser, some soldiers had died in the explosion. According to someone else it was a Proctor who had been killed, and God help us all if *that* was true. Mr. Kingsley next door said it was some new experiment at the defense plant that caused the explosion . . . but Joe Kingsley hadn't been in his right mind since his wife died last August; you could tell because he never washed his clothes anymore.

And so on. On Friday, Clifford picked up a single-sheet edition of the *Two Rivers Crier* from the stack at the corner of Beacon and Arbutus. The newspaper reported "hooliganism on the main street" but said no one had been seriously hurt, and Clifford decided to believe that, although you couldn't be sure of what they printed in the *Crier* anymore. The town's punishment had been fairly mild, considering what was possible, and the number of soldiers on the street declined over the course of the week; so it was probably true that no one had been killed. If a soldier or a Proctor had died, Clifford thought, things would be much worse.

It was good to think he hadn't hurt anyone. Still, the presence of the scanner in his closet continued to make him nervous. He lost sleep, thinking about it. His mother said, "Cliffy, are you sick? Your eyes are all puffy."

Friday night, Luke came to the house again. He brought rice and a half pound of fatty ground beef, plus the inevitable quart jar of barracks whiskey. Clifford's mother cooked the meat and rice for dinner, all of it at once. The whiskey she placed at the back of the counter next to the microwave oven, handling the bottle as reverently as if it were a piece of the True Cross.

Clifford ate a good share of food, although the conversation at the table was strained and halting. As usual, the talk picked up after he departed for his room. They always sent him to his room after dinner. Clifford only went as far as the halfway point on the stairs—close enough to the kitchen to hear what was being said; close enough to the bedroom to make good his escape when they left the table. What his mother said to Luke, or the soldier to his mother, sometimes bewildered him and sometimes made him blush. His mother seemed like a different person, a stranger with a hidden history and a new vocabulary. The soldier called her Ellen. That made him uneasy. Clifford had never thought of his mother as "Ellen." As she drank, she used more dirty words. She said, "No shit!" or "Well, fuck!" And Clifford always winced when this happened.

Luke drank, too, and in the long pauses between drinking he would talk about his work. It was this talk Clifford particularly wanted to hear. The disaster on Beacon Street should have cured him of eavesdropping, he thought. Eavesdropping with the scanner had almost gotten him killed. But he went on listening to Luke. It seemed important. He couldn't say why.

Tonight was a good example. Tonight Luke talked about all the bulldozers that had come in from Fort Le-Duc, and what the bulldozers were doing on the edge of town.

Tuesday was the first food depot day after the electricity came back on and Clifford volunteered to make the trip to pick up rations. His mother agreed. Which was no surprise. She seldom left the house if she could help it. Some days she didn't even leave her room.

The air outside was damp and cold. The pale sun at

noon was just warm enough to melt the skin of the
fallen snow and fill the gutters with frigid water. Clifford
passed the time during the long walk to the food depot
by trying to make perfect footprints in the crusty snow.
When he stepped straight down his boots left cookie-cut-
ter outlines behind him.

He carried an empty bag to fill up with food, and another bag—a plastic bag, into which he had placed the
radio scanner in its box. He held the bag with the scanner close to his body and hoped no one would pay it
any attention.

At the depot he collected the family allowance of
bread and cheese. Then he stood across the street under
the awning of the Two Rivers Thrift Shop, watching the
ration line grow as it hitched forward. The people in the
line looked unhappy and too thin. Some of them were
sick. The cold week had been hard on people, his
mother had told him. He paid attention to the faces of
the men in the line. Would he recognize the one he was
looking for? He thought so. But it was hard to wait. His
toes were numb inside his boots; the cold air made his
nose run.

The line lengthened until it was twenty people long;
then it began to shrink as the shadows grew. The soldiers
dispensing food were tired. They punched notches into
ration cards without really looking at them and paused to
take off their gloves and blow into their cupped hands.
Clifford was about to begin the walk home, disappointed,
when he saw the man he was waiting for.

The man looked skinnier than Clifford remembered—
and he had been a thin man to begin with—but it was
definitely the same one. The man joined the line and
waited with no particular expression on his thin face.
When he reached the front he offered his ration card for
clipping, then opened a dirty cloth bag for the bread and
cheese. Then he turned and walked away with his head
bent into the wind.

Clifford gathered his own food bag in one hand and the bag with the scanner in the other and followed the man west toward Commercial and River.

After a twisty walk among the slatboard houses of the west end of town, the man went into a shabby house. Clifford hesitated on the sidewalk. A shoal of cloud had hidden the low sun and meltwater was freezing in the gutters. There was a film of ice on the empty road.

He went to the door of the house and knocked.

Howard Poole opened the door and peered in obvious surprise from a dim hallway. The plume of his breath hung like a feather in the air.

Clifford, wanting to be sure, said, "You're the man on the hill at the defense plant that day. You're Howard."

He nodded slowly. "And you're Clifford. I remember." He looked around the snowbound yard. "Did you follow me here?"

Clifford said yes.

"But you're alone, right?"

"Yes."

"You need something? You need some help?"

"No," Clifford said. "I brought you something."

"Well, come in."

In the barely warm kitchen, Clifford took the radio scanner from its bag and set it on the table. He explained to Howard how it worked and how he was able to hear the soldiers talking on the marine band. He left out what had happened to the gas station. He didn't want even Howard to know about that.

Howard accepted the gift gravely. He said it would probably be useful, though he wasn't sure how. "Clifford, you want something to drink? There's milk powder. Even a little chocolate. I could probably manage cocoa."

It was tempting, but Clifford shook his head. "I have to get home. But there's something else. You remember when I told you about Luke?"

"Luke—?"

"The soldier my mother sees."

"Oh. Yes, I remember."

"He talked about something they're doing. He said the Proctors brought in a whole bunch of earth-movers from Fort LeDuc. Band saws, too, and stump cutters. They're using them all around the town, following the line where, you know, where *our* territory meets *their* territory—that whole circle. They're cutting down trees and digging up dirt. It's a big project. From my house, you can hear the noise all the way from Coldwater Road."

Howard looked very solemn. His eyes were big behind those taped-up glasses. "Clifford, did Luke say *why* they're doing this?"

"He says he doesn't know, and the Proctors won't talk about it . . . but it looks like what they're cutting is one big firebreak."

The boy went out into a windy dusk. Howard wanted to pass on this information about the Proctors to Dex, but curfew was too close and a visit might be dangerous in any case. He closed the door. Maybe tomorrow.

The house was dark. After months of hiding here, Howard was still reluctant to use the lights. But a little light was good. For a week the Cantwell house had been cold and dark and even more lonely than it had seemed in the autumn: a strange shore to have washed up on. He still felt like an intruder here.

He climbed the stairs to Paul Cantwell's study and loaded the last fifty pages of the Buchanan and Bayard counties white pages into the Hewlett-Packard PC. This work had been interrupted, maddeningly, by the week of darkness, and today by the need to pick up rations. He finished it now with more dread than excitement. The experiment for which he had risked so much—his life, his friend Dex's life—might be exactly as ephemeral as Dex had predicted. He had built an ornate palace of conjecture, and that delicate structure might well collapse under the weight of reality.

The telephone number Stern gave him hadn't appeared in the first hundred pages of the phone book—unless the optical reader had mistranslated it, or the program he was reading it into had some kind of flaw. But that was unlikely. More likely was that he simply hadn't found the number yet . . . or that it was unlisted.

Howard finished loading the directory and told the computer to sort for the target number. The disk drive chattered into the silent room.

It didn't take long. The machine announced success as prosaically as it had announced failure. The number simply appeared highlighted in blue; a name and address appeared at the left.

WINTERMEYER, R. 1230 HALTON ROAD, TWO RIVERS

Less than three blocks from here.


He spent a sleepless night thinking about Stern, his mind crowded with a hundred memories and a single image: Stern, so like his name, fiercely intelligent, eyes dark, lips pursed behind a curly beard. Generous but mysterious. Howard had been talking to Alan Stern for much of his life and every conversation had been a treasured event, but what had he learned about the man in back of the ideas? Only a few clues from his mother. Stern the enigmatic, Stern who was, his mother once said, "trying to secede from the human race."

Howard walked to the Halton Road address in the morning in a dizzy mixture of anticipation and dread.

The house itself was nothing special: an old two-story row house faced with pink aluminum siding. The tiny lawn and the narrow passway at the side were obscured by snow; a tin trash can peeked out from a drift. A path snaked to the front door. There was a light in a down-stairs window.

Howard pushed the doorbell and heard the buzzer ring inside.

A woman answered the door. She was in her fifties, Howard guessed; slim, small-boned, her gray hair long and loose. She looked at him warily, but that was how everyone looked at strangers nowadays.

He said, "Are you R. Wintermeyer?"

"Ruth. 'R' only to my tax form." She narrowed her eyes. "You look a little familiar. But only a little."

"I'm Howard Poole. I'm Alan Stern's nephew."

Her eyes widened and she took a step back. "Oh my God. I think you really *are*. You even look like him. He talked about you, of course, but I thought—"

"What?"

"You know. I thought you must have been killed at the lab."

"No. I wasn't there. They didn't have a place for me —I stayed in town that night." He looked past her into the dim interior of the house.

She said, "Well, please come in."

Warm air embraced him. He tried to restrain his curiosity but his eyes searched for evidence of Stern. The furniture in the sitting room—a sofa, side table, bookcases —was casual but clean. A book was splayed open on an easy chair but he couldn't read the title.

Howard said, "Is my uncle here?"

Ruth looked at him for a time. "Is that what you thought?"

"He gave me the telephone number but not the address. It took me a long time to find you."

"Howard . . . your uncle is dead. He died at the lab that night with everybody else. I'm sorry. I thought you would have assumed . . . I mean, he did spend most of his nights here, but there was something going on, some kind of work. . . . Did you really think he might be here after all this time?"

Howard felt breathless. "I was sure of it."

"Why?"

He shrugged. "It was a feeling."

She gave him another, longer look. Then she said, "I have that feeling, too. Sit down, please, Howard. Would you like coffee? I think we have a lot to talk about."

# CHAPTER 14

The clergy of Two Rivers had responded to the events of the summer by putting together what they called the Ad Hoc Ecumenical Council, a group of pastors representing the town's seven Christian churches and two synagogues. The group met in Brad Congreve's basement twice a month.

Congreve, an ordained Lutheran minister, was proud of his work. He had assembled a delegation from every religious group in town except for the Kingdom Hall of Jehovah's Witnesses and the Vedanta Buddhist Temple, which in any case was only Annie Stoller and some of her New Age friends sitting cross-legged in the back of Annie's self-help store. The churches had not always been on friendly terms, and it was still a chore to keep the Baptists talking to the Unitarians, for instance, but they all faced a common danger in this peculiar new world.

Certainly they had all shared a trial of faith. Congreve

often felt the way he supposed the Incas must have felt when Pizarro marched into town with banners flying— doomed, that is, at least in the long run. There was a Christianity here but it was like no Christian doctrine Congreve had ever imagined—it was not even monotheistic! The God of the Proctors presided over a cosmogony as crowded as the Super Bowl, Jesus being only one of the major players. Worse, these *faux* Christians were numerous and well armed.

Symeon Demarch had allowed the churches to carry on with services, which had been a morale booster, but it was Congreve's private conviction that the writing was on the wall. He might not go to his death a martyr, but he would probably go down as one of the last living Lutherans. There was not even history to sustain him. History had been erased, somehow.

The only thing that had not been challenged was his belief in miracles.

In the meantime he drew together the Christian community in Two Rivers and tried to set a dignified tone. There was argument tonight about the explosion at the filling station and the curious phenomena some people had seen there. Signs and wonders. Congreve shunted that aside when he called the meeting to order. It was not the kind of issue they could resolve; it only fostered disagreement.

Instead, he raised the more immediate and practical question of Christmas decorations. The electrical power would be restored by the beginning of next week, and it was already the first of December—although it felt more like January with all this snow. His youth group wanted to string Christmas lights on the church lawn. A few lights would make everybody feel better, Congreve supposed. But Christmas lights were a religious display and according to Demarch all such displays needed prior approval by the Proctors. That was where the problem arose. Symeon Demarch was out of town; the man in charge was an unpleasant bureaucrat named Clement Delafleur. Father Gregory of the Catholic church had already spoken to Delafleur and the meeting had not been a happy one; Delafleur had expressed a desire to close down the churches altogether and had called Father Gregory "an idolator and an alien."

But Christmas decorations were a secular tradition, too, and no doubt some of the private citizens in Two Rivers would be moved to dig out their strings of lights—so why not the churches?

A plausible argument, Congreve thought, but the Proctors might disagree. He counseled a prudent caution. Reverend Lockheed of the Mission Baptist said his young people were also anxious to do something to mark the season, so how about decorating the big pine in the Civic Gardens outside City Hall—as a kind of test case? If the Proctors objected, the lights could be unstrung. (Though not without vocal objections, if Congreve knew Terry Lockheed.)

Lockheed made it a formal motion. Congreve would have preferred to hold over the entire issue until Demarch was back. Why court trouble? But the show of hands overruled him.

The combined Lutheran and Baptist youth groups, plus interested parties from the Episcopalians and Catholics— about seventy-five young people in all—converged on the Civic Gardens east of City Hall the next Saturday morning.

Electrical power was still interdicted at the source, so no one brought lights—those could be added later. Instead there were ribbons, balls, colored string; spun-glass angels, gold and silver coronets; tinsel, brocade, and popcorn chains by the yard. A morning snow fell gently and there was room for everything among the capacious, snowy branches of the tree. Reverend Lockheed showed up with a cherry-picking ladder so that even the peaks of the big pine were not neglected.

Work went on for more than two hours despite the

cold. When the last ornament was installed, Pastor Congreve handed out songsheets printed on the Methodists' hand-crank mimeograph: *Silent Night,* to be followed by *O Come All Ye Faithful.*

Midway through the first carol, a military vehicle pulled up across the road and a single soldier emerged. The militiaman stood looking on without expression. Congreve wondered if he understood the purpose of the display.

The soldier watched, arms folded across his chest, but didn't interfere. Across the square, a crowd of townspeople had been watching the tree-trimming. They ignored the militiaman and clapped for the carolers.

Terry Lockheed looked at the soldier, then at Congreve, a mute enquiry: Should we carry on? Why not, Congreve thought. One more song. If this was a crisis, they were already well in it. He nodded his head. The faithful, the joyful, the triumphant were duly summoned.

Then, suddenly, there was nothing left of the morning. The young people adjourned to Tucker's Restaurant for hot milk. The crowd melted away. Before long the Civic Gardens were empty save for the soldier, the tree, and the falling snow.


The tree disappeared that night.

Sometime before dawn it was cut, thrown into the back of a military transport, and burned on the perpetual trash fire in the parking lot of the highway 7-Eleven. Only the stump remained, a snow-covered hummock by the dim light of morning.

The news traveled fast.


It was never clear who initiated the Youth Club picket. Forced to guess, Brad Congreve would have picked the thick-set Burmeister girl, Shelda—the one who wore bottle-glass lenses and quoted Gandhi during Sunday Discussion.

It was exactly the sort of febrile notion Shelda would have taken into her head.

She was certainly one of the twelve young people who had set up a picket line around the Civic Gardens, carrying stick-and-cardboard signs with such legends as

LET US WORSHIP AS WE CHOOSE

and

JESUS DOESN'T PLAY FAVORITES!

This time there was no pastoral guidance and no approving crowd of strangers. This wasn't fun or familiar. This was patently dangerous. Pedestrians who saw the picket line stared a moment, then turned away.

When the soldiers came, Shelda and her eleven compatriots filed submissively into the back of a dung-green transport truck. In best Gandhian fashion, they were willing to be arrested. Calmly, they appealed to the consciences of the soldiers. The soldiers, grim as stones, said nothing at all.

The trouble with being close to a man, Evelyn Woodward thought, is that you find out his secrets.

From hints and silences, from phone calls half-overheard and words half-pronounced and documents glimpsed as they crossed his desk, she had learned one of Symeon Demarch's secrets—a secret too terrible to contain and impossible to share.

It was a secret about what was going to happen to Two Rivers. No. Worse than that. Let's not be coy, Evelyn thought. It was a secret about the *last* thing that would happen to Two Rivers.

It was a secret about an atomic bomb. No one called it that; but she had discerned words like *nucleic* and *megaton* among the veiled discussion of what would be done with the town, the vexing and impossible town of Two Rivers.

Now, with Symeon away and the house empty and all this snow coming so relentlessly from a woolen sky, the secret was an awkward weight inside her. It was like having a terminal disease: no matter how hard she tried not to think about it, her thoughts came circling back.

Her only consolation was that Symeon had not originated the idea and even seemed to despise it. He hadn't argued when he talked to his superiors, but she heard the unhappiness in his voice. And when he told her she would be safe, he seemed to mean it. He would take her away. He might not live with her; he had a wife and child in the capital; but he would find a place for her out of harm's way. Maybe she would go on being his mistress.

But that left everybody else. Her neighbors, she thought, Dex Graham, the grocer, the schoolkids—*everybody*. How do you imagine so many deaths? If you went to Hiroshima before the bomb fell, and you told those people what was going to happen to them, they wouldn't believe you—not because it wasn't plausible but because the human mind can't contain such things.

There was plenty of food, and she dealt with the cold by burying herself in sweaters and blankets and lighting the propane stove Symeon had left. But she couldn't keep out the dark, and in the dark her thoughts were loudest. Sleep didn't help. One night she dreamed she was Hester Prynne from *The Scarlet Letter,* but the A on her breast stood for *Atom,* not *Adultery.*

She was gratified when, at the end of that unendurable week, the electricity came back. She woke up to a wave of new heat. The blankets were superfluous. The *room* was warm. The windows ran wet with condensation. She ate a hot breakfast and sat by the stove until it was time for a hot lunch. And then a hot dinner. And bright lights to batten out the night.

The morning after *that* she felt both restless and celebratory. She decided she would take a walk: not in any of the fine dresses Symeon had given her, which would mark her for abuse, but in her old clothes, her old jeans, her shabby blouse and heavy winter jacket.

Dressing in these things was like putting on a discarded skin. Old clothes have old memories inside. Briefly, she wondered what Dex was doing now. But Dex had moved out when the lieutenant came (Evelyn had chosen to stay in the house); Dex had been threatened by the Proctors; worst of all, Dex was going to die in the bomb blast (damn that hideous, unstoppable thought).

She walked along Beacon past Commercial until she reached the woody corner of Powell Creek Park, which was quite far enough: her cheeks were ruddy and her feet were cold.

The exercise helped to empty her mind. Evelyn hummed to herself from deep in her throat. There was not much traffic on the streets and it was better that way. She decided to go home by way of City Hall, a walk she had always enjoyed in winter when the skating rink was open. She didn't skate but she used to like seeing the people glide in looping curves, like beings from a better world, light as angels.

Of course the skating rink was closed. The Civic Gardens looked barren, too. City Hall itself was stony gray, and there was something odd about the lampposts lining the avenue.

When she saw the dead children she didn't understand what she was looking at. The bodies were stiff inside frozen clothing; they moved in the wind, but not like anything human. The ropes had been thrown over the angle brackets of the streetlights and knotted in timeless fashion around the children's necks. The children's hands had been tied behind their backs and their faces were hidden under shapeless hemp sacks.

Evelyn came closer without really meaning to, shocked beyond reason. The shock was purely physical, like putting your finger in a wall socket. She felt it in her arms and legs. *Somebody went and hung their laundry from the lampposts,* she thought, and then the world became suddenly much uglier: *No . . . those are children. Those are dead children.*

She stopped and stood for a long time looking at the dead children hanging from the lampposts outside City Hall. A delicate snow began to float down from the sky. The flakes of snow were large and perfect and they landed on the humped, frozen clothing of the dead children until the dead children were clothed all in white, a perfect unsullied purity.

A patrol car passed on the snowy street. Evelyn turned to look at the soldier who was driving, but he was hidden in the shadow of the car and had turned his head away: away from Evelyn, or away from what Evelyn had seen.


She walked without a destination and after a bleak passage found herself peering up through veils of snow to the window of Dex Graham's apartment. His light was on. The window was a yellow punctuation in the snow-scabbed brick wall. She went inside, walked up the stairs, knocked on his door.

Dex opened the door and looked at her with unconcealed surprise. Maybe he had been expecting someone else. That was natural, after so much time apart. But, seeing him, she was overwhelmed with memories that seemed terribly immediate: of his voice, his touch, his smell. There was that catalog of intimate knowledge still between them. She wasn't entitled to it but couldn't put it away.

He said, "Evelyn? Evelyn, what is it—are you all right?"

"I have to tell you a secret," she said.

# CHAPTER 15

**W**e met at a bar," Ruth Wintermeyer said. "Sounds tacky, doesn't it? But really, we met because he'd read my book."

She lit a cigarette, drew the smoke into her lungs, and closed her eyes a moment. After the accident at the lab, Ruth said, she had driven to the local grocery and filled a bag with cartons of cigarettes. Lately she had weaned herself to one cigarette a day—"Just a little taste of better times." She had two packs left.

Howard Poole sat in an easy chair opposite her, too warm in his jacket but cold without it. Like everyone else, Ruth Wintermeyer was cautious about turning up her heat —as if electricity could be hoarded, too.

She said, "I'm a member of the Historical Society. I wrote a book of Peninsula history from colonial times to the Civil War. Strictly amateur scholarship. My degrees are thirty years old and my publisher doesn't distribute east of the Great Lakes. But I guess in Two Rivers that makes me an intellectual.

"Your uncle called on the phone and we got together. He was interested in the history of the town. In a way, I think he was adopting it. He refused to live in government housing—when I met him he was renting a room at the Blue View. Very unorthodox. The government wanted him inside perimeters, but Stern wouldn't hear of it. He was a kind of scientific celebrity and he could get away with a little prima donna behavior. I think the price of *having* Stern was *indulging* Stern." She paused. "Not that the security people weren't busy. When he started seeing me, suddenly there were these, you know, *little men*, these guys in three-piece suits parked outside the house or asking questions at the bank, checking my credit record and so forth. I guess I passed the test. I'm not much of a security risk."

"You two were dating?"

"Does that surprise you?"

"No. It's just that I never saw much of his personal life. To be honest, I wasn't sure he had one."

"A private life?"

"A romantic life. I guess I imagined he was all intellect."

"I know what you mean. He didn't do intimacy very well. Part of him was always detached. Howard, have you always called him Stern?"

"Everybody in the family called him Stern. Except my mother, when they were together, and even then—she called him Alan, but I didn't sense a real connection. She said he always stood apart even as a child. The Sterns were a big family. Had a big house on Long Island. Not rich, but certainly not poor. There was some inherited money, I think."

Ruth said, "A religious family?"

"Agnostic at best."

"Because he talked a lot about religion."

"He had some odd ideas."

Ruth stubbed out her cigarette and cleared her throat. "Maybe we should talk about those odd ideas," she said.

The conversation wound into the afternoon. Ruth fed him sandwiches and coffee for lunch. ("Ground coffee from the Pine Street depot. It's stale, and there's more than a little chicory in it. But it's hot.") And as curfew approached and a new snow dappled the windows, a picture of Stern began to emerge.

Alan Stern, the outsider. The one who stood apart even in childhood. Stern the seeker. His religiosity wasn't so mysterious, Howard thought. It was not an uncommon motivation among the scientists Howard knew, though few of them would admit it. One of the things that drew people to cosmology was the promise that the universe might yield up a secret or two . . . maybe even *the* secret; a glimpse into the hidden order of things.

But the best science is always tentative, a grope into the darkness. "That was never enough for Stern. He wanted more. He was always playing with the grand systems: In his own field, he paid attention to people like Guth and Linde, the fearless theoreticians; or else it was Hegel, Platonism, the Gnostics—"

"Oh, Gnosticism—he *loved* to talk about Hellenic and Christian Gnosticism. And it was genuinely interesting. I borrowed some of his books. . . ."

"But it wasn't just a hobby. He saw something in it."

"Himself," Ruth said promptly. "He saw himself in it. What would you call the basic Gnostic idea, Howard? I think it's that there's a secret world, that it's hidden from us, but we can find our way to it—or *back* to it, because we're imperfect reflections of perfect souls, embedded in an imperfect world."

"Cast out from the Pleroma," Howard supplied. "The World of Light."

"Yes. The Gnostics said, 'You can find your way to this,

because you're part of it. You long for it. It's your original true home.' "

Howard pictured Stern as a lonely child, perhaps too aware of his own awkwardness and great intelligence. He must have felt it keenly, that lost imperium from which he had dropped into humble matter.

"And we *do* live in an unholy world," Ruth said. "He was always conscious of that. When he watched the news on TV, the wars and the starving children, he looked like he was in pain."

Howard said, "It became an obsession."

"Oh, at least."

"More than that? Ruth, are you questioning his sanity?"

"I don't want to judge. I knew him for a little more than a year, Howard. We were close. I loved him. Or I thought I did. All I can say is, during that time, he changed. Maybe something at the lab affected him. He started spending more time with his books. He picked up religious arguments everybody else abandoned centuries ago. Worse, he wanted to have these arguments with *me*." She held up her hands in a helpless gesture. "I don't have any particular faith in God. I don't know if evil is a creative force. I worry about, you know, *shopping*. Or the national debt, if I'm ambitious. Not theology."

The room was silent for a moment. Howard listened to the ticking of snow on a windowpane. He sipped coffee.

Ruth toyed with her cigarette pack but didn't light one. He said, "It's hard not to make the connection."

She nodded at once. "I've thought of that. It's a neat little scenario: Stern is obsessed with Gnosticism. He runs the Two Rivers Research Lab. Something happens out there, God knows what, and we're transplanted into a place where there's a powerful church that professes a version of Gnostic Christianity."

"I wasn't sure you knew about that."

"I've heard the soldiers at the food depot swearing by Samael and Sophia Achamoth. I don't know the details."

"If it's a meaningful connection," Howard said, "what are we saying? That Stern, somehow, *brought us here?*"

"Somehow. Yes, that's the implication. I can't imagine what it means in practical terms."

"Whatever happened at the lab may still be happening. There was that incident on Beacon Street."

"God in a pillar of blue light?"

"God or someone." Howard hesitated. "You know, I truly thought he would be here. Ruth, I had—I *still* have—a powerful feeling that Stern is alive."

"Yes. So do I."

They regarded one another.

"But if he's alive," Ruth said finally, "I don't know where he *can* be except at the lab, and I thought the lab had been destroyed."

Maybe not, Howard thought. He recalled the buildings trapped in light; the luminous forms roaming the old Ojibway land.

Ruth stood up. "Howard, it's getting late. Things being what they are, you shouldn't cut it too close to curfew. But before you go, there's something I want you to see."

She led him up the stairs to a door at the end of a dim corridor.

"It used to be a spare bedroom," Ruth said. "He made it into his study."

The door opened on a tiny room crowded with bookcases, the bookcases overflowing with volumes Howard supposed had been his uncle's. There were physics journals shelved with religious esoterica, philology texts next to photo reproductions of Aramaic codices. Had Stern taught himself to read Aramaic? It was unlikely, Howard thought, but far from impossible.

The room was obviously Stern's. There was a sweater hanging from the back of the wooden chair that faced an oak desk, an electric typewriter—no computer.

The room even smelled like Stern, a musty echo of pipe tobacco and crumbling paper. Howard felt dizzy with the memories it evoked.

"I never went in here much," Ruth said. "He didn't like me to. I didn't even clean. Even now, I don't go in here very often. It feels funny. But I've looked at a few things." She picked up a thick bundle of typewritten pages bound with a rubber band. "He left this."

Howard took the manuscript from her. "What is it?"

"His diary," she said. "The one he never showed the people at the lab."

The single word *JOURNAL* was typed on the top page. Howard regarded it with wide eyes.

He said, "Have you read it?"

"Only a little. It's technical. I don't understand it." She looked at him solemnly. "Maybe you will."

# Axis Mundi

## PART THREE

Our work yields a harvest of impossibilities. Speculation is that the fragment may not be matter as we conventionally know it—apart from its measurable mass and volume, it lacks qualities we would call material. It cannot be subdivided. Its structure is grainless, undifferentiated even at great magnification, though optical scanning might be misleading for several reasons. Its radiation violates the inverse-square law as if the curvature of local space were being disturbed by an immensely greater mass, though the fragment can be lifted by four reasonably strong men (although none of us would be so unwise as to touch it). It seems to conjure high-energy photons from the surrounding air and shifts them toward the red as it radiates them. The effect includes reflected light: the fragment actually seems disproportionately more distant as you back away; that is, it shrinks too quickly with distance! The inverse is also true and makes nearfield measurement almost impossible. At microscopic distances, the fragment appears as a homogeneous structure as large as the surface of a star, though fortunately not as energetic! Although this makes it hard to handle, perhaps the miracle is that it is not much harder.

What a privilege to be allowed to witness these mysteries. How strange that the fragment should have come from an excavation in a Middle Eastern desert. Draw a radius of a thousand miles around the dig site and it encloses centuries of religious thought: Moses, Jesus, Mithra, Mani, Valentinus. . . .

Recall Linde's idea of the observable cosmos arising from a chaotic "foam" of possible configurations of space and time: embedded in, tangled up with, other universes similar and dissimilar. In a dream I saw the fragment as something whole, as a sort of "wormhole boat" for traveling between adjacent islands of creation.

In the dream the vehicle was assembled by luminous beings, strange and unknowable: dwelling in the Pleroma? Using the device to penetrate the mystery of Created Matter—but unsuccessfully—broken fragments of ur-substance scattered through countless islands of space–time including our own. . . .

We mean to bombard the fragment with high-energy particles. Knocking on Heaven's door.

—from the secret journal of Alan Stern

# CHAPTER 16

When the Bureau de la Convenance collaborates with the War Department, Symeon Demarch thought, anything is possible.

The test gantry had been assembled in his absence. It rose from a bald patch of ground in the forest two miles west of the wreckage of the laboratory facility, and it looked deceptively simple: a steel tourelle that might have passed for a watchtower. A crane was in place to lift the weapon into its cradle.

The weapon itself—or its parts, prior to final assembly —had arrived on two fiercely guarded trucks from the airstrip in Fort LeDuc along with a cargo of nervous technicians. The bomb parts resided now under the roof of a tin shed nearby, tended under glaring banks of lights by the same white-smocked civilians.

Demarch walked the grounds with Clement Delafleur,

the Ideological Branch attaché who had become his chief
rival in Two Rivers.

A gentle snow encircled the two men and softened the
harsh angles of the gantry on its concrete pad. The snow
did nothing to soften the equally harsh lines of Clement
Delafleur. He was at least ten years older than Demarch and
much closer to confirmation as a fully fledged Censeur. The
lines of his face were a geology of ancient frowns and disap-
provals. Etched there by decades of political maneuvering,
no doubt. Delafleur had more friends at the Centrality than
Demarch himself—perhaps even including Censeur
Bisonette, whose branch loyalties ran in one direction and
personal loyalties, perhaps, in quite another.

All of which meant that Demarch could not openly
question the wisdom of hanging twelve of the town's children by the neck until dead. He could only allude to it—
delicately.

Delafleur chose to be more blunt. "What they were doing was insurrection and the actions I took were well within
our brief. You know that as well as I do."

The noon bell sounded across the camp. Demarch listened as the ringing faded into the perimeter of snowy
trees. He wondered what he ought to say. His own position
was still unclear. He remembered riding back into town
and seeing the small corpses dangling like wheat sacks from
the street lamps. He had ordered them cut down.

He said, "I won't debate the justice of it. Or your authority to give the order. Only whether it was wise to gener-
ate more ill feeling." He nodded at the test gantry.
"Especially now."

"I fail to see why I ought to be concerned about the
sensibilities of people who are next door to annihilation."

"To avoid provoking counterattacks, for one." A military
patrol had already taken rifle fire from a grieving parent.
The parent had gone the way of his offspring, but on a less
public gallows.

"We can deal with that," Delafleur said.

"But should we have to?"

"It's moot." And Delafleur looked at the test gantry as if it answered all objections.

Perhaps it did. Demarch had learned a few things about the nature of the weapon. "Difficult to believe . . ."

"That it can do what they say? Yes. I don't understand it myself. To think of everything within such a vast radius leveled or burned. The engineers have cleared a firebreak all around the perimeter, or else we might lose much of the forest—we might burn the entire Peninsula." He shook his head. "They say it operates on the same principle as the sun itself."

"Incredible." These trees would be kindling, Demarch thought; and the town a brick oven—an oven full of meat.

The image made him wince.

"You deserve some of the credit," Delafleur said, looking at him slyly. "It was your idea to plunder the libraries, was it not? Which, I'm given to understand, helped advance the work on the bomb. At least by a few months. They were already well along, of course. So it isn't *all* your fault." Delafleur's smile was bottomless. "You needn't look so startled, Lieutenant."

He consulted with Delafleur and an adjutant about evacuation plans. The agenda came from the capital, but there were details to be arranged. It was almost surrealistic, Demarch thought, to be negotiating escape timetables with this prim, endlessly fastidious Bureau functionary. Delafleur was like so many of the hierarchs Demarch had met, ambitious, loyal, and utterly innocent of conscience. The impending deaths of thousands of people mattered to him less than the protocol of this rush to the exits.

But wasn't that as it should be? If the deaths were sanctioned by Church and State, wasn't it absurd to question the decision? If Bureau functionaries made their own poli-

cies and obeyed their own consciences, surely the only result would be anarchy?

Still, there was something evil about Delafleur. According to the Church every soul possessed an *apospasma theion*
—a fragment of God. But if such a fragment existed in
Delafleur, it must be buried very deeply.

When the negotiations were finished, he drove through
a bitter dusk to the house where Evelyn was.

In the bedroom, she looked at him with a wounded
wariness—the way she had been looking at him every day
since his return. He knew she had seen the executed children, though she hadn't spoken of it.

Her wide, bruised eyes reminded him of Christof.

Upstairs, intimidated by her silence, Demarch showed
her the documents he had obtained from Guy Marris. Evelyn looked at them with no visible emotion. "This is me?"

"For certain purposes."

The travel permits were blue, registration yellow, citi-
zenship green, birth and baptism pink. Guy had been as
thorough as ever.

"I'm not as tall as it says."

"It won't matter, Evelyn. No one really looks."

She folded the papers and handed them back. "This is
for when we leave town."

"Yes." He knew she had surmised something of what
would happen. He didn't know how much. They hadn't
talked about it; only exchanged glances.

She said, "When?"

"The decision hasn't been made."

"How soon, Symeon?"

This was treasonous, he thought. But so were the documents. So were his thoughts. There was no turning back
now.

"Before the end of the month," he said.

# CHAPTER 17

Dex talked to Bob Hoskins, who sent him to one of the PTA parents, Terry Shoemaker, who introduced him in turn to a skinny ex-charter pilot named Calvin Shepperd.

They met in Tucker's Restaurant, in the small back room that had served as a pantry in the days when there was enough food to store. Dex shook the older man's hand and introduced himself.

"I know who you are," Shepperd said. "My brother's girl Cleo was in your history class couple years back." He seemed to hesitate. "Bob Hoskins vouched for you, but frankly I was reluctant to have you involved."

"May I ask why?"

"Oh, the obvious. For one thing, you're seeing that woman from outside."

"Her name is Linneth Stone."

"Her name doesn't matter. The point is, I don't know

what she says to you or you to her. And that raises a question. Plus, didn't you used to go out with Evelyn Woodward at the bed-and-breakfast? Who's been on the arm of the chief Proctor lately."

"Small town," Dex observed.

"Is, was, and will be. I'm not opposed to gossip, Mr. Graham, especially nowadays."

"As gossip, it's honest enough," Dex said. "All those things are true. Maybe they're liabilities, but they gave me access to some information you need."

"Meaning?"

"Bob Hoskins tells me you're trying to set up an escape route to ferry out some of the local families."

"Bob Hoskins must have a fair amount of confidence in you." Shepperd sighed and folded his arms. "Go on."

Evelyn had come to his apartment three times with fresh information, much of it gleaned from documents Demarch had left unattended on his desk. Dex described the firebreak, the bomb—the apocalypse bearing down on Two Rivers like a runaway train.

Shepperd leaned against a shelf that harbored a single gallon can of pinto beans and listened with a fixed expression. When Dex finished, he cleared his throat. "So what are we talking about—a week, two weeks?"

"I can't pin it down, but that sounds like the right range. We might not have much warning."

"They'll have to evacuate the soldiers."

"I don't think they're planning to."

"What, you mean leave 'em here? Let 'em burn?"

Dex nodded.

"Jesus," Shepperd said. "Cold-hearted bastards." He shook his head. "Bet any money the Proctors move out, though. So there's some warning there  .  .  .  if any of what you're telling me is true."

Dex said nothing.

Shepperd put his hands in the pockets of his jacket. "I suppose I should thank you."

Dex shrugged.

"Incidentally, Hoskins said he was surprised when you came to him with this. He figured you were mainly talk, not much action. So what changed your mind?"

"Twelve kids hanging from the City Hall lampposts."

"Yeah, well—that'll do it."

Twelve kids hanging from the lampposts, Dex thought as he walked the snowy streets.

Twelve kids, some of whom he had known personally; three of them his students.

Twelve kids: any one of whom might have been his son. Might have been David.

If David had lived.

"He didn't believe you?" Linneth asked.

She sat at Dex's kitchen table warming her hands over a pot of ration tea. The sky beyond the window was blue; a cold wind rattled the loose pane.

"He believed me," Dex said. "He didn't want me to know it, but he believed me."

"How large is his group?"

"Maybe thirty, forty adults plus their families. According to Bob Hoskins, they've scared up some hunting rifles and even a couple of automatic weapons. Amazing what some people keep in their basements."

"They hope to escape?"

"So I gather."

"It isn't very many people, considering the size of the town."

"There are other groups like Shepperd's, but they don't talk much to each other—and it may be better that way."

"Still, no matter what, too many people will die."

He nodded.

She said, "Even the scholars from outside. I don't think

they mean to let us leave. We've seen too much and we're too likely to talk about it."

Dex said, "We'll get out. A few lives saved is probably the best we can hope for." He shrugged into his jacket.

She said, "Where are you going now?"

"Unfinished business. I'm going to look for Howard Poole."

"Let me come with you."

He thought about it. "There's another jacket in the closet. Leave yours here. And keep a scarf around your head. I don't want us to be recognized."


She walked beside him in the street, head down, her arm in his. She was small and perfect, Dex thought, and probably doomed, like everybody else in these quiet winter houses.

# CHAPTER 18

So much had become clear in the last few days—Howard didn't know how to begin to tell Dex.

Dex had come out of a cold afternoon without warning. He brought a woman with him: Linneth Stone, an outsider but not a Proctor, Dex said. "You can talk in front of her. She's an academic, Howard—she has tenure."

He looked at her. "What's your subject?"

"Cultural ethnology."

"Oh. Kinship systems. Yuck."

"Howard's a physicist," Dex said.

"Oh," Linneth said. "Atomic particles. Yuck."

But the news was more important than all this. Howard turned to Dex and said, "Listen, I found her."

"Her?"

"The woman Stern was living with. She's only a couple of blocks away. And she has all his notes."

"Howard, that doesn't matter now."

"But it does. It matters a lot."

Dex exchanged a look with Linneth, then sighed. "All right," he said. "Tell me what you found out."


Stern wasn't the only physicist obsessed with God. Think about Einstein's objection to quantum theory, or Schrödinger's notion of the hidden unity of the human mind. If you look hard enough at the cosmos, Howard said, all these metaphysical questions emerge—*religious* questions.

But Stern's obsession was much stranger than that. He had been God-haunted from his earliest childhood, driven by what could only be called a compulsion: by dreams or visions or maybe even a hidden physical problem: a tumor, temporal-lobe epilepsy, borderline schizophrenia. Stern had studied the world's religious texts for clues to a mystery that must have seemed omnipresent, urgent, and taunting . . . the mystery of what might lie beyond the borders of human knowledge.

He had looked for answers with equal vigor in Einstein and the Talmud, in Heisenberg and Meister Eckehart. Physics gave him a career, but he never set aside his volumes of esoterica. He had been especially fascinated by the wild cosmogonies of the early Christian Gnostics, creation myths cobbled together from fragments of Judaism, Hellenic paganism, eastern mystery religions. In the flourishing mystical thought of the late Roman Empire Stern had perceived a fertile metaphor for the universe behind the quantum and before creation.

"He must have been a brilliant man," Linneth said.

"Terrifyingly brilliant. A little scornful of his colleagues. He was capable of eccentric behavior—he never wore any clothes but jeans and T-shirts, even when he accepted the Nobel prize. But he had the brains to get away with it."

"Intimidating," Linneth said.

"Always. It was part of his shtick. It made him a reputation. And it was his reputation that brought him here."

Dex said, "I'm surprised he accepted government work."

"He didn't want to. Especially during the Cold War, government research was often the equivalent of dropping into a black hole. If your work is classified, you can't publish, and if you can't publish, it ain't science. But they made him an offer he couldn't refuse. They promised him a long look into the heart of the mystery."

Howard described the Turkish fragment, an object so defiantly strange that it beggared comprehension.

"You can imagine how it fed Stern's obsessions. By day he took measurements and made cautious, rigorous hypotheses. By night he installed himself in the study in Ruth Wintermeyer's house and composed rambling notes about the Plenum, the fragment as a divine artifice, literally a piece of the Appennoia. The journal he left is partly autobiography, partly scientific chronicle, partly the ravings of a lunatic. He was losing the ability to distinguish speculation from fact. It all became one thing, the *mysterium tremendae* —the outer limit of rational thought."

Linneth said, "But ultimately, did he discover what the fragment *was*?"

"Not with any certainty. He came to believe it was a piece of what he called a 'wormhole boat.' "

"Wormhole?"

"Call it a device for traveling between parallel worlds. But that rests on some highly speculative physics and a lot of Stern's own bizarre ideation. He did prove one interesting thing—that the fragment responded in minute but detectable ways to the proximity of living beings. It knew when someone was close, in other words. Stern took this as evidence for another of his pet notions, that consciousness is tied to reality in some way more profound than we generally suppose. Whether it really proved any such thing is questionable, of course."

"And the accident?" Dex asked.

"Ah. Interesting. There's no way to reconstruct it from his notes, but he was talking about pouring radiation into the fragment to see how it responded. He had these enormous power lines installed. Ultimately, I guess he provoked a bigger response than he anticipated. Crossed some threshold."

"And brought us here?"

"Yes."

"You mean, *personally*?"

"Well," Howard said, "it's a puzzle, but the pieces are in place. The fragment responds to Stern's presence—to his mind, Stern would claim. He applies a tremendous amount of energy and some kind of catalysis takes place, and in some unimaginable way, we're transported here. But more than that. I think the process isn't finished. It's still happening."

"I don't understand."

"Isn't it obvious? The lab is still enclosed in that dome of light. And think about what happened when the filling station caught fire. Energy was liberated, and it took a strange form. People saw God or the Devil, but to me—" He looked at the table, then raised his eyes defiantly. "To me it looked like Stern himself."

Howard's reasoning had gone deeper than he wanted to admit.

From the scant evidence in the journal he had decided that Stern might be right: the fragment *was* part of a device meant to cross between avenues of creation, the infinite universes of Linde or the multiple alternatives of the uncollapsed wave function—or, somehow, both. And it had interacted with human consciousness, with Stern himself.

It was a boat, and Stern had become its pilot, had taken this piece of northern Michigan with him into a world that echoed, but imperfectly, all his stubborn obsessions.

He pictured Stern as a lingering presence inside the ruined lab, preserved somehow . . . as alive as he had seemed in Howard's dreams.

"When the Proctors were investigating the lab, they sent people inside in protective clothing. It must have helped, if only a little. I want to get hold of one of those suits."

"Howard, that's ludicrous," Dex said. "What could you possibly achieve?"

He hesitated. Did it make sense to say that he *knew* he should do this? Not only that he wanted to but that he felt asked to? Compelled to?

"I can't explain it," he said finally, "but I have to try."

Linneth said, "You don't have much time."

Howard looked blankly at her. "What do you mean?"

"She means the *town* doesn't have much time," Dex said. "The Proctors mean to destroy it. They have some kind of atom bomb out on the old Ojibway reserve. That's what we came to tell you. Howard, even if Stern *is* alive—there's no way to help him. All we can do is try to get out."


Howard thought of all that random energy, the white heat of nuclear fission, flooding the ruined lab and whatever mystery still pulsed at the heart of it.

He remembered a dream of his uncle in a globe of light.

Dex said, "We can't stop them. The only way out is to *get* out."

Howard took a breath, then shook his head. What he had heard in his dreams was a cry for help: Stern, lost at the edge of the world, looking for a way home. He had turned away from it once. Bad decision. "No," he said. "You're wrong, Dex. Maybe not for you. But for me. I think, for me, the only way out is in."

# CHAPTER 19

The temperature dropped steadily, but the clouds parted and for three days the sun shone from a flawless blue winter sky. Last week's snow receded from the streets and Clifford was able to take his bike out again.

He started early in the morning and rode eastward through the silent town. Each storefront, each dusty window, glittered in the sunlight. Clifford wore his warmest winter jacket, plus gloves, boots, and a knit cap. Pedaling was a little awkward under all these clothes. And he tired easily, but maybe that was because of his diet: there hadn't been meat for two weeks, except what Luke brought; no fresh vegetables for months.

The town, encased in winter, was doomed. Clifford knew what the firebreak meant. Two Rivers was going to burn. He had been certain of it as soon as he saw the teenagers hanging by their necks from the City Hall streetlights. If that could happen, Clifford thought, anything could happen.

He pedaled east toward the highway and the old Ojibway land. Luke had said the Proctors were building something out there. Something the soldiers weren't supposed to know about.

He reached the highway before noon and ate lunch—a sandwich of stale bread and old cheese. He stood off the road in a pine grove enclosed by snow, eating his sandwich in big bites. Bars of sunlight came through the pine branches and the moist air.

After lunch he rode in the direction of the ruined lab, but turned left where a new track had been cut into the woods. There was not much traffic here and he had plenty of warning when a truck or car approached; the roar of the motor and the crunch of tires on old snow carried a long way in the afternoon air. The rutted, wet road was difficult for his bike, however, so he left it in a shadowy copse and walked a distance among the trees.

He was about to turn back when he came to the crest of a low hill and saw the steel gantry above the distant pinetops. Clifford approached more cautiously now, aware of the din of voices and clatter of tools. He moved close enough to see all of the tower, its girders entwined like metal scrollwork against the sky.

He guessed its purpose. He had seen a movie about the first atomic bomb test and he knew the Los Alamos bomb had been dropped from a gantry like this one. Maybe this wasn't a bomb, maybe it was something else, but what else would burn a territory as large as Two Rivers?

He stood a long time looking at the gantry and the enclosure above it, which might contain the bomb itself, so much destruction to fit in a simple steel box. He half hoped the explosion would happen now; that it would carry him away in one white-hot instant.

But it didn't.

He thought of the town and all the people in it, all with no future. Including his mother—himself.

Then, suddenly tired, he turned and headed for home.


Shortly before curfew, he knocked at Howard Poole's door and told him what he had seen. But Howard had already heard about the bomb.

Clifford said, "Are you still trying to save the town?"

"In my own way."

"Maybe not much time left," Clifford said.

"Maybe not."

"Is there anything I can do?"

"No." Then, after a silence, "Or maybe there is. Clifford, this radio scanner." Howard took it from a kitchen cupboard. "I want you to take it to someone. Dex Graham. I'll write down his address. Take it to him and show him how it works."

"Dex Graham," Clifford repeated.

"And tell him how you and I met. Tell him you need to get out of town, and tell him I said he would help. Can you remember that?"

"Sure," Clifford said. The prospect of leaving Two Rivers intrigued him; he had not thought it was possible. "But what about you?"

Howard smiled in a strange way. "Don't worry about me."

# CHAPTER 20

John F. Kennedy High School had closed for the holidays and never reopened. The reasons were both political and practical.

Early in January, the words PROCTORS = MURDERERS were spray-painted across the school's brickwork where it faced La Salle Avenue. A military patrol arrived in the morning to splash whitewash over the slogan, but the words showed through, baleful and ghostly. The Proctors declared the school a property of the Bureau de la Convenance and welded a chain across the doors.

The gesture was largely symbolic. Parents had agreed among themselves that the risk of sending their children to school was not worth taking any longer. Anything might happen to children out of sight; the evidence of that had been ample. Besides, what were they learning? Ancient history. To what end? None.

∞

Evelyn had copied some of Symeon Demarch's written dispatches in her careful longhand. Dex passed them on to Shepperd in exchange for more information on the planned escape.

The plans were reasonably credible. All the military traffic moved on a north–south route that connected with the highway and led back to Fort LeDuc—obviously not a viable way out. But during the invasion in June a tank battalion had come in from the west along a seldom used corduroy road through the forest. Shepperd's scouts had established that this largely unguarded road was a logging trail that led to an evacuated timber camp twenty miles southeast. From there, a larger road led west—presumably toward civilization, but avoiding the bottleneck at what used to be the Mackinac Bridge. There was plenty of tree cover and even a large expedition might go undetected. "Provided we get out relatively clean and the weather's favorable—say, cloudy but not too snowy. If we land on our feet, a lot of folks are talking about heading farther west, maybe what we would have called Oregon or Washington State. It's supposed to be kind of a frontier out there. The Proctors are less powerful. Homesteading is a possibility, in the long run."

He told Dex, "We'll let you know when the times are final. But it's close, obviously. You'll need transportation, extra gasoline, snow tires—chains, if you can get 'em; rope, tools, food. Bob Hoskins says he can help you out on that account. And we prefer a fully occupied vehicle; we have more refugees than cars. If you don't have at least three passengers, come to me; there's a waiting list. Tell me, you ever do any shooting?"

Dex said, "In the Reserves. But that was years ago."

"Still handle a weapon?"

"I suppose so."

"Then take this." Shepperd pressed a .38 caliber military pistol into his hand and filled the pocket of Dex's jacket with spare clips. "I trust you won't have to use it. But I'm a trusting soul."

Dex Graham went home to Linneth. The Proctors had recently withdrawn their guards from the civilian wing of the Blue View Motel and it was easier now for her to spend the night.

After dark, blinds pulled, she sat beside Dex on the bed and unbuttoned his shirt. The bullet wound was a pink dimple in the meat of his arm. It was only intermittently painful. She touched it with the palm of her hand in a gesture that was probably unconscious but seemed to Dex full of significance, a healing caress she might have learned from her mother. Maybe a token of the strange religion she had grown up with, Hellenic paganism evolved through centuries of Europe. In London, she said, they still allowed temples in the city. Oracles of Apollo in Leicester Square.

She undressed in the dim light with a combination of modesty and glee that was half Puritan, half pagan. In spite of all the hardship—the arrest of her parents, three years in a gray nunnery in Utica, her long and arduous education—she still owned this hidden liveliness. It ran through her veins like blood.

And it struck a similar chord in Dex. Strange to realize, so close to what was liable to be his death, how much of himself he had lost. Invisibly. He was accustomed to the idea that he had seen the boundaries of the world and that he was lingering here by default, neglected by death for reasons he couldn't fathom. That belief had made him brave . . . or at least insolent, careless, grim.

But it was an addictive sort of courage. Teflon courage. He had glided through time, adhering nowhere. It was a courage, in any case, not much exercised. He had never been called on to face down a tank, like the murdered students of Tiananmen Square. He was an American and it was still possible, even at the ragged end of the twentieth century, to live a life insulated from evil—any evil but his own.

He had occasionally wondered what evil looked like. It was easy enough to find it on CNN, the bodies in the pits, the death squads in their dusty pickup trucks. But evil face to face: would he cower before it? Or would it have the same stale odor as his own guilt?

But now he *had* seen it. The small bodies hanging outside City Hall were its frank signature. What else to call it but evil? There was nothing to exonerate the hangman, no extenuating circumstances or plausible excuses; only a contrived, practiced cruelty.

And it was *not* frightening. It was offensive, banal, repellent, crude, tragic—everything *but* frightening. It could hurt him, certainly. Kill him. Probably it would. But its face was only the face of the Proctors, self-aggrandizing and completely superficial.

And here was Linneth, its opposite. Her smile repudiated oppression and her touch brought martyrs back to life. Prisons opened with every breath she took.

There was nothing complicated here, he thought, only a doorway with daylight beyond it and an opportunity after all these dry years to step forward and pass through, pass through.


Linneth was with Dex in the morning when the boy came to the apartment.

The boy was an ordinary-seeming child, large eyes under a cascade of unkempt blond hair, but Linneth thought she noticed a hint of recognition from Dex. Odd, because the boy was clearly a stranger: he had come with a strange sort of radio and instruction for its use from Howard Poole.

The boy must be twelve years old or so, Linneth thought. Blue-eyed, like Dex. He looked almost like a relative. Or a son. *Ah.*

How many agonizing times had that spark of recognition leaped to strangers? It must be terribly hard for him, she thought.

The boy said Howard had promised that Dex would help him when it was time to leave Two Rivers.

"Of course," Dex said.

"And my mother," Clifford said. "There's just the two of us. We have a car, if you need a car. A Honda. There's even some gas in it."

"Don't worry about it," Dex said. "We have room for two."

But a darker thought had occurred to Linneth. She said, "Clifford, when did you talk to Howard?"

"Yesterday—just before curfew."

"You told him about the tower in the forest, you said?"

"The bomb. He already knew about it."

"And he gave you the radio and told you to come here?"

"Yes."

"That sounds very final. Clifford . . . do you think he was getting ready to *go* somewhere?"

Clifford seemed to think it over. "Maybe. He had a big winter coat by the door. A backpack next to it. He could have been getting ready to go somewhere."

And Linneth looked at Dex, who knew at once what this meant.

Dex hurried to the house, but it was empty. The light had been turned off, the kitchen cleaned—a futile but typical gesture—and Howard's sleeping roll was missing from the basement where Dex had seen it last.

"I didn't think he would really do this," Dex said. "It's suicide. He *knows* that."

"Perhaps he didn't feel he had much to lose. Or perhaps he really thought it was a way out." Linneth shrugged unhappily. "I didn't know Howard well. But he seemed like a very religious man."

# CHAPTER 21

Because it was Friday night, Lukas Thibault borrowed a car from the motor pool and drove across town to Ellen's.

It was easier nowadays to borrow a vehicle and find someone to cover for him in the evenings. Not that it wasn't still dangerous: Nico Bourgoint, newly recovered from his flying-glass injuries at the gas depot explosion, had been stockaded for laying over with a woman from the road-house crowd. But Nico had few friends; no one would cover for him. It was a matter of protocol, really. The purely mechanical aspects of an assignation—vehicles, duty rosters —had lately been less problematic. All the commanding officers seemed distracted.

Thibault parked his car in the shadow of Ellen's garage. The neighbors would know he was here, of course; discretion was only a gesture. But he doubted Ellen spoke often to her neighbors.

She opened the door at his knock, her eyes traveling to the bag that contained a quart of barracks whiskey in a glass jar—the real object of her desire.

She waved him inside. They sat together at the kitchen table. Thibault had grown almost accustomed to the strange unkempt sybaritic luxury of the house, with its broadloom (stained), sleek machines (dusty), glittering countertops (chipped). Still, it struck him every time he crossed the threshold, a dizzy feeling. How mysteriously these people had lived!

He had found Ellen at the roadhouse on the highway not long after the occupation began. The roadhouse had become notorious as the place where a soldier might meet a woman who would barter her virtue for ration coupons. It quickly became a brothel in all but name.

In a sense, Thibault had rescued Ellen from that. She had worked tables there when the roadhouse was respectable and she had been unhappy with the new clientele: crude farmhands, mostly, dragged unwilling from their provincial pigpens. Thibault, who took pride in his Manhattan pedigree, had saved her from an amorous private who was trying to impress her by showing off his glass eye—"the only one-eyed gunner in the Army of God," though he was more likely to be found on latrine duty than near the artillery. Samael, what an army they had brought here!—battalions of the halt, the lame, the blind.

Thibault had driven Ellen home, his first illicit journey through the town of Two Rivers. She had been grateful. Would he stay the night? He would stay the night. Would he come back? He would come back. Would he bring some food? Of course.

Tonight the boy was away somewhere, which was all right with Thibault. Ellen cooked a desultory supper and advanced directly to the jar of copper-kettle drink-me-down. Her drinking was heavier and faster these winter nights. Too bad. There was something unappetizing about a drunken woman. Not that Thibault was about to turn and leave.

"Clifford's staying at a friend's house," Ellen said. "We have the place to ourselves." And she ducked her head in a gesture she probably imagined was coquettish.

Thibault nodded.

"That boy," Ellen said. "His ideas. Luke." She stroked his cheek. "Are you really going to burn us all up?"

"What do you mean?"

"Digging ditches around the town. *He* says. To keep in the fire. To keep it from spreading."

She stood and leaned against the kitchen counter. Thibault was not really drunk yet, only a little loose in his skin, as the farmers said. His eyes traced the curve of her hip. She wasn't young enough to be genuinely beautiful . . . but she was pretty enough.

He was only vaguely alarmed by what she was saying. "A person hears rumors," he said. "All kinds of rumors . . ."

"A bomb, Cliffy says."

"Bomb?"

"An *atomic* bomb."

"I don't understand."

"To burn us all up."

He was genuinely baffled by the word *atomic,* but otherwise this was old news—though he was surprised it had traveled as far as Ellen. No doubt Two Rivers was going to be razed; the firebreak wasn't hard to figure out. Perhaps it did involve an "atomic" bomb. Maybe that was what the Proctors had built out in the forest. Anything was possible, Thibault supposed.

She wanted to be reassured. He said, "I'll take care of you, Ellen—don't worry."

"Cliffy says you won't be able to." She took a long, deliberate drink of the barracks whiskey. "Soldiers get burned up too, Cliffy said."

"What?"

"The Proctors don't care. They really *don't,* you know. They'll burn up everyone. Even you, lovely Luke. Even you, my charming soldier."


He woke the next morning with a headache and a sour stomach. Ellen, unconscious next to him, looked to Thibault like a lump of stale flesh, slightly greasy in the daylight. He glanced at the bedside clock, then moaned. He was late! He was on watchtower duty this morning. Maybe Maroix or Eberhardt had signed on for him. But maybe not. He had the nagging thought that he already owed too many favors.

He dressed without waking Ellen and drove away into a chilly gray dawn. At quarters, he signed the car back into the motor pool and ran for the barracks. He needed today's duty chit and a plausible excuse—but all he had was the chit.

It didn't matter. Two roster police and a fat Proctor were waiting at the barracks.


The Proctor was named Delafleur.

Thibault recognized him. Delafleur had been everywhere lately, fluttering about in his black pardessus and Bureau uniform. The new chief Proctor, people said. The voice of the Centrality.

Thibault swept his cap off and nodded his head. Delafleur came nearer, his jowly face swinging close to Thibault's, the expression on his face a mixture of contempt and sorrow. "Things have changed," he said, "and I think you were caught unawares, Monsieur Thibault."

"Patron, I know I'm late—"

"You spent the night at the house of—" And Delafleur made a show of consulting his notebook. "Madame Ellen Stockton."

Thibault flushed. Which of these pig farmers had be-trayed him? His head throbbed mercilessly. He couldn't force himself to raise his eyes to meet Delafleur's. He felt the Proctor's breath on his face—the man was that close.

"Tell me what you talk about with the woman."

"Nothing of any consequence," Thibault said, grimly aware that he was begging now. He tried to smile. "I wasn't there to talk!"

"That won't do. You don't understand, Monsieur Thibault. The town is on the verge of panic. We want to prevent lies from spreading. Two infantrymen were at-tacked in their car on night patrol while you were in bed with this woman—did you know that? You're lucky you weren't killed yourself." He shook his head as if he had been personally insulted. "Worse, there are rumors being repeated even in the barracks. Which could have tragic consequences. This isn't an ordinary offense."

In the end Thibault told him what Ellen had said about the bomb—the "atomic" bomb—but he was careful to de-fend her honor: Ellen didn't really know anything about this, he said; it all came from the boy, from Clifford, who behaved oddly, who was often out of the house. And De-lafleur nodded, making notes.

Thibault had never liked the boy, anyway. The boy would not be a loss.

The Proctors took him to the makeshift stockade in the City Hall basement and locked him in a cell there.

Thibault, who hated confinement, paced his cage and remembered what Ellen had said.

*They'll burn up everyone,* she had said. *Even you.*

Was that possible? It was true, there had been some muttering in the barracks and at mess hall—Thibault had never taken such things seriously. But there was the firebreak. That was real enough. And the tower in the forest. And his imprisonment.

Lukas Thibault's head felt as if it had been cracked like a walnut. He wished he could see the sky.

*Even you, my charming soldier.*

# CHAPTER 22

**W**ork at the test site peaked and ebbed. Many of the civilian workers had been sent back to Fort LeDuc. A battalion of physicists and engineers remained behind to initiate the bomb sequence and study the results. The stillness of completion had descended on the circle of cleared land; the air was cold and tense.

Clearly, Demarch thought, these were the final hours. Censeur Bisonette had flown in from the capital for a one-day tour: Two Rivers, before the end. Demarch stood on the snowy margin of the test grounds while Bisonette marched about with his press of Bureau personnel, Delafleur unctuously proclaiming each tedious landmark. This was followed by a lunch in one of the freshly emptied tin sheds, trestle tables stocked with the only decent food ever to be trucked into town: breads, meats, fresh cheeses, leek and potato soup in steaming bouilloires.

Demarch sat at the Censeur's left, Delafleur to his right. Despite this ostensible equity, conversation flowed mainly between Bisonette and the Ideological Branch attaché. More evidence of a shift of patronage, Demarch thought, or an even deeper movement in the geology of the Bureau de la Convenance. He felt left out but was too numb to care. The wine helped. Red wine from what had once been Spanish cellars in California. Spoils of war.

After the meal he had Bisonette's attention exclusively, which was really no improvement. Demarch rode in the Censeur's car during what was meant to be a tour of the town itself, though it was difficult to see much beyond the bustle of security cars on every side. The procession wound eastward from the fragmentary highway, over roads full of potholes, past drab businesses and gray houses under a sunless sky. The wealth of the town and its impoverishment were both much in evidence.

Bisonette was unimpressed. "I notice there are no public buildings."

"Only the school, the courthouse—City Hall."

"Not much civic spirit."

"Well, this wasn't a city of any proportion, Censeur. You might say the same of Montmagny or Sur-Mer."

"At least at Montmagny there are temples."

"The churches here—"

"Aggrandized peasant huts. Their theology is impoverished, too. Like a line drawing of Christianity, all the details left out."

Well, Demarch had thought as much himself. He nodded.

The cavalcade wound through Beacon Street and back to the motor hotel the Bureau had appropriated as headquarters. The chauffeur parked and stood outside without offering to open the doors. Demarch moved to get out, but Bisonette touched his arm. "A moment."

He tensed now, waiting.

"News from the capital," Bisonette said. "Your friend Guy Marris has left the Bureau."

"Oh?"

"Yes. With three fingers missing."

Demarch stiffened. Three fingers was the traditional penalty for stealing Bureau property. Or lying to a hierarch.

Bisonette said, "I understand the two of you were close."

Nauseated, weightless, Demarch could only nod.

"Fortunately you have other friends. Your father-in-law, for instance. He's fondly remembered. Though very old. No one would want to insult him or his family. Not while he's alive." Bisonette paused to let this wisdom sink in. "Lieutenant, I assume you want to keep your fingers."

He nodded again.

"You have the forged papers Guy Marris gave you?"

They were in his breast pocket. Demarch said nothing, but his hand strayed there.

"Give them to me. No more need be said. At least for now."

Demarch caught and held the Censeur's eyes. His eyes were a mild blue, the color of a hazy sky. Demarch had wanted to find something there, the *apospasma theion,* or its opposite, the *antimimon pneuma,* a visible absence of the soul. But he was disappointed.

He took Evelyn's pass papers from his breast pocket and put them in the Censeur's ancient hand.

# CHAPTER 23

Bisonette's visit was more troublesome than Delafleur had expected. It distracted his attention from the situation developing in the military barracks.

Two militiamen had been caught trying to bluff past the checkpoints out of town. Questioned, they admitted that they had heard the town would be burned with the soldiers still in it; that the Proctors had decided they were expendable.

Which was true but not for public consumption. It was a dangerous rumor and needed to be stopped. Today three more militiamen had disappeared on routine patrol: perhaps killed or captured by townspeople, more likely on the run.

All this would be taken care of in less than twenty-four hours, but a lot could happen in that time. If the soldiers rioted it would make everything problematic. Delafleur had taken over City Hall as his quartier général and made the basement storage rooms into a kind of stockade; Lukas Thibault was down there, but Lukas was not the only font of this poisoned water.

Delafleur moved restlessly through what had once been the office of the mayor, with its commanding view of the town. The town was deceptively still. Motionless, except for the wind and the falling snow. The trouble was subterranean, but for how long? And the weather was a problem in itself. Would snow postpone the bomb test? He listened to the chatter on the radio monitor the military men had installed for him, but it was only technical caquetage. The countdown hadn't begun.

Delafleur wished he could hurry time onward, push the hours until they tumbled over.

There was a knock at the door. Delafleur said, "Come in!" And turned to see a soldier waiting.

"The woman you wanted us to pick up was out, Censeur," the man said.

"I'm not a Censeur," Delafleur said irritably. "Call me Patron. It's in your handbook, for God's sake."

The soldier ducked his head. "Yes, Patron. But the boy. We found the boy."

Delafleur looked past the soldier and saw the boy in the waiting room: a nothing-in-particular marmot wearing spectacles and a rag of a shirt. So this was Clifford Stockton, Lukas Thibault's nemesis.

"Lock him downstairs," Delafleur said.

Perhaps the rumors could no longer be contained. Maybe it was too late for that. But it couldn't hurt to try.

He shooed out the soldier. Then he picked up the telephone and called the military commander, Corporal Trebach, and told him to keep his troops confined to quarters today. There had been gunfire from the townspeople, he said, and he didn't want anyone hurt. It was a lie, of course. Two lies: no gunfire, at least not yet, and he didn't care who got hurt. Whether Trebach was fooled . . . who could say?

It was strange work, Delafleur thought, like plugging holes in a dike until the dike can be destroyed.

"It's tomorrow," Evelyn Woodward said. "I don't know what time. Probably around noon. I heard him talking to Delafleur on the phone. There are some problems with the soldiers, so no one wants to wait."

Dex nodded. Evelyn had shown up at his door for what he supposed was the last time, bearing this final nugget of information. She looked cold, he thought; gaunt, though there was no doubt plenty to eat while she was under Demarch's wing. Her eyes took in the room without expression; she never smiled—but why should she?

He promised he would pass on the news. Then he said, "You can come with us, Evie—there's room in the car."

He had told her about Linneth, about his escape plans. She had not seemed jealous and Dex supposed she didn't have the emotional capacity for it, after so much else. She had only looked at him a little wistfully. As she looked at him now.

She shook her head. "I'll go with the lieutenant," she said. "It's safer."

"I hope so."

"Thank you, Dex. I mean, really—thank you." She touched his arm. "You've changed, you know."

He watched from the window as she walked into the falling snow.

Shepperd came by later with essentially the same information from a source of his own: D-Day was tomorrow; the convoy would begin an hour before dawn. "Bless you if you aren't ready, but we can't wait; everybody just head west up what used to be Coldwater Road and pray for luck. And carry that damned pistol! Don't leave it lying on your kitchen table, for God's sake."

Dex offered him the use of the scanner, but Shepperd shook his head. "We have a few. Useful items. Check the marine band, though, if you're curious, and a signal up around thirteen hundred megahertz—we think that's coming from the bomb people. Mostly it's incomprehensible, but you might pick up a clue. Mainly, though, don't worry about that. Set out on time is the main thing. I would like us all on that corduroy road westbound by daybreak. You have a car, I gather."

He did, an aging Ford in a basement lot, the car he used to drive to work on days when the weather made walking a chore. He had already stashed a couple of jerricans of black market gasoline in the trunk.

Shepperd offered his hand. Dex shook it. "Good luck," he said.

"To us all," Shepperd told him.


Linneth came before curfew—AWOL, though nobody cared anymore; the guards had been posted elsewhere. There was no question of sleep. She helped Dex carry supplies down to the car; he filled the tank with acrid-smelling American petrol.

Three hours after midnight they ate a final meal in Dex's kitchen. A granular snow was still gathering and blowing in the street. The wind rattled the casements of the window.

Dex raised a glass of tepid water in a toast.

"To an old world," he said. "And a new one."

"Both stranger than we thought."

They had not finished drinking when they heard the sound of distant gunfire.

# CHAPTER 24

Among the Huichol Indians of the Sierra Madre Occidental it was called a *nierika:* a passageway—and simultaneously a barrier—between the everyday world and the world of the spirits.

The *nierika* is also a ceremonial disk, both mirror and face of God. It resembles a mandala. The four cardinal directions radiate from the sacred center.

In Huichol paintings, the axis always rests in a field of fire.

Howard reached the highway before dark but was barred from crossing it by an uninterrupted stream of traffic, mainly trucks and automobiles—the Proctors and their possessions, a few military commanders, the last looting of the town; all bound south for Fort LeDuc and safety. It can't be long now, Howard thought.

He broke into an abandoned shack, off the road and out of the snow, and pulled his sleeping bag around him for warmth while he waited. There was no possibility of sleep and probably no time for it. He rested in an ancient bentwood rocker made brittle by the cold. The windows were choked with dust.

Waiting was the hard part. He was all right while he was moving; there wasn't time to think beyond the next step. But while he waited he began to grow frightened.

He was as close to death as he had ever been.

For a time, the immediacy of the danger paralyzed him. Fear seemed to fall as inexorably as the snow, in icy crystals from a dark sky. Howard shivered and closed his eyes.

After midnight the sound of the traffic lapsed. He stirred, rose on cold and aching legs, and folded his sleeping bag into his backpack to carry with him.

He jogged across the highway. Multiple tire tracks were already dimming under fresh grains of snow, the asphalt slick and treacherous beneath. The woods on the far side, the old Ojibway land, were black with shadow. Howard used a watchman's flashlight to find his way along the dirt track eastward among the trees. The trees were tall and he listened to the snow sifting among the pine needles. Each ripple of wind sent snow showers cascading around him and made a flickering ice tunnel of the flashlight beam.

He passed a fork in the road. To the left was the way to the testing ground. Ahead, the way to the ruined lab. He pressed forward, though this road was less traveled, old snow still frozen under the new, a difficult walk.

As he approached the near radius of the lab he saw more of the ethereal forms he had glimpsed in the night last autumn. They were less frightening now, though not less mysterious. They seemed disinterested in him, disinterested in anything but their own stately motion, perhaps a circle around the ruined buildings: restless ghosts, he thought. Chained here.

In fact they were strangely beautiful, nearly human flags of light casting very real shadows among the trees, their reflections glinting from countless prisms of fallen snow. It was as if the trees themselves were moving, performing oddly graceful pirouettes against the blackness of the night. Howard's eyes blurred with tears at the sight, though he could not say what moved him. He walked for what seemed hours among the shifting shadows. It was hard to remember to follow the road. It was hard to remember anything at all.

He paused when one of these creatures (if it could be called that) came near him. He held his breath as it moved across his path. He felt a prickling heat on his skin; the snow nearby melted to gloss. He looked deep inside it, past translucencies of green and fiery gold to inner complexities of indigo and luminous purple evolving outward like the corona of a star, then fading and falling back like the arc of a solar prominence. Its eyes were shadows, dark as the night. It didn't pause or look at him.

It moved on. Howard took a deep, ragged breath and did the same.


He reached the laboratory grounds as dawn was lightening the sky.

He walked fearlessly past the wire fence and guardpost the Proctors had erected and abandoned. There was no one here; there hadn't been for months. This was the mystery the Proctors had declared too frightening to contemplate and too dangerous to endure.

Their works lay scattered under softening dunes of snow: earth-moving machinery, rusted tin sheds, a few ve-

hicles stripped to the axle and open to the sky. The largest
intact structure the Proctors had left was a windowless
brick box with wide tin doors, sealed with a bar and padlock. Howard moved that way.

The dome of blue light surrounding the original Two
Rivers Physical Research Laboratory loomed above his
head. He had never been this close. It interested him. The
border of light, the passage between *inside* and *outside,* was
crisp and distinct. Within that border, no snow had fallen;
the grass was still an eerie green, a single tree still held its
leaves . . . though all these things began to change and
mutate if he stared very long. Strange, Howard thought. But
had the phenomenon at the lab cast a subtler effect beyond
its borders? Those creatures in the forest, for instance. And
even here, in the dawning light, the snow-humped detritus
looked oddly bright, as if his peripheral vision had grown
prismatic, flensing rainbows from every acute angle—as if a
junkyard had been strewn with jewels.

In his last days Stern had viewed the fragment in the
laboratory as a new sort of matter: quantum matter, its
material volume only a fraction of its true size, which was
incalculable because it lay outside the observable universe.
It was a piece of the Protennoia and therefore unknowable;
its effects on surrounding matter were quantum effects, acting on the collapsing wave function of reality in ways un-
predictable and often bizarre.

Was that true, Howard wondered? If he stepped past
that border of blue light, would he be in some sense *inside*
the fragment? Or was he already inside it? Perhaps the
Proctors and their world, all their universe to its farthest
limits, was *inside the fragment already*—the illusion was that
the *universe* contained *it.*

It was a gateway, a barrier—a *nierika.*

*Axis mundi,* his uncle had called it.

∞

The Proctors had left much of their equipment and salvage protected from the weather in this shed. Files, boxes of paper retrieved from the nearest of the laboratory buildings; notebooks abandoned, tables strewn with aerial photographs of the site, books of physics, books of the Bible. There was a tumble of white smocks and lead aprons in the corner. And in a doorless closet, three of the suits Clifford had described to him in the autumn: heavy, quilted vests with a sort of hood, a smoked-glass helmet. The vests to ward off radiation, Howard supposed. He remembered hearing that the fire chief Dick Haldane had died after driving his truck into the glow. The helmets he guessed were to diffuse a glare he had not yet seen . . . some unimaginable radiance, the blinding light of creation . . . but what could protect you from that?

He took the outfit off its shelf and draped it over himself, no doubt a futile gesture, but it made him feel less vulnerable.

Then he stepped out into the cold air. The sun had only begun to rise and the air was gray under gusts of low cloud. He walked past this deserted building, past diamond fields of rusting machinery, onto the flat snow-contoured surface of the road and into the nimbus of blue light.

# CHAPTER 25

Morning found the test site hushed and vacant.

The last technician had left at midnight. The observation bunker was miles to the east, a slit-windowed slab of reinforced concrete. Remote monitors communicated the status of the weapon to banks of telemetry consoles inside, their anodized faceplates glittering with jewel-faceted lights. The telltales showed amber or green in reassuring patterns. Everything was going according to plan. Everything was as it should be, Milos Fabrikant thought—at least within the narrow compass of these machines.

Fabrikant had been invited here as an observer, and he still had not received a convincing explanation why the Proctors had chosen this particular place to test the weapon: was Cartagena a snowbound target? Was Spain so full of pine woods?

But the Proctors, inevitably, followed their own logic.

He hadn't pressed the issue. All Fabrikant had done was his duty, which was to extract enriched uranium isotopes and apply them to the manufacture of a bomb. Three functional implosion-type weapons had been constructed, with more on the way; one of them rested on the gantry in the forest. The other two had been shipped to some Atlantic airbase or other, and if this test was successful the bombs would be dropped on belligerent Europe. And then God help us all.

He had seen the yield prediction from the Bureau Centrality, and it was even more prodigious than his own calculation. He wondered who was right. In either case, the numbers defied imagination. Divining energy from mass, he thought, as if we were Archons ourselves: the sheer hubris of it!

He was privileged to be here. And not a little frightened.

He turned to the Censeur in charge, that unpleasant man Bisonette. "How long—"

"Two or three hours yet, Monsieur Fabrikant. Please be patient."

*I wasn't trying to hurry it,* Fabrikant thought.

Symeon Demarch had stayed close to the telephone all night, talking in relay rounds to Bisonette at the test bunker, Delafleur at City Hall, Trebach at the soldiers' quarters, and the commandant at Fort LeDuc. From the dim light of Evelyn's study he had watched the parade of lights along the far shore of Lake Merced, a huge detachment of Proctors and senior military men in a convoy bound for safety and the south. The traffic had possessed a strange beauty in the falling snow. It looked like a candlelight procession, like a body of Renunciates making a midnight pilgrimage on Ascension Eve.

The procession of automobile lights faded long before dawn. Of those leaving Two Rivers, only Trebach and Delafleur and himself (and their chauffeurs) were left. Delafleur was worried about some unrest at the military barracks; he tied up the line to Bisonette and Demarch's phone was quiet for an hour before sunrise. Demarch sat motionless in the silence, not asleep but not really awake . . . only sitting.

A military car came for him at dawn.

He answered the knock at the front door and told the driver, "All right. Yes. Just wait a moment."

"Sir, we don't have much time." The driver was a young man and worried. "There's trouble in town. You can hear the shooting. And this snow is a problem, too."

"I won't be long."

He trudged upstairs to the bedroom. Evelyn was inside. Perhaps she hadn't slept, either. She was wearing the dress he had imported from the capital so many months ago. She looked frail in that confection. Frail and beautiful. The bedroom window faced the wind, and the snow had covered it completely; Evelyn looked up at him from a dimness of silk and ice. Her eyes were wide.

She said, "Is this it? Are we leaving now?"

Demarch felt as if something had lurched inside him. *Incipit vita nova,* he thought dazedly. A new life begins: not when he joined the Bureau but now, here in this room. Now something is left behind; now something is forsaken.

He thought of Dorothea and the memory was so vivid that her face seemed to float in front of him. He thought of Christof and of Christof's wary eyes. He had left home for a place less real, a makeshift and temporary place, he thought; it would only exist for a few hours more.

He thought of Guy Marris, missing three fingers from his right hand.

Downstairs, the driver was calling his name.

Evelyn frowned.

"It's only a chore," he told her. "They want me at City Hall. I'll be back before long."

He left the room before she could answer. He didn't want to know whether or not she believed him.

∞

Evelyn hurried downstairs and reached the big window in the front room just as the car was pulling away. It skidded on the snow-slick surface of Beacon Street, then picked up speed as it headed east and out of sight.

When the sound of the motor faded she was able to hear another sound—popcorn bursts of distant gunfire, faint but unmistakable.

Was there still time to reach Dex Graham? Evelyn doubted it . . . and anyway, that wasn't what she felt like doing.

Mainly she wanted to watch the snow. It looked lovely as it fell, she thought. It absorbed the attention. She would sit in her bedroom and watch the morning snow shaped into ripples and dunes by the wind that blew across the frozen surface of Lake Merced.

That would be a fine thing to be doing, Evelyn thought, when the bright light finally came. But first she wanted to change her clothes. She didn't like this dress anymore. She didn't want it touching her.


Clement Delafleur lost the phone line with Corporal Trebach and reached him moments later by radio. Trebach was shouting something about the barracks, about his men, but it was unintelligible in gusts of static; Delafleur told him, "Leave, for God's sake—it doesn't matter now! Just leave." But there was no response. Trebach's radio had failed, too.

Delafleur went to search for his own driver. He had fulfilled his duties with what he thought was considerable élan under pressure, and any inconvenience would soon be erased: as in the joke about doctors, he would bury his mistakes. If Trebach ran into trouble and was forced to stay, then Delafleur would be the last to leave . . . and that might impress Censeur Bisonette, who seemed to have overcome his distaste for the Ideological Branch. Delafleur was attracting patronage these days the way sugar attracts insects. It was a consoling thought.

He walked to the outer office where his chauffeur should have been. There was another radio here, tuned to the broadcast from the test bunker. It emitted a high-pitched whistle punctuated by bursts of incomprehensible data or mechanical time checks. Less than three hours to the detonation, Delafleur noted, and a little late to be leaving, but this messiness with Trebach had delayed him.

Where had the driver gone? The rest of the office was empty, of course. He had dismissed the staff, all faithful Proctors and pions, and sent them off in a midnight cortege. The driver had stayed behind, drinking black coffee from the strange cafetière in the corner. But now the room was empty.

Delafleur roamed the carpeted hallways with an increasing but carefully suppressed anxiety. He checked the toilet, but the driver wasn't there. Nor in the empty offices, their doors all ajar, nor in the marbled foyer on the first floor. There wasn't time for this! He was suddenly conscious of the ebbing minutes, to which he had been oblivious only an hour ago. There was snow on the roads and some of it had drifted dangerously deep. They *must* leave soon.

He heard the sound of gunfire from the west. According to Trebach's last dispatches, that was some disturbance at the edge of town: a guardpost had exchanged gunfire with civilian automobiles, presumably refugees attempting to escape on one of the logging roads. Trebach had sent out a few more troops, and that should have ended it. But the sporadic firing went on and on—a bad sign.

Maybe the driver was in the basement, Delafleur thought, down among the water pipes and concrete walls and the steel cages where Thibault and the boy Clifford Stockton were imprisoned. But no, that wasn't likely. In any case, Delafleur was reluctant to go down there. He was afraid of being trapped. All these walls seemed suddenly too close.

He pulled on his winter pardessus and went out through the main doors to the allée: damn the man, let him burn, he would drive the car himself if necessary! But as he hurried down the snow-rounded steps he saw that it was not just the driver who was missing. The car was gone, too.

Delafleur was mute with outrage.

He'll pay more than three fingers for this, Delafleur thought. He'll pay with his head! There had not been a beheading in the capital since the Depression, but there were still men in the Committees for Public Safety who knew what to do with a traitor.

But that was irrelevant; he needed transportation more than he needed revenge. No vehicles had been left behind. His cowardly chauffeur had taken the last. Delafleur felt a surge of panic but instructed himself to think, to be constructive. There was still the radio. Maybe Bisonette could send someone from the bunker. There might be time for that.

He was about to march back up the steps of City Hall when a black van came roaring around the corner past the Civic Gardens, and for a moment Delafleur felt a blossoming hope: somehow, they had come for him already! But the van had taken the corner too quickly; it wavered drunkenly from side to side and finally skidded off its wheels and over the curb.

Delafleur stared. The van was silent a moment, then armed men began to leap from the outflung doors like ants from a disturbed nest. They were soldiers, and they were obviously drunk and dangerous.

One man aimed a rifle at a streetlight, fired a single shot and sent a flurry of shattered glass to join the falling snow. The others began to shout incoherently. Not just drunken, they were also terrified. They know what's about to happen, Delafleur thought. They know they're doomed.

He thought: *And they know who to blame.*

A window shattered somewhere over his head. Had he been seen, here in the shadow of City Hall? Perhaps not. Delafleur ran back inside and barred the big door behind him.

# CHAPTER 26

Dex didn't like the idea of driving into gunfire, but Shepperd's plan was the only real option: make for the logging road and pray for confusion. The snow was deep enough now to be a real impediment, bad enough on the streets of Two Rivers and certain to be worse on a one-lane track through the forest. But he would worry about that later. His first task was to pick up Clifford Stockton and his mother, and his second was to put distance between himself and the fission weapon in the Ojibway land.

Linneth sat beside him with her attention focused on the predawn gloom beyond the windows. The streetlights burned pale amber overhead. There were lights in many of these houses, as if the buildings themselves had been startled awake. Dex wondered how much of the population had been warned about the escape. Lots of the parents had been contacted, Shepperd had said. Getting kids out was a priority, and school staff had been generous with names. The black community around Hart Avenue had been nervous ever since the Proctors forced them to register as "Negroes or Mulattos" on the town rolls; that was another substantial fraction of the convoy.

But Two Rivers was too big for a genuine mass evacuation. Word had spread rapidly in the last couple of days, but there must be many who simply hadn't heard. Dex saw them peering cautiously from the draped windows of their houses, no doubt wondering at the sound of gunfire and all the unaccustomed traffic. Dex's car was not the only one on the road. Several sped past him, too panicked for caution, and at least one ended up in the ditch beside La Salle Avenue with its wheels spinning vainly.

Dex pulled over at the address Clifford had given him, a house not far from Coldwater Road, and left the motor running as he ran to the door. He knocked, waited, knocked again. No answer. Was it possible that Clifford and his mother had somehow *slept late*? Or left early? In desperation he pounded his fist on the door.

Ellen Stockton opened it. She wore a housecoat and her eyes were red with weeping. She held in one hand what appeared to be a mason jar of oily water—but it smelled like bathtub hooch.

Dex said, "Mrs. Stockton, I need you and Clifford in the car right away. We really don't have time to wait."

"They took him," she said.

The falling snow clung to her dark hair. Her eyes were red and unfocused. Dex said, "I don't understand—you're talking about Clifford? *Who* took him?"

"The soldiers! The soldiers took him. So go away. Fuck you. We don't need you. We're not going anywhere."


Linneth helped get the drunken woman dressed and into the car. Despite the occasional obscenity, Mrs. Stockton was too tired to fight and too intoxicated to offer more than a token objection. In the back seat she became a malleable object under a woolen blanket.

Dex sat at the wheel of the car. It was fully morning now. There were plumes of smoke all over town, Linneth saw, and still that sporadic *crack-crack* of gunfire—sometimes distant, sometimes much too close.

She said, "The boy is probably at City Hall. They have a makeshift prison there." Unless he was dead. Which was possible, even likely. But Dex must surely know that, and Linneth didn't want to say more in front of the mother.

The Stockton woman said something about a neighbor who had seen the soldiers taking her boy into City Hall—so at least Clifford *had* been there, not long ago.

Dex said slowly, "There may not be much of a guard. All the Proctors are gone by now. Soldiers, though, maybe." He looked at Linneth.

She thought, *He wants me to decide.* Then: *No . . . he wants my* permission.

Because it was her life at risk, too, not just his own.

She thought, *But we might die.* But surely that was true no matter what. People were *already* dying. More would die very soon, and she would probably be among that unfortunate majority—and so what?

The Renunciates had taught her that if she died outside the Church she would be scourged by the angel Tartarouchis with whips of fire, forever. So be it, Linneth thought. No doubt Tartarouchis would be busy, with the war and all.

City Hall was five blocks behind them. She told Dex, "We should hurry," wanting to get the words out before her courage failed.

He smiled as he turned the car around.


Symeon Demarch sat braced against the plushly upholstered rear bench of the Bureau car as his chauffeur mumbled to himself and drove at a dangerous clip east toward the highway.

Demarch had stopped thinking about Evelyn. He had stopped thinking about Dorothea, or Christof, or Guy Marris, or the Bureau de la Convenance . . . he wasn't really thinking at all, only gazing from this sheltered space at the pine-green and cloud-gray shape of the exterior world. He faced the window, where each flake of snow that lighted would cling a moment before it slid into wind-driven dew.

"Some trouble at the military barracks," the chauffeur said. The chauffeur was a young man with pomaded hair and a Nahanni drawl: a civilian employee, not a pion. Demarch saw the nervous way his eyes flicked to the rear-view mirror.

They turned onto the highway heading south. This road connected with the route to Fort LeDuc, but it also passed the motor hotel that had been commandeered as a military garrison. Demarch said, "Is that a threat to us?"

"I don't know, Lieutenant, but it may be. See that smoke up ahead?"

Demarch peered forward and saw nothing but snow, the same snow that sent the wheels askew whenever the car turned a corner. "Must you go so quickly?"

"Sir, if I slow down we might end up spinning our wheels for traction. I prefer a little momentum."

"Do what you think best."

A few moments later the driver said: "God and Samael!" And the car lurched sickeningly as he pressed the brake.

Ahead, on the left-hand side of the road, the military barracks was burning. It was a strange sight in the falling snow and Demarch was mute, marveling at it. Black smoke billowed from the many windows of what had once been the Days Inn. The flames rising from the embrasures looked almost like faces.

The road was blackened with soot but passable. "Don't stop," Demarch said. "Not *here,* for God's sake!"

Then a window shattered. It was the front window,

driver's side. The chauffeur jerked and turned as if to look
back, but his visible eye was full of blood. His foot
convulsed against the gasoline pedal and the car bucked
sharply as he slid away from the wheel.

The car rolled into a mile marker. Demarch was thrown
forward by the sudden stop, and before he could right himself he saw the chauffeur's bullet-cracked skull staining the
upholstery with slurries of blood. A cold wind came
through the broken window. Demarch looked past the
clinging tines of glass to the pine woods opposite the burning motel, where soldiers were emerging through flags of
smoke. They carried rifles. Most of their rifles were aimed at
the car.

The soldiers took aim as Demarch scrambled from the
right-side rear door. He was wearing his Bureau uniform;
even at this distance they would know him for a Proctor.
Glass exploded all around him in brittle showers, and he
heard the whine of bullets and their hammering impact on
the snowbound roadway. When he stood to run, he felt the
bullets enter his body.

Then he was on the ground. The soldiers shouted and
waved their weapons, but that sound faded into noise.
Breathless, Demarch turned his head to look at the burning
building. The roar of it was all around him. The fire had
melted the snow into mirrors of ice: mirrors full of sky, fire,
ash, the world, himself.


Clifford Stockton had slept a little during the night.
Lukas Thibault had not.

Each had been given his own cage in the basement jail
at City Hall. They were separated by a dusty space in a
room that had once been the building's archives. All the
filing cabinets had been moved out and their contents
burned when Delafleur took over the building. The walls
were concrete. The ceiling was white acoustic tile. The floor
was green linoleum, and it was as cold as winter earth.

Clifford had learned to keep his feet off it; his snow boots were scant protection. He spent most of his time on the tiny hemp cloth cot the Proctors had provided.

He woke to the sound of Lukas Thibault's cursing.

"I want my breakfast," Luke was shouting. "Assholes! We're starving down here!"

Brief silence, then the rhythmic banging of Luke's fist against the bars. Clifford didn't bother to look. He could see Luke's cell only by forcing his head against the bars of his own cage and peering around an L-bend where the cages followed the wall. It wasn't worth the effort.

He was grateful for the relative privacy. Clifford emptied his bladder into the crockery pot provided for the purpose, embarrassed by the sound. It was cold enough this morning that the pot steamed for a few minutes after he was finished.

He sat back down on the cot and wrapped the blanket around himself.

"Fuckers!" Luke was screeching. "Cretins! Bastards!"

Clifford waited until the soldier had lapsed back into silence. Then he said, "They aren't here."

Luke said, *"What?"*—startled, as if he had forgotten Clifford was in the basement with him.

"They're not here!" It was obvious. For hours after dark the building had been full of sound: legions of feet upstairs, doors opening and closing, motors roaring and then fading away beyond the high, dust-clogged windows that vented the basement. "They're gone. They evacuated. Today must be the day."

The day of the bomb, he didn't need to add. That was why Luke was here: for talking about the bomb.

That was also why Clifford was here, though no one had told him so—no one had talked to him. The soldiers had just put him in this cage and gone away.

It was too late now to do anything but wait, and he told Luke so.

Thibault called him a little idiot, a criminal, a liar.

"They can't leave me here. Sons of Samael! Even the Proctors wouldn't do that!"

But the morning ticked on and Luke lapsed into a despairing silence. Clifford knew it was past dawn by the faint light in the vent windows. That was his only clock. The shadowy fluorescent tubes overhead were the only other light—and most of those were burned out.

Clifford gazed at that patch of daylight far up at the margin of the ceiling for a time he could not calculate; it was interrupted only by the sound of Lukas Thibault's sobbing.

Then there was another sound: gunshots, and not far away.

"Sophia Mother!" Luke cried out.

This was a new threat. Clifford was dismayed: better the bomb, Clifford thought, than a gun. He had read about Hiroshima and Nagasaki. The bomb washed everything away in a tidal wave of light. The people were gone with only their shadows left behind. He had resigned himself to dying in the bomb blast, but this gunfire was different. It worried him.

The shooting paused, crackled for a time, paused again.

Then the door marked FIRE EXIT swung open, and here was the Proctor Delafleur wide-eyed and with a pistol in his hand.

# CHAPTER 27

In the beginning was the Ennoia, and the world was made of light.

Then Sophia, a thought of the Uncreated God, committed the sin of creation. Cast out from the primordial Nous, she fashioned base matter, the *hyle,* and fertilized it with her spiritual principle, the *dynamis,* which is both seed and image of the World of Light.

Thus the world was both created and separated from its origins; it was matter with a kernel of spirit in it, neither *kenoma* nor *pleroma.* It was incomplete, less than whole; it was asymmetric.

Here was the metaphor Stern had found so compelling. It resonated with modern cosmology: pull a linchpin from primordial symmetry and everything cascades forth: quarks, leptons, atomic nuclei, stars; eventually kittens, dung beetles, physicists.

And in all this there is embedded an unquenchable *epignosis*, the memory of that ancient isotropic unity of all things in the uncreated world.

Sophia, abandoned, wanders the infinite shoals of hylic matter with her terrible longing for the light. And yet—

And yet . . . Sophia laughed.

Howard had found the phrase in Stern's notebook, circled and underlined and crowned with question marks.

*Sophia laughed.*


Howard calculated that he had to walk a hundred yards across the parking lot of the Two Rivers Physical Research Laboratory to reach its central building, the collapsed concrete-block structure where—perhaps—Stern had died.

It was not a long distance, ordinarily. But this was no longer an ordinary place. He had passed the boundaries of the ordinary. He was inside the glow.

No snow fell here. The air was suddenly moist and warm; the neat bordered lawns near the workers' quarters were green, though the grass had not grown since the spring. Did time pass more slowly here? If so, Howard thought, his attempt to reach Stern might be futile; the bomb would detonate between one footstep and the next.

But he could see the snow falling only a few paces behind him, and it was falling at its usual pace. So time didn't pass especially slowly here, though he supposed it might pass *differently* . . . and he took another step forward.

His vision was obscured. The eye didn't like this environment. Nor did the other senses; he felt dizzy, awkward, alternately too hot and too cold. Most confusing, though, was this refusal of any solid object to hold still and be seen. Images curved and lost proportion as if the act of seeing them challenged their reality.

Observation, Howard thought, was a kind of quantum guillotine: it sliced uncertainty into *this* or *that,* particle or wave. Here there seemed to be no such effect. The collaps-

278 Robert Charles Wilson

ing wavefront, the moment of isness, was imprecise, too
fluid, as if he were experiencing time a fraction of a second
*before* anything happened. For instance, this asphalt under
his feet. Glimpsed briefly, it was the lab parking lot, spaces
marked with whitewashed numbers, 26, 27. Stare too long
and it became granite or glass or grains of crystalline sand.
And the temptation to stare was immense.

He understood why the firefighters had beat such a
hasty retreat: too much exposure to this would surely affect
more than the senses. Madness must look like this, Howard
thought.

But he took another step and another after that.

The light around him was bright but sourceless. It
wasn't daylight. It pervaded everything; everything was lit
up from within. Colors were divided, split as if by a prism
into countless bands. Every motion was a blur.

He took another step and another, though his stomach
was churning. There was a turbulence all around him. The
air itself seemed to solidify and take form, as if translucent
bodies were moving through it. More ghosts, he supposed.
Maybe they really *were* ghosts, the restless remains of the
men and women who had died in these bunkers the night
of the explosion.

But Howard doubted it. There was something purposive
in the way they crossed his path, circling the laboratory
buildings as if they were trapped here, and perhaps they
were: maybe these were the creators of the fragment, still
attached to it, orbiting it a helpless half step out of time.

He shook his head. Too much speculation: that had
been Stern's downfall.

Stern, who was calling him onward. Set aside the ratio-
nalization and that was why he was here: Stern had called
him. And Stern was calling him yet.


*You might be as smart as your uncle,* Howard's mother
used to say. It was a compliment, a suspicion, a fear.

Stern had always loomed over him like a monument, stony and unapproachable. In Howard's family no one talked much about the important things. But Stern always came with a baggage of big ideas and he always shared them with Howard. Teased him with them: You like this morsel? Then how about this? And *this*?

Howard remembered his uncle leaning forward from the cane chair on the porch, on a summer evening alight with stars and fireflies, his voice obscuring the faint rattle of china dishes on a faraway table: "Your dog sees the same world we do, Howard. Your dog sees those stars. But we know what they are. Because we can ask the right questions. And that's knowledge the dog can never share. By his nature: never. So, then, Howard—do you suppose there are questions even *we* can't ask?"

Fireflies here, too: sparks in his vision.

He was approaching the central building. Its roof had collapsed, but the concrete-block frame was intact. A crack ran through the steel door. On closer inspection, the brickwork was filleted with jewels; diamonds clung like barnacles to every wall. There was something seductive about these faceted surfaces and Howard was careful not to stare too long. There were other horizons here, not his own.

He touched the door. It was hot. This was real heat, and he was probably close enough to the core event that he was being bathed with real radiation. Enough to kill him, probably, but that was of no concern any longer.

He had used the word *awestruck* in the past without knowing what it meant, but now he understood it. He was stricken by awe, consumed by it; it obliterated even his fear.

This was the place where his uncle had crossed the border of the world.

∞

If Stern had brought them all here, did that make Stern a Demiurge?

Had he found this world or actually *made* it? Constructed it, consciously or unconsciously, with the aid of the Turkish fragment, from his own fears and hopes?

If so . . . then, like Sophia, he had made an imperfect thing.

Everything he had wanted from his ancient books, a key to the pain and the longing he felt, a cosmogony beyond physics, here in the world of the Proctors it was all transmuted into something base: a lifeless dogma. Everything noble in it had grown calcified and oppressive.

Maybe Stern was lost, Howard thought. Trapped in his own creation and helpless to redeem it.

*Am I prepared to face a god?*

He shuddered at the thought.

But he opened the cracked and jeweled door.

# CHAPTER 28

With daylight the town surrendered to panic.

Fire broke out in the Beacon Street business district and there was no one to control it; Tom Stubbs had headed west, along with most of the Volunteer Fire Department. Flames swept through the Emily Dee Large-Size Fashion Shop, the New Day Bookstore, and an empty corner property with boarded windows on which the faint words COMING SOON! ANOTHER FRY CASTLE FAMILY RESTAURANT were still faintly legible.

Refugees approaching Coldwater Road encountered a roadblock manned by a detachment of soldiers—word of the escape attempt had leaked—but the lead cars, including Calvin Shepperd's, each carried three sharpshooters and the cream of Virgil Wilson's collection of semiautomatic rifles. The gunfire began before dawn and continued sporadically through the morning.

Three truckloads of soldiers, turned back from the road to Fort LeDuc by steel gabions and a skirmish line of tanks, passed through town at high speed.

One truck made it nearly to Coldwater Road before a rear guard of armed civilians caught it in a crossfire. The driver was killed instantly and spared the knowledge that his last act had been to steer the vehicle over a barricade and down a vertical embankment into the shallow ice of Powell Creek.

The second truck headed north in a vain attempt to cross the firebreak and reach safety; it broke an axle in a snowy hydroelectric right-of-way. Twenty-five soldiers without winter clothes or adequate supplies formed a line and marched into the dark woods, hoping to outrun the angel Tartarouchis.

The third truck turned over in front of City Hall, spilling a cargo of angry draftees who fanned out and began to empty their rifles into the unblinking facades of these alien houses, in this town on the edge of the Abyss, this Temple of Grief.


Dex started a turn onto Municipal Avenue when he saw the soldiers among the trees on the City Hall promenade— and the soldiers saw him.

Taken by surprise, he twisted the steering wheel hard right. The road surface was too slick for traction. The car slid at a skewed angle toward the sidewalk and Dex fought to keep the wheels out of a drainage ditch. Something *pinged* from the hood: he saw the new dent and a gleam of steel where the paint had been scoured by a bullet.

He told Linneth to get down. "And keep *her* down, too!"—Ellen Stockton, who was gawking at the soldiers with boozy incomprehension.

The car stopped shy of the ditch. Dex threw it into reverse and stepped on the gas with as much restraint as he could muster—but the wheels only raced on a slick of compressed snow.

He worked the gear shift, rocking the car forward and back. When he spared a glance down the street he saw a soldier maybe a hundred yards away—a kid, it looked like, barely voting age, aiming a big blue-barreled rifle at him. It was a mesmerizing sight. The soldier's aim wobbled and then seemed to steady. Dex hunkered down and goosed the gas pedal again.

A bullet popped two of their windows—back seat, left and right. The safety glass fell away in a rain of white powder. Linneth emitted a stifled scream. Dex stomped the accelerator; the car roared and leaped forward in a cloud of blue exhaust.

He worked the vehicle into a turn and steered away from the soldiers. He heard more bullets strike the trunk and bumper, harmless *pings* and *thunks*—unless one of them happened to find the gas tank.

He steered left on Oak, still fighting the wheel. The car danced but moved approximately north.

He was two blocks gone and around another corner before he dared slow down.

"Christ Jesus!" Ellen Stockton said suddenly, as if all this had only just registered. *"What are they doing to Cliffy!"*

"It's all right, Mrs. Stockton," Dex said. He looked at Linneth. She was pale with anxiety, but she nodded at him. "They don't seem to have any particular interest in the municipal building. We'll just have to go in from the back."

Time was a precious commodity, and worse, there was no way to know exactly how precious it really was. Nevertheless, he waited in the car until the sound of the soldiers' sporadic gunfire had moved away.

He was two streets beyond City Hall, in a quiet residential neighborhood—quieter than ever, except for the pop and echo of the gunshots. The road was flanked on either side by tall row houses, old buildings but carefully preserved. Some of these houses were empty; some, undoubtedly, were still occupied, but the occupants weren't showing themselves. The snow fell in gentle gusts. On some distant porch, a wind chime tinkled.

It was cold, Ellen Stockton said, with the wind coming in these shot-out windows.

"Get under the blanket," Dex said. "I want you to stay here while we're gone. Can you do that?"

"You're going to get Cliffy?"

"I mean to try." Though it looked more and more like a futile effort, or worse, a gesture. City Hall had been evacuated. Clifford Stockton, in all likelihood, had been killed or carried off to Fort LeDuc.

He told Linneth, "Maybe you should stay here with Ellen."

"I'm sure she'll be all right." She looked at him steadily. "It's a misplaced chivalry. I'm not baggage, Dex. I want to find him, too."

He nodded. "We should go on foot. It's less conspicuous."

"A good idea. And don't forget about that pistol in your jacket."

The funny thing was, he had. He took it from the vest pocket and slid the safety off. The grip was cold in his hand.


They moved across a snow-humped backyard, over a cane fence collapsed and unrepaired, across another quiet street. The wind swirled snow into exposed skin and sifted it like sand against Dex's vinyl jacket.

He reminded himself that Clifford was not David. It was tempting to yield to that obvious parallel: back into another doomed building to save another doomed child. Tempting, Dex thought, but we're not allowed to reenact our sins. It doesn't work that way.

But the memory came back more powerfully than it had in a long, long time, and he made room for it. Some part of him welcomed it. It was possible to smell the reek of burning in all this cold snow.

There were no soldiers in the space behind City Hall, only a narrow corner of the Civic Gardens and the white wasteland of Permit Parking Only. No one had been here lately, Dex thought. The snow was pristine. He hurried into the shadow of the building with Linneth next to him.

City Hall was not a large building under all its stone facades and sculpted lintels. It contained an assembly room, a rotunda, and a battery of offices on two floors. And the basement. In better times he had visited this building sporadically, to renew his driver's license and pay his rates.

The employees' entrance was unlocked. Dex stepped inside with his pistol drawn, then beckoned Linneth after him. He listened for voices but heard only the rush of the wind through some distant vent. To his left, stairs led upward. He followed them to the second floor and out into an empty broadloomed hallway.

He passed doors marked OMBUDSMAN, LICENSE BUREAU, LAND MANAGEMENT. All these doors were wide open, as if the rooms had already been searched. "All abandoned," Linneth whispered. She was right. Papers had been strewn everywhere, many with the letterhead of the Bureau de la Convenance plainly visible. Some of the office windows were broken; the wind rattled vertical blinds and rolled plastic cups like tumbleweeds over the carpet.

Dex touched Linneth's arm and they both stood still. He said, "You hear that?"

She cocked her head. "A voice."

He held the pistol forward. A marksmanship course in the Reserves had not prepared him for this. His hand was shaking—a gentle tremor, as if an electric current were running through him.

He located the source of the voice in the anteroom of the Office of the Mayor: it was a radio . . . one of the

Proctors' radios, an enormous box of perforated metal and glowing vacuum tubes. It was plugged into a voltage converter that was plugged into the wall.

It spoke French.

*"Quarante-cinq minutes."* And a continuous metallic beeping, as of a time clock, once per second. Dex looked at Linneth.

*"Quarante-quatre minutes,"* the radio shrilled.

He said, "What is this?"

"They're counting down the time."

There was another burst of speech, indecipherable with static, but Dex heard the word *détonation*.

He said, "How long?"

She took his hand. "Forty-four minutes." *Quarante-trois minutes.* "Forty-three."


Clifford recognized the man who came through the FIRE EXIT door. This was the Proctor the others had called Delafleur. An important man. Lukas Thibault drew a sharp breath at the sight of him.

Delafleur wore an overcoat nearly long enough to touch his ankles, and he reached into the depths of that garment and took out a gun—one of the long-barreled pistols the Proctors sometimes carried; a revolver, not an automatic weapon like the one Luke once showed him. The handle was polished wood inlaid with pearl. None of these refinements seemed to matter to Delafleur, who was sweating and breathing through his mouth.

Luke said, "Patron! Let me out of here, for God's sake!"

Delafleur looked startled, as if he had forgotten about his prisoners. Maybe he had. "Shut up," he said.

There was the sound of more gunfire outside the building, but was it growing more distant? Clifford thought it might be.

Delafleur stalked down the length of this basement room between the stockade cages and the wall with his long coat swinging behind him. He carried the pistol loosely in his left hand. In his right hand was a pocket watch, attached by a silver chain to his blue vest. His eyes kept traveling to the watch, as if he couldn't resist looking at it—but he plainly didn't like what he saw.

He pulled a wooden crate under one of the high, tiny windows, and stood on the crate in a vain attempt to look outside. But the window was too high and louvered shut. Anyway, Clifford thought, it opened at ground level. There wouldn't be much of a view.

Delafleur seemed to arrive at the same conclusion. He sat down on the crate and fixed a baleful stare at the door where he had come in.

Luke said, "*Please,* Patron! Let me out!"

Delafleur turned in that direction. In a prim voice he said, "If you speak again, I'll kill you."

He sounded like he meant it. Luke fell silent, though if Clifford listened carefully he could hear his labored breathing.

Luke had often been silent in the last few hours. But never for very long. Would Delafleur really shoot him if he made a sound? Clifford was sure of it. The Proctor looked too frightened to make idle threats.

And if he shot Luke, would he then shoot Clifford? It was possible. Once shooting started, who could tell what might happen?

But he didn't want to think about that. If he thought about it, the cage began to seem much smaller—as tight as a rope around his neck—and Clifford worried that *he* might make a sound, that the terror might leap uncontrollably from his throat.

Time passed. Delafleur looked at his watch as if he were hypnotized by it. At the sound of each fading gunshot he cocked his head.

"They're going away," Delafleur said once—to himself.

More fidgeting with the watch. But the Proctor seemed to regain a degree of composure as the seconds ticked past.

Finally he stood up and adjusted his vest. Without looking at the cells, he began to walk toward the FIRE EXIT.

Lukas Thibault panicked. Clifford heard the soldier throw himself against the bars of his cage. "FUCK YOU!" he screamed. "DON'T YOU LEAVE ME HERE! GODDAMN YOU!"

And that was the wrong thing to say, because Clifford saw Delafleur hesitate and turn back.

The Proctor shifted the long-barreled pistol into his right hand.

Clifford cowered in the corner of his cell, as far away from the Proctor as he could force himself—which was not very far. He had ceased thinking coherently as soon as Delafleur turned back from the door.

Delafleur walked past him with a steely expression, around the L-bend to where Luke was. Both men were out of Clifford's sight now. But he could hear them.

Lukas Thibault had stopped shouting. Now his voice was low and feverish and hoarse with panic. "Bastard! I'll kill you, you bastard!" But it was the other way around, Clifford thought.

Delafleur's pistol sounded like a cannon in this stony basement room.

Lukas Thibault gave a choked scream. Clifford heard him fall against the cold floor. It was the terrible muted sound of bones and soft tissue striking concrete. A limp, dead sound.

Now the Proctor came back within the compass of Clifford's sight. Delafleur was pale and grim. The pistol in his hand trailed wafts of blue smoke. His eyes roamed a moment before they fixed on Clifford.

Clifford felt the pressure of that gaze, as dangerous as the gun itself. The eyes as deadly as the weapon. He couldn't look away.

But then there was another sound, and Delafleur's eyes widened and he jerked his head toward the door.

FIRE EXIT opened. Dex Graham stepped into the room.

Dex fired a handgun at the Proctor and missed. Now the Proctor's weapon came sweeping up and Clifford had time to cover his ears before the batteringly loud bang. No telling where that bullet went.

Dex fired a second time and the Proctor sat down on the floor. The pistol dropped from his hand. He slumped against the bars of the cage, moaning.

Dex came striding forward. Linneth Stone came through the door behind him. She picked up the weapon the Proctor had dropped.

Dex found a length of copper piping and used it to pry the lock from the door of Clifford's cell. The lock burst and the door rattled open and Clifford ran to the schoolteacher without thinking.

He noticed Dex Graham's eyes, how strangely calm they seemed.


Linneth took the boy to the stairway.

Dex lingered a moment longer.

He looked at Delafleur, who was still alive. The bullet had shattered his hip. He was paralyzed below the waist. The wound was bleeding freely into the silk-lined folds of his long winter coat.

"I can't move," the Proctor said.

Dex turned to leave.

Delafleur said, "You don't have time. It's hopeless."

"I know," Dex said.

# CHAPTER 29

**S**ome of the cinder-block walls of the high-energy laboratory had melted to slag and most of the roof was gone. A sky of blue sheet lightning illuminated a maze of corridors.

Howard walked through the rubble. During the brief intervals when his vision cleared he saw structural rods protruding from concrete forms, broken electrical cables as thick as his arm, ceramic insulators scattered like strange pottery all around him.

When his vision was *not* clear he saw these things through endlessly multiplied prisms, as if a snow of faceted crystal had filled the air.

He moved toward the heart of the building. He felt its heat like sunlight on his face.

Stern's last coherent scientific writings had leaned toward the idea of chaotic inflation: a cosmological scenario in which quantum fluctuation in the primordial void gives birth to universes in endless profusion. Not a single creation but infinite creations. And no universe accessible to any other, except perhaps through quantum tunnels known as wormholes.

In this schema, a universe might even *contain* a universe. If you could somehow compress an ounce of matter inside the orbit of an electron, it would blossom into a new avenue of time and space—someone else's Big Bang; someone else's quarks and leptons and stars and skies.

In other words, it was possible to contemplate the technology of becoming a god.

Stern thought it had already been done. The Turkish fragment was the result of an effort, perhaps, to connect two branches of the World Tree. These ghosts (they moved through Howard and around him with clockwork regularity) might be its makers. Mortal gods. Demiurges. Archons, but trapped: chained to this vortex of creation.


Here at the center of the building the ruins were more chaotic. Howard climbed a bank of broken brick and tile. He was dizzy, or perhaps the world really was spinning around this axis. He fixed his eyes rigidly ahead. Everything he saw seemed to swarm with iridescence.

Blackened walls rose above him like broken teeth. He passed markers and signs, some words still faintly legible: WARNING and AUTHORIZATION and FORBIDDEN.

The core of the building had been a containment unit surrounded by two layers of reinforced steel. This was the matrix into which all the cabling and conduits had run; this was where Stern had focused immense energies on the fragment, particle beams hotter than the surface of the sun.

The containing walls had been breached, but sections were still standing. Everything else—debris, dust, shrapnel

—had been scoured away by the explosion. The containment unit stood alone in a sort of black slag crater within the larger ruins of the laboratory building. Howard stepped into that circle, reached the tattered containment room, felt a new wash of terrible heat as he moved through air thick with ghosts and stars, to the crenellated walls, through a vacancy that had once been a doorway, and inside, to the heart of the world: *axis mundi*.

Inside, Stern was waiting for him.

It was Stern, even though it was not human any longer.

He must have been here when the fragment was bombarded with energy—closer than he should have been, by design or by accident.

The fragment had become an egg of blue-green phosphorescence. It was perhaps twenty feet in diameter, or seemed to be—appearances, Howard knew, were immensely deceptive. It was hot and vividly alive. It looked as fragile as a bubble but much more menacing, a bubble of spun glass containing the substance of a thousand stars.

It was patently radioactive and Howard assumed it had already killed him. No matter what happened here—even if a miracle happened here—he would not live longer than another few hours.

Alan Stern stood outside the sphere. He was touching it.

Howard knew this was Stern, although there was not much left of him. In some sense Stern probably *was* dead; some incomprehensible event or process had preserved only a fraction of him here: his mind, but not much of his body. What Howard saw against the glare of the sphere was a body as translucent as a jellyfish. The nervous system—the brain and bundles of nerves—pulsed with a strange luminosity. Stern's arms touched the sphere and seemed to merge with it, and so did a dozen other limblike projections that had grown into and from his body, fixing him in place like the roots of a tree.

Stern's *presence* was more nebulous; it enveloped Howard and seemed to speak to him. Howard sensed a terrible stasis, an entrapment, a speechless fear. If the sphere was a doorway, Stern was powerless to pass through it and couldn't retreat. He was caught between flesh and spirit.

He turned his head—a fleshless bulb in which even the skull was only a dim shadow—and, somehow, eyeless, *looked at Howard*.

He was pleading for help.


Howard hesitated for a time he couldn't count or calculate.

All his speculation, and all of Stern's, had circled around a truth: that the object in this room was a passage between worlds—or even a means of creating a world. The idea seemed to flow from the object itself. Wordlessly, the sphere announced its nature.

But if that was so, the only way he could help Stern (this thing, this tortured essence of Stern) was to step into that doorway, perhaps to open it wider. To succeed where Stern had failed.

And how could he do that? Stern was the genius—not Howard. Stern had revised and elaborated the work of Hawking and Guth and Linde. Howard had barely understood them.

Stern was the wizard. Howard was only an apprentice.

The intangible bodies of the ghosts pressed closer around him now, as if the question interested them. Howard took a dizzy breath. The air was blisteringly hot.


The memory that came to him was of his mother at the kitchen sink washing dishes while Howard dried. Years ago. How old was he? Fifteen, sixteen. Better days.

Stern had just accepted the Nobel prize—his picture

had been on television—and Howard was babbling about how great it was to know this man, this genius.

His mother rinsed the last porcelain dish and began to drain the soapy water. "Alan is smart all right. But he's also . . . I don't know a word for it." She frowned. "For him, everything was always a puzzle. A trick. Show him a stone, he could tell you what it was made of and how it came to be at your feet, or how its atoms worked or what it would weigh on Mars. But just to pick it up? To look at it, to hold it in his hand, to *feel* it? Never. It was beneath him. It was a distraction. Worse, an illusion." She shook her head. "He understands the world, Howard, but I will tell you this: he does not love it."

*Contemptus mundi:* contempt for the world and the things of the world. When Howard read the words in an undergraduate philosophy text, he thought immediately of Stern.


He hesitated, but there was nothing to turn back to; only the Proctors, their terror, a fiery wasteland. He was surprised the detonation hadn't come sooner.

The entity that had been Stern regarded him with a pain as tangible as this awful heat.

Howard put out his hand. The skin of it pulsed with new veins of light.

Now the light was all around him, a sudden presence of it.

A world of light.

*The bomb,* Howard thought.


Sophia wept, and was in pain, because she had been abandoned alone in the darkness and void; but when she thought of the light that had abandoned her, she took comfort, and she laughed.

∞

A field of fire.


He touched something. Everything. He held it in his hands, a stone.

# CHAPTER 30

**E**llen Stockton cried when she saw Clifford running for the car. The cold air had made her sober; she knew how unlikely this reunion was. She opened the door for him and he ran into her arms.

Dex stood outside with Linneth. She looked at him as if awaiting some verdict. He said, "Fifteen minutes—if the countdown can be trusted." He lowered his voice so the boy and his mother wouldn't hear. "We're too far east. These roads, the snow . . . we can't make the town limits in that time, much less a safe perimeter."

Linneth was almost ethereally calm. "I agree. Is there anything else we can do?"

"Drive and hope for a miracle."

"The Proctors won't delay this explosion. Not if they have a choice. Too much has gone wrong already."

"Drive and pray," Dex said, "or else—"

"What?"

"I keep thinking about Howard. You remember what he said? 'The only way out is in.'"

"He meant the ruined laboratory. Do you think that would offer us some sort of protection?"

"I can't imagine how. But maybe. Who knows?" He touched her shoulder and said, "Something else we should think about is that it's closer to the bomb."

"Hardly an advantage."

"Linneth, it might be. If the worst happens—it would be faster."

She looked into his eyes. Irreclaimable seconds ticked away. She said, "You may be right. But I want this to be because there's a chance. Do you understand? Not just suicide. I think some part of you wants that. But I don't."

*Did* he want to die, out there on the wooded Ojibway reserve? The strange fact was, he did not. For the first time in many years, he would have preferred to go on living. Wanted desperately to live.

But the roads were thick with snow, and he remembered the yield predictions Evelyn had smuggled out of Symeon Demarch's study. He remembered everything he had ever read about Hiroshima and Nagasaki. A quick death would surely be better than some lingering, blistered agony. He couldn't bear to see Linneth die like that.

And there *was* a chance, he thought; at least a long shot —at least, Howard had seemed to think so.

The snow was soft and seemed suspended in the air. The air itself seemed to tremble with anticipation. He said, "We're wasting time." The research lab was not much closer than Coldwater Road. It would take some fancy driving to get them there in—what? He checked his watch. Thirteen minutes.

∞

Linneth pressed her face to the window as the car passed along Beacon Road. Much of the commercial district was on fire. The flames reflected wildly on the snow. Smoke fanned across the road.

Dex was driving at a perilous speed, but he knew the route. She avoided looking at the strange digital clock on the dashboard. She couldn't change the time and didn't want it to obsess her.

Instead, oddly, she thought of her mother, dead years ago in some Bureau prison. *Something lives in everything,* she had said. Perhaps something lived in that tangle of ruins Dex was driving toward; perhaps it was the man Howard had called Stern. Who was a sort of Demiurge, if she had understood correctly. A mortal god.

A good or malevolent angel.

Low clouds rolled across the sky. The snow fell in a gentle curtain. The car turned onto the highway.


Clifford understood soon enough where they were headed.

He didn't question it. He had seen enough to know Dex Graham meant him no harm. But when the car left the highway for the narrow road into the forest—a road Clifford knew too well—he could not contain a sigh of resignation.

"It's all right, Cliffy," his mother said, as a roof of pine boughs closed over the car. "It'll be okay now."

She didn't know any better.


The trees had sheltered this road from much of the snow, but the road itself was deeply rutted. The military vehicles had a wider wheelbase than Dex's car, which kept wandering in and out of the ruts. The old snow here had been beaten down to black ice. More than once, the wheels began to spin freely and the car slowed and Dex had to fight it forward, patiently, carefully.

Like Linneth, he tried to ignore the clock. Not as successfully. The time available had slipped below five minutes.

Clifford had guessed their destination. He said, "There's a hill before you get to the lab where the road cuts through the escarpment. It might be slippery."

Dex saw it ahead. Not a steep rise, but a long one. The angle was maybe thirty degrees. He eased his foot down on the accelerator, carefully, carefully. The car picked up speed. It wobbled alarmingly from side to side, but he kept the nose pointed forward.

The car was doing sixty through the snow when it reached the foot of the hill. He was counting on the momentum to carry them forward, and it took them a long way up before he began to lose traction. Linneth held her breath as Dex worked the gas pedal and the car slowed to a crawl.

Now the front wheels lurched sideways and the car slid back a foot or so. Dex stepped on the gas. Let the wheels spin: maybe they would grind down to a solid surface. Blue smoke roared from the exhaust pipe. The car jumped forward, hesitated, jumped another yard or two. The peak of the hill was tantalizingly close.

Dex made the mistake of glancing at the dash clock.

They were on overtime now, and the bomb was less than half a mile away. Clifford had been staring out the back window. From here, he could see the gantry above the trees.

Linneth's hands were clenched into fists in her lap.

Another yard forward and another. The motor screeched as if it had been burned clean of oil—which was possible, by the look of the steely blue smoke in his rearview mirror.

Almost there now. He pushed the gas pedal all the way

down. This wasn't strategy, it was panic—but the car surged over the summit of the hill in a series of spastic leaps, and suddenly it was the brake he was fighting.

The ruined Two Rivers Physical Research Laboratory lay ahead. This blister of strange light was more energetic than Dex had expected from Howard's description of it. It was like liquid lightning—frightening to drive into. More accurately, to *slide* into. The car was gathering speed and he was on the verge of losing control.

"Everybody hold on," he said.

Linneth whispered something about *"time."* Ellen Stockton held her son against her. Dex took his foot off the brake. If the wheels locked now the car would tumble. We're a sled, Dex thought madly. This is free-fall.

A timeless moment passed. Then the sky was full of light, and the pine trees caught fire and burned in an instant.

# CHAPTER 31

Milos Fabrikant followed the Censeur, M. Bisonette, to a trench that had been carved into the cold, bare hillock in front of the bunker.

The snow had stopped. The clouds were high and thinning. The countdown proceeded with a relentless precision, and Fabrikant listened to the numbers unreel from the mouth of a metal-horn loudspeaker. When the count reached twenty seconds, Fabrikant and Bisonette and a half dozen other privileged observers crouched with their backs to the west wall of the revetment.

The light from the detonation was sudden and shockingly bright. Shadows flared to the east. A revision of nature, Fabrikant thought. Silent at first. It was his thoughts that were loud.

Bisonette stood up immediately, cupping his hands

around his amber-colored goggles. Fabrikant's joints were agonized by the cold; he was slower to stand.

The fireball glowed like sunset in the far undulations of the pine forest. Incredibly, the clouds above the blast had been torn open. A pillar of smoke boiled into the sundered heavens.

The sound came at last, a battering roar, like the outrage of the offended Protennoia.

Fabrikant touched the sleeve of the Censeur's greatcoat. He felt Bisonette's unconcealed tremor of delight. *He is as full,* Fabrikant thought, *as I am empty.*

"We should take cover again, Censeur," he said.

Bisonette nodded and ducked into the trench.

The wind came next, as hot as the wind from Tartaros.


Evelyn Woodward was blinded at once. The new sun devoured her eyes. Briefly, the sensation was beyond pain.

Then Lake Merced turned to steam as the shock wave crossed the water, and suddenly the window was gone. And the house. And the town.


Clement Delafleur had tried to staunch his bullet wound with the silk lining of his torn pardessus, but he had lost a great deal of blood despite his best efforts. In the time it took Dexter Graham to drive to the Ojibway reserve, Delafleur managed to drag the insensate meat of his legs as far as the door marked FIRE EXIT. From there, his plans were vague. Perhaps to lift himself to salvation. But time was short.

He was panting and only dimly conscious when the high basement windows admitted a column of superheated steam, and the stone walls of City Hall were crushed and carried away above him.

Calvin Shepperd listened to the countdown on a portable scanner, up at the limits around 1300 MHz. When the count approached zero, Shepperd stopped the lead car and flashed his blinkers. The signal went down the long line of the convoy: it meant, *Take cover.* That is, hunker down on the upholstery and turn your engine off. Which he did. His friend Ted Bartlett huddled next to him, and in the back a sharpshooter named Paige. Shepperd's wife Sarah was seven cars back, riding with a woman named Ruth and five-year-old Damion, Sarah's nephew. He hoped they were all right, but he hadn't been able to check. No time to stop. It was slow driving on this old log-truck road, even with chains.

The flash was distant, but it penetrated the cathedral pines like slow lightning.

The sound came later, a basso thunder that barreled out of the troubled sky. And then a hot, whipping wind. The car was buffeted. "Christ Jesus!" Paige exclaimed. Then a series of hard but muffled thuds against the roof, the windshield, the hood. *Some kind of bomb debris,* Shepperd thought wildly, but it was only snow, huge mounds of snow shaken out of the crossed boughs of the trees. It slid against the window glass, already wet in this unnatural heat.

"Drive on," Ted Bartlett said as soon as the roar abated. "This can't be healthy."

Shepperd started up his engine and heard others revving behind him. *Hang on, Sarah,* he thought, and put the car in gear.

Shepperd's convoy reached the abandoned logging camp, which was three tin-roofed wooden longhouses and a potbelly stove, at dusk.

He calculated that this expedition had saved maybe one hundred families out of the thousands in Two Rivers. The rest were smoke and ashes . . . and that was a crime so grievous it beggared comprehension.

But the people with him had been saved, no small accomplishment, and that included a lot of kids. He watched them filing out of the cars as they were parked in a defile between the tallest trees. The kids were cold, stunned, but alive. It was the kids he had some hope for. They knew how to adjust.

Not that the future looked especially rosy. One of his scouts had come back from the south with a road map, and sales of hoarded bottle liquor and bathtub hooch to the soldiers had built up the gasoline fund, in local currency, to a respectable size. But they were marked strangers. Even their cars were strange. No amount of paint or pretense would allow a Honda Civic or a Jeep 4×4 to pass for one of those cumbersome boats the natives drove.

Still . . . the few roads west were said to be lightly traveled (if passable!) this time of year, and if they made it over the unthinkable obstacle of the Rocky Mountains, even if it took until June . . . the northwest was supposed to be wide open, hardly a policeman or Proctor to be seen outside the biggest towns.

He held that thought. It was comforting.


The clouds were gone by sunset. Even the towering mushroom cloud had dispersed, though there was still a column of sooty black smoke, which he supposed was the incinerated remnant of Two Rivers, Michigan, drawn up like a migrant soul into the blue ink of the sky.

Sarah joined him under the shadow of a longhouse roof and Shepperd put his arm around her. Neither of them spoke. There were no words for this. A military aircraft passed overhead—amazing how much those things resembled P-51's, Shepperd thought—but it didn't circle, and he doubted they had been seen. It was a safe bet, he thought, that they would all live to see morning.

# After

Mr. Graham says it's important to keep this diary. He wants me to keep up with my English, although that's not what they speak here, and with history, although they have a different history, here, too.

Today, although still winter by our calendar, is warm. Almost as warm as the day we came here. I don't remember all of that, which is just as well, my mother says.

Mainly I remember how green everything seemed after we came through the light. The lab looked very strange, a few ruined buildings in a clearing as round as a crater, all surrounded by green, the bushes with long pointed leaves and the trees that looked like green feathers. A few snowflakes were still in the air around us! Of course, they melted quickly.

The blue light was gone.

For a few days after that we stayed in a partly collapsed dormitory building at the edge of the forest, but Mr. Graham said we couldn't stay too long because there might still be radiation. We had the food and supplies in the car but no road to drive on, only trails.

Then the new people came and took us to their town.

The town is really as big as a city, Mr. Graham says, if you count the underground part.

The people have been good to us. Their skin is mostly dark, sometimes even a shade of dark green. The green of shadows in a forest. Most of them are not as tall as Mr. Graham. About the size of Miss Stone. Their language is hard to learn, but I already know several words. When I learn a new word I write it the way it sounds in my "language" notebook.

They treat us well and are curious about us. We're not prisoners. But everything is very strange.

Above ground, the buildings are as green as the trees. The ceilings are arched, like church ceilings.

I saw an airplane yesterday. Its wings were painted purple and white, like butterfly wings.


Mr. Graham and Miss Stone talk a lot about all the things that have happened to us. Last night we went up to what we call the courtyard, an open space with stone benches not far from the market square. You hear music there some nights and it's never crowded.

The stars were out. The stars are the same, Miss Stone says, even if everything else is different.

She thinks it was Howard Poole who created this world. She says he is a "Demiurge" now.

Mr. Graham said he didn't think so. "I think this world's gods are a little more distant. It's not a haunted place. But I think Howard may have steered us here, at least."

"A godlike act itself," Miss Stone said. Her voice was quiet, and she was looking at the stars.

*I don't know if I believe in God. My mother says if you believe in Jesus it doesn't matter if you go to church or not. She never did.*

*Miss Stone says something lives in everything.*

*I don't know what the new people believe. But I am curious to find out, and as soon as I learn more of their language I hope to ask them.*

*About the Author*

ROBERT CHARLES WILSON is a native of California who now resides in Nanaimo, British Columbia, with his wife and son. His short fiction has appeared in *The Magazine of Fantasy & Science Fiction* and *Isaac Asimov's Science Fiction Magazine*. His other novels include *A Hidden Place*, *Memory Wire*, *Gypsies*, *The Divide*, *A Bridge of Years*, and *The Harvest*.

# BANTAM SPECTRA

## CELEBRATES ITS TENTH ANNIVERSARY IN 1995!

With more Hugo and Nebula Award winners
than any other science fiction and fantasy publisher

With more classic and cutting- edge fiction
coming every month

Bantam Spectra is proud to be the leading publisher
in fantasy and science fiction.

KEVIN ANDERSON • ISAAC ASIMOV • IAIN M. BANKS • GREGORY BENFORD • BEN BOVA • RAY BRADBURY • MARION ZIMMER BRADLEY • DAVID BRIN • ARTHUR C. CLARKE • THOMAS DEHAVEN • STEPHEN R. DONALDSON • RAYMOND FEIST • JOHN FORD • MAGGIE FUREY • DAVID GERROLD • WILLIAM GIBSON • STEPHAN GRUNDY • ELIZABETH HAND • HARRY HARRISON • ROBIN HOBB • JAMES HOGAN • KATHARINE KERR • GENTRY LEE • URSULA K. LE GUIN • VONDA N. MCINTYRE • LISA MASON • ANNE MCCAFFREY • IAN MCDONALD • DENNIS MCKIERNAN • WALTER M. MILLER, JR. • DAN MORAN • LINDA NAGATA • KIM STANLEY ROBINSON • ROBERT SILVERBERG • DAN SIMMONS • MICHAEL STACKPOLE • NEAL STEPHENSON • SHERI S. TEPPER • PAULA VOLSKY • MARGARET WEIS AND TRACY HICKMAN • ELISABETH VONARBURG • ANGUS WELLS • CONNIE WILLIS • DAVE WOLVERTON • TIMOTHY ZAHN • ROGER ZELAZNY AND ROBERT SHECKLEY

Bantam Spectra publishes more Hugo and Nebula Award-winning
novels than any other science fiction and fantasy imprint.
Celebrate the Tenth Anniversary of Spectra—read them all!

## HUGO WINNERS

| | |
|---|---|
| A CANTICLE FOR LEIBOWITZ, Walter M. Miller, Jr. | _____27381-7 $5.99/$6.99 |
| THE GODS THEMSELVES, Isaac Asimov | _____28810-5 $5.99/$6.99 |
| RENDEZVOUS WITH RAMA, Arthur C. Clarke | _____28789-3 $5.99/$6.99 |
| DREAMSNAKE, Vonda N. McIntyre | _____29659-0 $5.99/$7.50 |
| THE FOUNTAINS OF PARADISE, Arthur C. Clarke | _____28819-9 $5.99/$6.99 |
| FOUNDATION'S EDGE, Isaac Asimov | _____29338-9 $5.99/$6.99 |
| STARTIDE RISING, David Brin | _____27418-X $5.99/$6.99 |
| THE UPLIFT WAR, David Brin | _____27971-8 $5.99/$6.99 |
| HYPERION, Dan Simmons | _____28368-5 $5.99/$6.99 |
| DOOMSDAY BOOK, Connie Willis | _____56273-8 $5.99/$6.99 |
| GREEN MARS, Kim Stanley Robinson | _____37335-8 $12.95/$16.95 |

## NEBULA WINNERS

| | |
|---|---|
| THE GODS THEMSELVES, Isaac Asimov | _____28810-5 $5.99/$6.99 |
| RENDEZVOUS WITH RAMA, Arthur C. Clarke | _____28789-3 $5.99/$6.99 |
| DREAMSNAKE, Vonda N. McIntyre | _____29659-0 $5.99/$7.50 |
| THE FOUNTAINS OF PARADISE, Arthur C. Clarke | _____28819-9 $5.99/$6.99 |
| TIMESCAPE, Gregory Benford | _____27709-0 $5.99/$6.99 |
| STARTIDE RISING, David Brin | _____27418-X $5.99/$6.99 |
| TEHANU, Ursula K. Le Guin | _____28873-3 $5.50/$6.99 |
| DOOMSDAY BOOK, Connie Willis | _____56273-8 $5.99/$6.99 |
| RED MARS, Kim Stanley Robinson | _____56073-5 $5.99/$7.50 |